WHEN WE CAUGHT FIRE

Also by Anna Godbersen

The Luxe
Rumors
Envy
Splendor

Bright Young Things
Beautiful Days
The Lucky Ones

When We Caught Fire

NEW YORK TIMES BESTSELLING AUTHOR
ANNA GODBERSEN

HARPER TEEN
An Imprint of HarperCollinsPublishers

For Marty,
who told me the best love story

HarperTeen is an imprint of HarperCollins Publishers.

When We Caught Fire
Copyright © 2018 by Alloy Entertainment
All rights reserved. Printed in the United States of America.
No part of this book may be used or reproduced in any manner whatsoever
without written permission except in the case of brief quotations embodied
in critical articles and reviews. For information address HarperCollins
Children's Books, a division of HarperCollins Publishers, 195 Broadway,
New York, NY 10007.
www.epicreads.com

Library of Congress Control Number: 2018939977
ISBN 978-0-06-267982-6
Typography by Aurora Parlagreco
18 19 20 21 22 PC/LSCH 10 9 8 7 6 5 4 3 2 1

First Edition

BEFORE AND AFTER

By morning the city had fallen. We had not seen the sky in a long time; even the sky was made of fire. The State Street Bridge was impassable, they said. The Rush Street Bridge, too. The streets were littered with objects that had once seemed valuable enough to carry, but now lay abandoned. The explosions did not frighten us anymore, for they came too frequently—sounds rang out, like a battle being waged one block over, every time a building went down.

Some would never recover, while for others it was the beginning of everything. For the ruined and reborn alike, there was simply *before* and *after*. And the moment that divided these two eras—the moment that old barn turned to tinder—would become a source of wild speculation and grand mythology.

Despite all the talk, it had been just us three when the fire started, and we would remain, forever, the only ones who knew what really happened.

BEFORE

ONE

The pleasure of your company
is kindly requested
for a small luncheon to inaugurate the celebration
of the Carter-Tree wedding
at the Carter residence
Wednesday, October 4, 1871
Noon

The room was full of her name.

In the two years that Emmeline Carter had lived with her father in the limestone mansion on Dearborn, north of the river, the big front parlor had never been as full as this—full of people, and full of iced delicacies, and full of servants lifting golden trays laden with champagne flutes above the heads of the guests. Full of ruffled skirts cascading over extravagant bustles, full of the confident talk of men in tail-coats custom-cut just for them. But mostly it was full of the name *Emmeline*, whispered with envy and approval from every corner, so that the edges of her ears went pink and her eyes became bright. Her step was light and her laugh was easy and her dress, of blush crepe de chine, floated around her slender limbs like a summer cloud. She did not think she had ever been so happy. By week's end she would have everything she ever wanted.

"Miss Carter, my dear, come along," said Mrs. Garrison, whose name at birth had been Ada Arles Tree.

Emmeline, never overfond of being told what to do, chafed at this command. But come Sunday she would be calling Ada "sister," and now did not seem an advantageous time to contradict her wishes. So Emmeline banished her pout, clasped the hand of young Mrs. Palmer—to whom she had just been introduced—bowed her head, and made a low curtsy. "Thank you, truly, for coming to our little party," she said with a modest fluttering of eyelashes. "It is such a pleasure to meet you."

"No, no, contrary-wise, the pleasure is mine," said Mrs. Palmer, who was sitting on the divan with the silk sapphire upholstery. Although the piece was quite old—Father had recently become something of a collector—the wooden armrests were polished to a high shine. "I find you quite charming. Will you come for a tea at the house tomorrow?

I have a little afternoon every week, all the best girls. You must be one of us."

Although Emmeline wanted to clarify that by "house" Mrs. Palmer meant the massive hotel that bore her married name, she sensed that it would be gauche to do so. Rich people were always referring to mansions as cottages, to enormous carriages as buggies. And to be one of them, a girl had to adopt their funny way of talking.

As they continued through the throng, Ada clutched Emmeline by the elbow and said in a hushed, excited way, "I cannot tell you what a coveted invitation that is. She would never have you into her set if she weren't confident of your future success. *Nobody* is more discerning than Bertha."

Emmeline replied with a vague smile and a guileless tilt of the head, although she hardly needed any explication of Mrs. Palmer's importance. The name *Potter Palmer* was carved with gold leaf into the lintels of several big buildings in the shopping district—all the ladies knew him, because of his department store—and when he married Bertha Honoré a year ago it was all anyone had talked about. As a wedding present, he'd given her an actual *hotel*, the brand-new and very grand Palmer House, on State Street.

At this time last year, nobody had sent invitations to the Carters, a family of two who had installed themselves four seasons prior in the block-wide property between Huron and Superior, without having any social connection to the place. Emmeline had spent that fall greedy for every detail: of Bertha's trousseau; the names of those invited to her wedding, and what they ate; the pattern on the specially designed luggage for the round-the-world honeymoon via ocean liner. And she had vowed that by the time she was Bertha's age—twenty-one—she would have a wedding just as spectacular. But here she was, quite ahead of her goal—just eighteen and engaged to be married to Frederick Arles Tree, who was an even better groom than Potter Palmer: at twenty-four, he was two decades younger, and such a good dancer, and the son of a banker, besides. His uncle was a senator, and so might Freddy be one day.

Senator Frederick Tree, didn't that sound just perfect? She thought of him as Freddy, everybody did, although she would not say the nickname in his hearing. He preferred Frederick, and insisted on being called by his proper name.

Married! She could hardly believe it. He had only proposed three months prior; she knew the date exactly. It had been July third—moody weather, with big drops pelting the windowpanes—and he had come calling at the Carter residence, and said that he wanted to announce their engagement at the Ogdens' Independence Day picnic. The ring was a great cluster of diamonds that covered her finger from knuckle to joint, and she didn't hear half of what Freddy said, so distracted was she by its shimmery light.

She knew she'd never forget that day. It was the last she remembered rain.

A servant in burgundy livery—he must have been hired for the party, for Emmeline did not recognize him—passed then with a plate of strawberries, and Emmeline took one and put it in her mouth. "Who shall we introduce me to now?" she asked Ada, lifting an eyebrow in giddy anticipation. She had just met the most socially discerning woman in Chicago, and was aflutter wondering who would be next.

"Let us pause here a spell," Mrs. Garrison replied, drawing herself up and casting her keen gaze across the parlor. They had reached the doorway onto the foyer. The clatter and bustle of preparations for a lavish luncheon could be heard from the dining room on the foyer's far side.

Everything before her was new, except the objects that were expensively old. The herringbone floor gleamed, as did the gilt frames of the giant mirrors that hung on every wall. Emmeline caught herself in one of these, and admired the narrow waist and drooping sleeves of her gown, her full pink lips and sloe-eyed glance. Her brass-colored hair was parted at the middle and plaited at the crown, and it curled in little wisps along her forehead. Guests were still arriving, coming up the wide stone steps from the vast front lawn, and she felt annoyed with Ada, who could be so old and meddling and married sometimes. Emmeline had practiced for several solitary years to be the center of attention, and now that she had arrived there, she was impatient to meet absolutely everybody.

"Goodness, what a showing." Emmeline overheard one of the new arrivals saying from just outside the parlor. "The whole world is here."

"How the curious do flock to the scene of the crime," replied another in an arid tone.

"My darling Miss Russell, don't be bitter," admonished the first speaker. "In time, it will ruin your face. Look around you. What a fabulous to-do!" She stepped into the doorway, revealing herself as a petite woman clothed in widow's black. "Mark my words, these nuptials will be the most talked about event in Chicago this year."

Ada leaned in toward Emmeline and whispered, "Mrs. Fletcher Fleming," in quiet reverence. "The most admired beauty of her day," she went on in a murmur. "In the drawing rooms of this city, her word is absolute."

Emmeline turned with naked curiosity to see the second speaker, who passed through the open pocket doors to join her interlocutor upon a sweep of vermilion skirt. She did not need to be told her name: it was Cora Russell, who had been escorted by Freddy at her coming out four years before, and who gossips said had waited too long for his proposal. In the spring, she had absented herself on a trip to

Paris in order that his heart grow fonder, which was when it found Emmeline instead.

"I don't care what you say," Cora said as she took Mrs. Fleming's arm. "What's all the fuss about? She's new, that's all. Freddy is always distracted by anything new."

"Pay no heed to that," Ada whispered as the two women were absorbed into the crowd. "She is jealous, of course."

But Emmeline was untroubled by Cora's words. They meant that she, Emmeline Carter, who two years ago had been a nameless nobody, was worth envying. There were so many eyes in that room, and they all seemed to search for her. The girls who had known Freddy since childhood and the men who frequented his club and the long-married women who entertained themselves by speculatively matchmaking the younger generation. On the far side of the room was Father, in a jacket of charcoal velvet, glancing at her now and then as though looking at his most prized possession. In another doorway Fiona hovered in her plain black pinafore, watchful to see if she were needed, her eyes shiny with excitement to match Emmeline's own. But mostly there was Freddy, in a cutaway jacket of dashing blue, his tall, lean body forging a path through the crowd as he strode in her direction.

Although Freddy had not called for the room's attention, he had it, just by walking. He was six feet tall and his blond hair grew long—he had to tuck it behind his ears to keep it away from his sable brown eyes. *Frederick*, she reminded herself, but that sounded so angular and self-serious, and Freddy wasn't like that at all. Freddy was wonderful. Whenever he came to see her he brought a dozen roses and afterward he'd take her out for rides in his fast little horse trap. People on the street stared, remarking, "There goes a handsome couple," for Freddy always dressed with care. He had his clothes made for him in Europe, a place they would go together, he said, once they were married.

Everybody turned toward him, ceasing their previous conversations. Upon reaching Emmeline's side he took her hand. As she gazed up at him, he put his free hand inside his jacket's lapel, and removed a leather-bound case—his every action smooth, as though for him the world contained no mysteries, and nothing he could not possess. With a flick of his thumb, the case popped open. Inside, resting on silk, was a golden diadem with a little ruby-dotted peak. Emmeline's feet suddenly seemed very far away; the jeweled crown was the stuff of little girls' dreams, almost too grand to believe. In the next moment, Freddy had placed it on her head.

"It belonged to my late grandmother," he said, adding, in an impressive tone: "to Genevieve Gage Arles."

The elegant guests were regarding her wide-eyed, as they had all afternoon, although perhaps more reverently. They very nearly gaped, as at a princess at her coronation.

She beamed at her fiancé, unable to disguise her sense of triumph.

"Oh, Freddy, thank you." She gasped. "It's perfect!"

He was staring down at her with a look she'd never seen before. His lips parted and his eyebrows went together, as though on the verge of a very serious thought. A fear arose, that he was angry at her for saying his nickname out loud. Then she saw it wasn't that at all. He wanted to kiss her; he actually might! He had never kissed her before— only on the hand and cheek, and that when no one was watching—although she had on occasion sensed that he wanted something more. But she had been careful, and always modestly demurred, the better to hold his interest, which had been Father's advice. *The trick is to have them always coming to you*, Father said.

Only once in her life had she been kissed for real.

For a moment, the memory of that kiss was more vivid than her surroundings, than any of the people watching her, more vivid than Freddy himself, and Emmeline was afraid that the girl she used to be was plain for all to see, and that they would know she was an impostor.

"A toast!" Emmeline heard her father's voice, booming from the far side of the room. "To the affianced couple, and the merging of our families."

Freddy was smiling like nothing had happened, and he took her hand chastely in his. A fleet of liveried servants appeared with fresh glasses and bottles of champagne. Emmeline was given a glass, and she tried to smile. From every corner people were shouting.

"To Frederick and Emmeline!"

"To happiness!"

"To love!"

Emmeline knew she ought to be joyful. But she could not shake a sudden feeling that something, somehow, was all wrong. She was surrounded by so many bodies, and the room was warm with their breath. The air was stale and heated by the sun on the big windows. Her skin prickled. She raised her glass, not quite to her lips, and tipped it.

"Oh!" she exclaimed, as though surprised. The champagne was cool down the front of her dress.

Freddy glanced at her, sidelong. "Are you all right?"

"A little overwhelmed, perhaps. How clumsy of me. Allow me just a few minutes to clean up."

A stark quiet came over the parlor as she hurried toward the doorway. Just as she reached it, she heard Cora Russell say, "Of course one *can* take the pigs off the farm. That is how ham is made."

There were many reasons that Emmeline was glad to have reached the door, the most pressing of which being that only a few people were positioned to see how Cora's comment inflamed her cheeks. But she did not yet regret spilling champagne on herself, did not regret making a scene. All she wanted was to be alone with Fiona, and to discuss the precise wording of the message that Fiona must deliver. The memory of that kiss had opened a window onto her previous life, and she knew that, however perfectly she had conducted herself since meeting Freddy, she had left unfinished some business of her old self, with its old desires. But, with Fiona's help, she could seal all that up and bury it for good.

And then her true life would finally begin.

TWO

When Clotilde felt Guillaume's stare scorch the skin of her bare shoulder from across the room, she knew how it was for Joan of Arc—engulfed in passion, consumed by flames, eternally grateful to be in this way reduced to ash.
—*Aurelie Auber,* The Loves of Clotilde

"Why are you standing there like a fool? It isn't happening to you, you know."

To Fiona Byrne, half hiding behind the mahogany doorframe onto the parlor, these words had the sound of a whip cracked at her ear. She had almost forgotten herself, so absorbed in reverie had she been, watching the Carters' guests, trying to match them in her mind with the names on the list of invitees.

"It *is* happening to me, too," she shot back before she had a chance to think.

The girl was unfamiliar, and just a maid like herself, outfitted in a white shirtwaist and long, plain black skirt much like Fiona's, and carrying two richly embroidered wraps folded over her arms. Her lips twisted in mirth, but she did not laugh outright.

"Oh, is it? How nice for you." Her gaze shifted in the direction of the parlor and she pointed to a young woman, in a skirt of brilliant red with a little matching jacket, newly arrived and making her way to the center of things. "That one's mine. Miss Cora Russell—just as fancy as she sounds. Everything that happens to her happens to me, too. You wouldn't believe how exhausting it is being fitted for all those gowns."

For a moment, Fiona's moss-green eyes got big. In the three years she'd worked as Emmeline's lady's maid, she had never had an item of clothing made for her. She was a good seamstress, and often repaired or improved the dressmaker's creations for Emmeline, but she never had spare hours to make anything nice for herself. But a second later she realized that the other girl was being ironical, and blushed at her own stupidity. "I suppose it would be" was all she could think to say.

The other maid appraised her. "Show me where the

coatroom is," she said, "and I'll tell you the way of things."

By the time they arrived in the basement, Fiona had resolved not to say much. She knew that her situation was difficult to explain—it was really only she and Emmeline who understood it—and there was no reason to tell Cora Russell's lady's maid that, although Fiona was the one who helped Emmeline dress in the morning, and also later in the day if she was going to a party, and arranged her hair, and drew her bath, and served her tea if she was being called upon by somebody of importance, she didn't think of Emmeline as her mistress. They were best friends, and had been as far back as Fiona could remember. The two of them, and Anders.

When Mr. Carter came into enough money to purchase the big house in the north section of town, and decided to make a go of a new way of life, Emmeline had a fit of temper and insisted she would not be moving away from her friends. They were almost sixteen, and changing fast, though still an inseparable band of three. Anders had been in love with Emmeline since they were children—if she had stayed, they would surely be married now. In the end, Mr. Carter convinced his daughter by saying that Fiona could come and live with them if she learned quickly how to comport herself as a lady's maid.

At first it had been strange to do things for Emmeline that they both knew she could do for herself. But at least the girls got to spend every day together, kept busy and excited by the task of transforming themselves into proper young ladies. Fiona was glad to live in bright, clean rooms that smelled of greenhouse flowers, and grateful to finally have a way of making some money of her own. Her family, back in the old neighborhood, was always in need of money.

"My name is Mary," said Miss Russell's maid.

"Fiona."

"Irish?" Mary asked.

Fiona shrugged. She knew Mr. Carter was sensitive on this point—he would have preferred to hire no Irish—and it was easy to answer inconclusively.

As they moved through the house, Mary made little clucking noises and let her fingers graze marble end tables and porcelain doorknobs. This annoyed Fiona—surely she would not behave that way in her own employer's house—but she tried to tell herself it was only natural. The Carters were new, and how they lived was a topic of interest. Her own family was always curious for such details. And it was certainly possible that Mary was *trying* to be friendly.

In the basement, beneath the parlor, the light of a few high windows illuminated a plain room with a long table, around which sat the few servants who had accompanied the Carters' guests. Most had come without help, but some of those who had traveled from the South Side or from estates outside of the city limits had brought along a footman or a girl to hold their things. They glanced up at Fiona and Mary, and watched as they pulled wooden chairs up to the table.

"So you're Emmeline Carter's girl?" Mary sat and removed a book and a small leather case from the pockets of her skirt and placed them on the table. *The Loves of Clotilde* was printed across the cover, by *Aurelie Auber*—Fiona always tried to read whatever sentences she came across, to keep up what letters she had. "If you could hear what Miss Russell says about Miss Carter, my word, your ears would burn. I rather like her, though. If she can crawl out of the swamp and convince Frederick Tree to marry her, it could happen to any of us. She must have some pluck. Not that I'd say anything of the kind to Cora, of course."

"Did you get that idea from your novel there?" said another maid, sitting a few chairs down with her elbows propped on the table to examine her needlepoint. She was older than Mary, with gray sprouts in her dark hair and purse lines around her lips. Without looking up, she continued, "That it could happen to any of us. That girl's father is Ochs Carter. Yes, if my father were a cunning businessman and ran things as Ochs Carter does, I suppose I might buy a lot of pretty clothes and catch a rich husband, too."

Mary made a show of stifling a giggle, and opened the leather case to offer Fiona a rolled cigarette. "Want one?"

"No, I . . ." Fiona began. Since they had left the old

neighborhood, the two girls had spent countless days learning to walk and talk and dress in the manner of fashionable young ladies. They had learned that smoking was for gentlemen, that only certain kinds of women indulged in them. Not the kind of women she and Emmeline were trying to be.

"Miss Russell developed a taste for them on the continent but she knows her mother would cut her allowance in half if she did it in public, so she has me carry them, and allows me as many as I like."

"Then it will be you that's caught," said the maid at her needlepoint. "And you that pays the price."

"Ignore her. They're delightful." Mary spoke loud enough that the whole room heard, and struck a match to light the cigarette between her lips. "She's no fun. Though she's right, of course. It's just daydreaming to say that what happened to your mistress could happen to me, or you, or that one there with the sour face. What's happening to little Miss Carter is not happening to you in the slightest bit, and don't forget it. You should do as I do and catch what crumbs you can. For instance, when your mistress is bored of a dress, ask if you can alter it—not the really fine stuff, that they'll never part with, but an old day dress, something she wears around the house—and if she asks you to hold her cigarette case, be sure that you're allowed one from time to time. Here, try it."

Fiona disliked the smell of smoke, but she had grown up in a hard place and she knew what happened when you were new and showed you were afraid of something: The pack turned against you in an instant. Upstairs, the heels of dress shoes sounded across the floor. There was applause and awed gasps. Mary ceased her chatter, and—perhaps sensing Fiona's reluctance—met her eyes with an intent stare. But Fiona took the cigarette expertly, balancing it between her middle and index fingers, and inhaled without so much as a cough. "That's all right, I suppose," she said with a shrug of indifference, and passed it back.

Mary seemed perturbed that the cigarette had not more impressed Fiona. "I got this in Paris," she said, gesturing to her novel. "When I accompanied Miss Russell to France. It's about a noblewoman who is married to an old yawn of a colonel and she falls in love with this gallant young cavalry fellow but it's a disaster and she doesn't realize all along her cousin is in love with her, and he's quite rich and has all kinds of castles and things. . . ."

Fiona smiled vaguely. She didn't mind if Mary wanted to prattle on. Upstairs in the parlor they were cheering now, stomping their feet and calling out the names of the bride and groom to be. "To love!" someone shouted, and Fiona's heart surged, and she thought: *It's happening, it's really happening, everything we've worked for is finally happening.* Emmeline was a success, and would soon be quite advantageously matched. In a week she would be married to Frederick Arles Tree, of the Wabash Avenue Trees, and ascend to the ranks of Chicago's very best people. Fiona found she was smiling. She was happy for her friend, truly, for Emmeline was finally to have everything she had worked so hard for, and Fiona was also happy for herself. For once Emmeline was Mrs. Tree, there would be no reason for her to think about Anders Magnuson, her sweetheart from the old neighborhood, in a proprietary way.

The union of Emmeline and Anders had been a favorite story of their childhood, when they were a tribe of three, planning a future in some faraway place where Anders and Emmeline would be wed. It was only when they were older that Fiona began to wonder what that would mean for her. But then the Carters picked up and left the neighborhood. Emmeline cried every day and said she would die without Anders, until she began transforming herself into a young lady of fashion, and became enthralled with her new role. Fiona saw Anders in the old neighborhood, but of course she never mentioned Anders to Emmeline, nor Emmeline to Anders—it would be too painful for both of them.

And then one evening, half a year ago, following the wake of one of Anders's uncles—his mother's youngest brother, the one who had died working on the construction of a big building downtown—he said he would escort Fiona home. They went on a walk at least once a week in those days, although they were careful not to talk of Emmeline, careful not to talk of the change that had come over their lives. As they walked, he talked meanderingly of all manner of things. Mostly how his father had met his mother—in Galway, after he left Stockholm, en route to America—and convinced her in a matter of days that they should be married.

"She wasn't from Sweden like my dad, did you know that? She was an Irish rose, like you."

Fiona's face flushed in confusion, because of course she'd known his mother—who never lost her accent, the way Fiona's mother and father had—but mostly because she hadn't realized Anders thought of her as any kind of rose.

"Are you cold?" he asked.

The night was bitter, and the tip of her nose felt near frozen, but he seemed to mean something else, and she watched him and waited to know what it was.

"I must be drunk," he'd said, and stepped closer. She was so surprised by the longing in his eyes that she would have fallen over had the wall not caught her. His forehead pressed her forehead, and his hands spread over her waist. For the first time, she understood how strong he was. Then he kissed her, and she forgot the cold, and everything else. She thought her body might melt, but that it didn't matter, as long as he kept kissing her just like that. As long as the kiss continued, they were one being, with no names or reputations to separate them. "I'm sorry," he'd muttered, pulling away. He had seemed to want to look at her again, but didn't. Instead he said he was sorry three more times, and disappeared down the darkened street.

She couldn't sleep that night, nor the night after. For several days she didn't want to eat, but neither did she want to feel better. She wanted the agony to go on forever. She was in love with him—what else could this feeling be? Maybe she always had been. Every idle moment became a time to imagine his swaggering gait, the way a dimple appeared in his cheek when he told a joke, to fill her mind with any detail of Anders, no matter how minute. When she saw him in the old neighborhood and he spoke a familiar word, her face would turn a shameful shade of scarlet. But there was nothing to do: He was Emmeline's first and always. It was only fate that had parted them, and Fiona was miserable with guilt over how much she had loved being kissed by the boy once promised to Emmeline. No, Fiona could never tell Emmeline about the kiss. She began avoiding their weekly walks for fear she would once again entice Anders into betraying their friend. But then Frederick Arles Tree began courting Emmeline, and Emmeline herself was thrilled by his attentions and never once let Anders's name pass her lips, and Fiona saw how everything might end happily for her, just as everything was ending happily for her best friend.

The joyful toasting sounded to Fiona like a celebration of her love, too. Her face tingled with it, and she smiled, and let Mary go on about some French people with a lot of desperate emotions a world away. She had no need for that kind of romance. She and Anders were simple people, but they knew each other well, and how to be happy, in simple ways, together. They would, if only she could find a way to tell him the truth.

Ever since the engagement, she had been avoiding Anders—she was holding her breath for the week to be over and for Emmeline to be married. Then Fiona's conscience would be clear. Then she could finally ask her friend's permission to want Anders as she did. She resisted the places she might have run into him; she was afraid if she saw him she would blush, and it would be obvious how often he was in her thoughts. She did not want him to know her true feelings before she had Emmeline's blessing.

"Anyway, when I finish, I'll lend it to you," Mary concluded with satisfaction.

"Fiona!"

The servants sitting at the long table glanced toward the stairs. The party above them had gone quiet. Mary's eyes rolled toward the ceiling and back at Fiona.

"Fiona?" It was Emmeline, closer now. The stairs to the first floor groaned. "Fiona, are you down there? I need to talk to you!"

Fiona was on her feet, unable to contain a spasm of pride over this show of familiarity between Emmeline and herself. She glanced at the other servants, startled and stone-faced at this intrusion upon their realm. Fiona thought how unmistakable her true situation was now—that she and Emmeline really were friends, despite their difference in station. She rushed to meet Emmeline on the top step.

"Oh, Fiona, look what I've done," Emmeline wailed, gesturing to the wetness that spread across the bodice of her dress.

"Are you all right?" Fiona could not hide her surprise—Emmeline was not usually a victim of nerves.

"Well." A mischievous light played in Emmeline's eyes, but they became earnest as she glanced up at her friend. Standing close together like this, Fiona always felt awkward and large—she was several inches taller than Emmeline, and not as fine-boned—even though Emmeline claimed it was *she* who was jealous of Fiona, with her full chest and long waist. "I might have been clumsy a little bit on purpose."

At the bottom of the stairs, Mary was leaning against the doorframe. The bald curiosity of her expression made Fiona's palms sweat. The pride of the previous moment was gone, overwhelmed by a presentiment of things going terribly wrong.

"Come," said Fiona. "Let me clean you up."

"Yes." Emmeline clasped Fiona's hand. "Let's get cleaned up quickly, and while we do, there's something I need to ask you to do for me."

"What is it?" Her dress stuck to the damp skin underneath the arms and her pulse became noisy while she waited for Emmeline to respond.

Emmeline bit her bottom lip. Her gaze shifted. "I must see him," she whispered.

Fiona stared at her friend. She knew in an instant who *him* was. Her heart ached with the meaning of *him*.

"Just once, to explain. Before it's done. We did always promise each other. Can you find him?"

Him. Him with the sideways smile, the stride and glint. Him with the strong hands. Him who had always been as dutiful to his family as she to hers. She would not have thought Emmeline had remembered that promise, not since Frederick proposed. But Emmeline was her best friend—Fiona had to agree to whatever she asked. And she was the one who paid her way—Emmeline never mentioned this, but the fact was always there, tugging at Fiona, telling her what she ought.

After a moment Fiona nodded. "I'll find him for you," she replied, hoping that the dimness of the hall hid the dread in her eyes.

THREE

What charming weather we are having! The long, dry summer has given way to sun-drenched fall, and the elegant families of our fine city have been afforded the opportunity to host lovely lawn parties and picnics and the like late into the season. . . . Let us hope the invitations keep arriving and that the rain stays away.
—*"Leisure Life" column,* Chicago Crier,
October 4, 1871

"Is it real?"

Emmeline's eyes rose to meet Fiona's in the mirror, but Fiona, transfixed by the gems shimmering in Emmeline's hair, did not look back. She had just finished pinning errant strands beneath the diadem, and helped Emmeline into a new dress of mauve silk that gave a lovely contrast to the warm pink blooms on her cheeks.

"Of course it's real!" Emmeline touched the dainty crown and appraised her reflection. She knew it was vain, but she couldn't help it—her reflection pleased her beyond words. With the ruby crown and the diamond engagement ring, the girls might have been posing for a royal portrait. Behind them Emmeline's bedroom spread out, with its tall, third-floor windows pouring light over the canopied bed and Persian carpet and fur throws and magenta chaise longue. The room was full of rich objects, but none were as fine as Freddy's gifts. "You should have seen Cora Russell's face when he put it on me!"

"I saw her, from the hallway, and then her maid came over and couldn't stop chatting. She talked and talked about how jealous her mistress was of you."

"Did she really say that?" Emmeline bit her bottom lip in delight. "And they say *our* manners are rough. But there's her, gossiping away about me. Isn't that rich?"

"Terribly rich," Fiona agreed. "You look very beautiful, Miss Carter. If I may say so myself."

"You look very beautiful as well, Miss Byrne." She did, too, Emmeline thought. Even with no special adornments Fiona was lovely, with her pale oval face and the constellation of freckles that spread across her nose, and the black pinafore tied tight so that it showed off her small waist. The sunlight brought out the russet tones in her hair where it frizzed. "And you *may*."

"We ought to go back, now."

"Must we?" Emmeline revolved on the velvet stool at her vanity, so that her heaping skirt twisted with her, and flicked her gaze upward at her friend. Fiona was right, of course. Lunch would be served soon, and there would be more toasts, and Cora Russell was probably chatting up Freddy by now. But at the moment what she really wanted was not to talk to all the fine people downstairs, but to talk *about* them with Fiona. It was so humid in the parlor with all those people crowded inside, and the atmosphere confused her thoughts. She couldn't help picturing the way Freddy had looked when he had seemed to want to kiss her, and the memory that moment had ignited.

Her mind kept wandering to a day when she and Fiona were doing laundry outside the Byrnes' apartment and Anders had appeared and taken her by the hand and led her up the fire escape and onto the roof. They could see the whole neighborhood from there, and the wind pressed her skirt against her legs, and she felt a little frightened to be up so high. He knelt, and took the claddagh his mother used to wear out of his pocket. While he waited, his eyes grew wide and earnest. When she nodded, he stood, placed the ring on her finger, and took her face in his hands to kiss. He had gazed at her with such strong emotion that she was surprised by his lips, so soft and gentle when they met hers.

A few weeks later, Father said the Carter household

would be making a permanent move. Emmeline still had that ring, somewhere with her other jewelry. They had never said aloud what that ring meant, but it would be dishonest to claim she didn't know. Certainly both of them thought of it as an engagement. In order to marry Freddy properly, didn't she need to break off that other engagement first?

"I'll feel much better," she said, trying to put away those confusing memories, "once I've seen Anders and explained things."

Fiona had been giving Emmeline her usual easy, encouraging smile, but now she frowned and glanced away. Was something wrong? Emmeline had been so lost in thought that she hadn't noticed Fiona's mood at all. She was about to ask what the trouble was, but in the next moment she understood.

The door was flung open, and the heels of Father's boots clacked against the floor. When he saw their cozy postures he paused, and his shoulders flared. Fiona stepped away, straightening up in a hurry.

Father grunted and buttoned his jacket. "Fiona," he said tersely. Her name never sounded as pretty when he said it. "What is taking so long?"

"The dress could not be dried off, Mr. Carter. We had to put Emmeline in a new one, and that meant—"

Father silenced her with a hand gesture. "I don't need

the details." After that, he seemed not to see Fiona. His attention became fixed upon his daughter. "Emmeline, you are being very rude. All of Chicago is here to see who Frederick Tree is marrying, and you're hiding in your bedroom. They will think you were raised wrong."

I was *raised wrong*, Emmeline was ready to say. That was the argument she always made when she was at odds with Father and wanted to get her way. "But—"

"Miss Carter." His voice went low and raspy, as it did when he would not be disobeyed. Such was their game. He averted his gaze and gripped the doorknob, opening the door to indicate where she should go. This angered her— but she knew that when she was willful with Father, Fiona was often in trouble with him later.

"Oh, all right." She pulled her skirt away from her feet. Fiona was holding very still, and Emmeline rolled her eyes and flounced out of the room to show her she need not be afraid. Emmeline hated it when her friend felt afraid. She did not acknowledge Father until she had passed the second-floor landing and felt his fingers on her arm, twisting her so that she was forced to turn toward him.

"Listen to me, Emmeline," he whispered, gripping her arm. "I held this luncheon for *you*, so that *you* might be introduced to a better class of people. Every last person whose opinion matters is downstairs wondering where you went off to, guessing at what has gone wrong. And hear me, they'd love for something to go wrong. It would give them gossip for the rest of the year. But I didn't sell my family farm, didn't buy this house, didn't pay for tutors to give you a finishing worthy of a princess, so that you could sit upstairs giggling with Fiona."

"You're hurting me," she whispered.

His hair, silvery now and kept respectable-looking with pomade, had become disheveled. That was how she remembered him looking sometimes when she was a little girl. He was slimmer then, but broad as ever. His temper used to come on quick whenever he sensed he might be wronged. After he sold most of his father's homestead to the railroad companies to build stockyards on—the land was swampy, and never yielded much—he built a hotel where farmers stayed when bringing their hogs into the city to sell for slaughter. Often, a man would drink too much and get in trouble at the card table, and Ochs Carter would show that he was not to be cheated, snarling and threatening to call his man at the Pinkerton Detective Agency if the bill was not paid promptly. As a little girl, Emmeline had found her father's moods frightening, but he had seemed to mellow with age, and she had not seen that volatile version of her father since they moved north of the river.

"I'm sorry." He released her. He sighed, and went on. "When my father came west there was nothing here, an old fort and less than a thousand people. But he was born into a fine family back east, and we will be a fine family again. Everything depends upon this week being perfect. Next year, there will be other newcomers, and we will be the people whose favor everyone strives for. Don't you want that?"

Emmeline glanced in the direction of the first floor, where a procession of rich fabrics in bright colors was passing out of the parlor and toward the dining room. The staff was leading the guests into luncheon. They prattled on, oblivious to the fact that their hosts were standing at the top of the stairs. Soon they would be seated around the many tables that had been decorated with arrangements of purple hydrangea, being served iced tea and lobster salad, waiting for her return. It was her dream of what life should be, it was everything she had worked for over two long years. "Of course I do."

Just then Freddy ambled into the foyer, and Emmeline remembered how handsome he was in blue. The fearful, shrinking moment had passed, and with it the longing for old comforts. The world was so much more than she had thought. She only wanted to stand next to him and have everyone admire how well they complemented each other. She smoothed her skirt and touched the diadem, to make sure it was in place.

"Frederick!" she called, and descended a few steps.

"Oh," he said. He swallowed when he saw her form in the new dress and a smile broke on his face. "Where have you been?"

She smiled back. "Getting ready. Did you miss me terribly?" she asked, descending the stairs two at a time, hands outstretched for him to take.

FOUR

What hustle and bustle! What excessive wealth and degrading
poverty! What a lot of speculation! What giddy building up and
ruthless tearing down! What a lot of railroads, wheat, hogs,
gadgets! Chicago—I have never seen anything alike to her.
The whole of her civic enterprise is built on a swamp, so they
simply lifted it up, bricking the streets with pine blocks, raising
sidewalks of plank. The residents call it heaven, but I should say it
reminded me more of that other place.
—Lord Rathbone, Travels in America

The lake was a dreamy blue and the clouds were shaded
peach by the low sun when Fiona slipped down the back
stairs and cut through the stables toward Clark Street. It
was all very lovely, and all very melancholy, she thought—
a picturesque view always just out of reach. Emmeline

was sleeping off the afternoon's excitement in her bedroom, and the door to Ochs Carter's second-floor study had closed, signaling he was not to be disturbed. The cook and her assistants were cleaning the lower regions of the house, and Malcolm, who had been Mr. Carter's man in the old neighborhood too, was nowhere to be seen. Although it was understood that Fiona had permission to visit her family one evening a week, she did not like to bring attention to her leaving. It was a privilege the rest of the household staff resented. This time, however, Fiona was at least able to justify herself with the notion that she was acting on Miss Carter's behalf.

Misery thickened in her throat every time she thought of Emmeline's request, but she had no choice but to do as Emmeline wished. She tried to tell herself that she had waited a long time already, that Emmeline's desire to tell Anders about her wedding was perfectly sensible, that it would be done soon and everything might still end just as she hoped. And yet, she had been friends with Emmeline a long time, and lived by the general principle that what Emmeline wanted, Emmeline got. If she should decide she wanted Anders again . . .

Fiona tried not to think that way. Anyway, it was unlikely. Since she was a little girl, Emmeline had possessed hair of spun gold and high cheekbones and a regal bearing as though she knew already she was destined to arrive in the fancy world. Here the air was full of leaves, and from the top floors of the elegant mansions you could see vessels on the water, the small sailboats out for pleasure cruises and the big steamers bound for New York or the Mississippi. Tasteful wrought-iron gates told passersby that only the right kind of people were allowed inside. In the old neighborhood, blocks like these seemed as far away as New York, as far away as Dublin. But, in fact, only a few miles separated them from where she was born.

Soon she was in another place. She smelled the river before she saw it, and approached the bridge with a sleeve covering her face. The river contained the refuse of the whole city, all its hustling and all its secrets, and in the years she had lived as Emmeline's lady's maid, she had become accustomed to rooms with big windows and a cross breeze. Once she was on the far side, the buildings she passed were taller, and they cast long shadows and left cold canyons in between. Men wearing brimmed hats hustled in and out of double doors. She walked fast and kept her head down, so that she would appear like any maid: invisible in her long black high-necked dress. The big bell at the courthouse rang seven o'clock. A few blocks later she turned west.

When she saw the ship masts of the south branch rising above the rooftops, she knew she was home. The buildings were low again, two or three stories packed close together, as though they had gone up in a day. This was where she had been born. These structures seemed to her as permanent as monuments, although they were quite the opposite.

The alley down which her family lived had recently been bought by a shirtwaist manufacturer, and would be razed to make way for a factory. She couldn't really believe that the tenements she'd known all her life could disappear like that—and in any case, everybody was acting as though things would go on, always the same, on this particular evening. Families soon to be displaced spilled onto the ramshackle wooden porches, enjoying the warm fall night air.

"Fiona!"

Running to catch up was her younger brother, Jack. He threw his arm around her middle jauntily, and they continued on together. "Hello, my darlingest," she said. "How was your day?"

"Good. There was a murder last night." He grinned up at her. "Sold a lot."

When Jack shouted headlines telling of city hall scandal and barroom violence from street corners he sounded tough, like he knew of what he spoke. He'd be nine in November, so perhaps he did. Fiona hoped not—Jack was her favorite. Even so she couldn't help but feel a little relieved that he'd had a good day. She brought an envelope for her family every week, but always worried that her parents weren't saving enough for the inevitable move.

"Since you know all the gossip, tell me this. Have you

seen Anders around lately?" Just saying his name aloud brought blood rushing to her cheeks, and she couldn't help picturing a future where they sat on porches together at the end of day.

"He's at Jem Gallagher's every day now. There's a big fight tomorrow, everyone's been making bets."

"He's fighting at Jem's already?" Fiona felt betrayed somehow. She knew that Anders had taken up boxing, but he never talked about it much, and it surprised her that he'd be in a fight like that, with the whole neighborhood speculating on the outcome.

"Don't act surprised. He's the best boxer around. Things keep happening even if you aren't here to see them."

"Of course. I know that. But it was only a month ago I saw him. . . ." Was it longer? Her sense of time was skewed when it came to Anders. Although she could not remember the exact day, she knew all the details—she had been carrying an armful of irises and day-old bread that the Carters would otherwise have thrown away, and he had called out to her from a doorway and insisted on carrying her spoils home. "I think you've been avoiding me," he had said with a glint in his eye, and she had hoped he meant something significant by it, and hoped he did not, for her desire for everything to be settled with Emmeline and Frederick before he kissed her again was absolute. He had asked if they could take a walk soon, saying there was something he wanted to talk over with her. And she had grabbed the bread and irises back from his arms and said yes, but that she was very busy, and it would have to wait. "He didn't mention anything about a fight."

"That's Anders Mag—doesn't brag. Lets his fists talk."

"Oh."

"He's been around, though, asking after you. . . ."

She wanted Jack to tell her more, wanted to know what he meant by that, exactly, but they had arrived home, and their mother, as though sensing her children's approach, flung open the door and ushered them inside. "Hello, Ma."

"Hello, my Fiona." Her mother drew her into her arms, and on into the front room of their first-floor flat, which was redolent of stew. "You shouldn't have," she added, as always, when Fiona handed her the envelope with that week's earnings.

The front room was the main room of the house, and always seemed crowded with wooden furniture. Her father had built the furniture himself, for their previous apartment, and when he lost the arm working for the railroad, they had been forced to move to a smaller place—he could neither make the same wages nor build furniture that would fit this room. His hair had gone white in the last year, and this made his eyes more vividly blue. "Hello, Fiona dearest," he called to her, and she went to him and kissed his forehead.

"Have you heard from the shirtwaist company again?" she asked her mother, coming around to the stove and lifting a bowl to help her ladle out their supper. Every week she expected the new landlords to have sent out eviction notices.

Her mother's eyes glistened and darted. "No," she said. "Why are you thinking of that? It may be another ten years before they build that factory, and in the meantime they are happy to have our rent. Don't frown, Fiona. Even if they do, well, perhaps you could get a job there, and then you would not be so far away from us all the time."

Fiona's chest tightened, and her thoughts became an anxious jumble. Of course she *could* get a job like that, but her family would still be out of a home, and where would they get another one, and she would make half as much in a factory, and the work would be twice as hard, and all day she would have to imagine Emmeline off somewhere in gowns from the dressmaker that cost a whole year's wages—and what kind of choice was that?

"But please, let's not talk of that now," her mother whispered. "We have so little of you as it is." Fiona looked at the wooden table, its wear less visible in lantern light; at her middle siblings, Kate and Brian, sitting expectantly; and Jack with his cap hung on the back of the chair. Upstairs, the neighbors could be heard dragging chairs up to their evening meal.

Fiona wanted to protest that they must think of the future, but decided that for this evening at least, her mother was right. Tomorrow would have its way no matter what they did. What could she do but make as much as possible with the Carters, and be ready when they had to find another place? Tonight the room smelled pleasantly of wood burning in the potbelly stove, and the lantern's flame cast everything a cozy shade. In the morning she would go to Anders—not to tell him, as she had long planned, that it was she who could make him happy, but as Emmeline's emissary. The prospect unsettled her stomach. She was frightened, and she also couldn't wait. But for now there was only this room, there was only her family. "All right," she said, setting the bowl of stew before her father. Steam rose up, bringing wetness to his eyes, and he raised his hand to give her shoulder a pat.

That night, while Fiona slept in the old room beside her sister, Kate, the city went about its ceaseless business. The barges arrived off the lake and the grain elevators began to fill up for the cold months. In the all-night churches voices surged together in hymn while the saloons filled with men who would be glad a little while, and sorry tomorrow. At half past two, a fire broke out on the South Side, and the local alderman dressed in a hurry to ring the alarm. By the time his signal came through, however, the watchman who perched high up on the courthouse cupola had already spotted the blaze through his binoculars, and guessed the location.

The watchman's name was Gabriel, and he was related to Anders Magnuson on his mother's side, and he had a natural affinity for the city map, the pattern by which the streets fit together even as they stretched out to the prairie. He was at ease on high, unlike in the neighborhood where he and Fiona and Anders grew up. There, people were rarely what they seemed—the grocer took bets, and the butcher was a murderer—and though the area was only, practically speaking, a few blocks wide and a few blocks long, it was a whole world, dense with the hundreds of lives trapped in its hovels, the alleys crooked and illogical, the rules ever-shifting. Gabriel's guess was accurate, and the Maverick Hook and Ladder Company had arrived and managed to douse the flames before they spread beyond a single building. The criminals locked up in the courthouse jail, six stories below the cupola, never even knew of the disturbance, nor did most of the city, and it was only later that the little blaze took on any significance. It was still early morning, three days before everything changed. Only afterward would people make much of the fact that there had been a fire every night that first week of October.

The hours passed peacefully and the men who lived in shanties down on the banks of the south branch went about their night fishing in the deep darkness before dawn, noting a shooting star that hung briefly against the eastern sky, and disagreeing on whether this was a good omen or bad. Morning came, much as it ever did, and Fiona woke with the same thought as everyone else in Chicago: Today was going to be like yesterday, and unreasonably hot.

Ordinarily, Fiona would have risen early and returned to the Carters' just as the cook was lighting the kitchen fires. But instead she dressed with care in her siblings' bedroom, as she would to play the part of Emmeline's maid, and walked through the neighborhood at an hour when she should have been at work a long time already. Although Jem Gallagher's was legendary—mostly as the cause of many an argument between husband and wife in the neighborhood—she had never gone herself. She wandered, trying to remember which alley it was down, her heeled boots clip-clopping against the sidewalk's wooden planks.

When she saw it, she wondered how she could have ever been unsure. The place had a flat front, no windows, and a big sign with the proprietor's name nailed above the entrance.

The black dress she wore had made her feel pretty before, but inside Jem's the fabric seemed too fine, the waist and bust too fitted, and she wished that she had not done her hair the way she sometimes did Emmeline's, in an elaborate, upswept bun with wispy waves framing her face. The row of men sitting along the bar inside Jem's saloon watched her, curling their lips, and one spit on the floor, where it was absorbed in sawdust.

"I'm looking for Anders Magnuson," she said to no one in particular.

"In the back," called the barman, not glancing up.

She hurried past the whistles and stares, down a long hallway, and emerged into a rear courtyard. Two men ran back and forth, lunging to smack a red ball against the brick face of the next building. The sweat made their shirtless backs shine, and the sound of the ball against the brick echoed over their grunting. When the bigger of the two missed, he shouted a word Fiona had grown unaccustomed to hearing.

The other man laughed, and when he turned to see where the ball went Fiona smiled at him, more than she had meant to. He was already smiling, and breathing hard.

Nobody said anything, and Fiona stood mute, eyes fixed on Anders. She tried, but failed, not to think of the night he'd kissed her. Several speechless seconds passed, and the reason she had come here at all escaped her. Then she remembered—Emmeline, of course, always Emmeline— and wondered what the famous Miss Carter would think if she saw Anders like this. The last time the three of them were together, Anders wasn't much taller than Emmeline, and almost as slender. Now his chest was broad and his jaw was square. A scar made two halves of his bottom lip, where it had been busted more than once. His arms were muscled and his tobacco-leaf hair was shaved on the sides so that it grew, brush-like, over his forehead. Only his eyes were the same, that light blue like the noon sky down at the horizon line.

"And who might this be?" said the other man. He was older, with a full beard and a belly that overhung his trousers, and he spoke with the old country accent, as though he kept all his words in his jowls.

Anders grinned. "Fiona Byrne, all dolled up."

The ball had rolled to her feet. To hide her blush, she bent to pick it up.

"Fiona, meet Jem Gallager. He's training me."

She glanced at the older man, gripped her skirts, and bent her head in a half-curtsy. "Pleased to meet you, Mr. Gallagher."

"Fine manners on that one," Jem Gallagher said in such a way that it was hard to tell if he was praising or mocking her.

Anders tilted his head. "What *are* you doing in a place like this, Miss Fiona?"

"Emmeline—"

"Emmeline?" he said, pronouncing the name slowly as though he were afraid of what it might conjure.

"Miss Carter—she sent me. She wants to see you."

"See me?" He lowered his eyes and touched the place on his lip where it had split. "Why?"

"She wants to tell you . . ." she began. She had planned what to say, but it was difficult to remember the precise words now. Anders was holding his breath, and his eyes widened while he waited for her to finish. If he cared that Emmeline was engaged, she thought her heart might just stop. "She has something she has to tell you."

"Ah. Emmeline Carter has something to tell me." In an instant, Anders lost his easy, smiling manner. His shoulders drew taut and his eyes became dark and she saw the truth in what Jack said—Anders might well be the best boxer anywhere. He had fight. "That she's engaged? I know. The whole city knows. It was in the papers."

His voice was so forceful, Fiona had to glance away. "Yes. Of course. I think she just wanted to . . ." she mumbled. She felt embarrassed by the older man's presence, over in the corner of the courtyard, but Anders seemed not to care if he overheard. "To tell you herself. Because it was always you two who were supposed to be married. . . ."

Anders was nodding, not quite in agreement. His throat worked, and she felt sorry for him. She wished he would say that was all childish nonsense, that that was all a long time ago. But he didn't. For a while he didn't say anything, and then he went on in a quiet way. "I suppose she might.

She would want that now. But it's been two years since I had a lone word from her, and she ought to have thought of that before. I've got a match tonight, so I'll tell you plain: I don't care what Emmeline wants."

"Oh." For a moment Fiona had no idea what she felt. She was only conscious of feeling presumptuous, and a little stupid, on Emmeline's behalf. She nodded stiffly, and extended her hand with the ball for him to take. "I'll tell her."

Anders's body relaxed again when he came toward her. His hand closed over hers, taking the ball, and she felt the press of his fingertips down the backs of her legs. "Tell her whatever you like. Or nothing. You, on the other hand—you are a welcome sight." He grinned, tossed the ball in a high arc, and caught it. "Though you're a hard one to get a word with."

Like that, Emmeline was out of mind—that morning's mission, the many tasks Fiona would perform over the long day ahead. All she knew was Anders, with his sharp dimples and taste for pranks; Anders who had been trying to make her smile since she was a little girl. They were just two children of the neighborhood, striving as best they could, laughing when they were able. They understood each other, and always had. With a courtly nod of his head, Anders turned back to the game. But he glanced over his shoulder, winked, and called out: "Don't you make yourself a stranger around here, Miss Byrne."

Fiona had no idea what she looked like then. His suggestion—that he had noticed her absence, and wanted more of her—caused such a riot of joy within that it was impossible to know what her outsides were up to. The best she could manage was a quick nod and a murmured "All right, then." As she fled back through Jem's, she scarcely noticed her surroundings, and when she crossed the threshold into the bright afternoon, she put her hand over her mouth to hide the smile that had spread quite involuntarily all over her face.

FIVE

The newly opened Palmer House shall soon be Chicago's choice place to strike a deal or exhibit a new gown. Eight stories, two hundred and twenty-five rooms, the gathering places impeccably decorated with Carrara marble and French chandeliers. It is not only luxurious, but also a safe haven in a combustible city. Mr. Palmer has installed fire hoses on every floor, telegraphic alarms in every room, and claims it is the only fireproof hotel in the country.
—Foley's Guide to American Hotels for Businessmen of Taste

"And for the honeymoon?" asked Bertha Palmer.

"We will go to the Riviera," Emmeline replied. "Frederick has never been to that part of France," she added hastily, to obscure the fact that she had never been anywhere.

"Very good," said Daisy Fleming, over a low murmur of approval.

The drawing room in the penthouse suite of the Palmer House, where Bertha Palmer held her afternoons, was a study in gold. The damask wallpaper was gold and the sofas and divans were gold and the carpet was a pattern of interlocking ivory and gold lilies. Bertha and her guests—ten young women whose fathers controlled railroads and stockyards and newspapers—were wearing pale day dresses, and arrayed in twos and threes across the furniture. Emmeline sat opposite them, on an upholstered wing chair, in a dress of bright blue polka-dotted chiffon with billowing sleeves and a high neck. She had never understood before this afternoon how it could flay the nerves to be the focus of so much attention.

"And where will you live?"

"When we return from Europe we plan to take a suite at one of the hotels downtown," Emmeline began. "Perhaps here." Bertha nodded encouragingly, so Emmeline pressed on: "Eventually we shall build our own house, but that will take time, and we don't yet know what part of town we prefer. The style will depend, I suppose, on what we see while we're on the continent. . . ." Emmeline had never discussed this with Freddy—she was just making it up as she went along—but the other ladies' faces lit up in admiration and approval. With every breath her voice became more sure, her plans more bold. "I intend to tour many grand estates, and learn a great deal about the decoration and maintenance of elegant homes. I don't want to make any permanent decisions before I have absorbed all Europe has to offer. I want our home to be exquisite, and we will host a lot of parties and balls, so it ought to be pleasing to the eye and senses. You must all come!"

Bertha Palmer smiled. Daisy Fleming smiled. Ada Garrison very nearly split her face with smiling. Only Cora Russell glowered.

"And the dress?" Cora asked ironically as she lifted her gold-rimmed teacup to her lips.

"My wedding dress? Oh, it's divine! I modeled it on Queen Victoria's, with heaps and heaps of lace, and bare shoulders, and a very full hoop skirt and pink trim and . . ."

"My." Cora placed her teacup in its saucer, so that it rang out like an alarm. A fraught hush came over the room. Cora's mouth twisted at the corners. With chilly delight, she continued, "Now doesn't that sound . . . *interesting.*"

Emmeline bit her lip and glanced at the others, waiting to see who would defend her against Cora's bitterness. Several seconds passed in which no one would meet her eye.

"Well." Bertha put down her plate and brushed her hands together, as though purifying them of crumbs. "You know you can't wear that."

Emmeline wasn't sure if she was actually dying, or if she just wanted to die very, very badly. "What?"

Daisy was looking at her now, and it was worse than not

being looked at. "You'll seem old, dear."

Ada's gaze had been fixed on her lap, but she lifted her eyes—one twitching a little—to meet Emmeline's. "That is a very old-fashioned style, Emmeline," she said carefully. "It was thirty years ago that Victoria was married. You really ought to have a narrower skirt nowadays."

"And a bustle." Bertha picked up the small poodle that had been sleeping at her feet. "Not a hoop."

"And the bare shoulders? Everyone will think Freddy found you in a house of New Orleans." Cora giggled. "But then, maybe he did."

"There's still time," Ada ventured, glancing at the others.

"Yes, but not much." Bertha sighed. "She must go to Mr. Polk at Field and Leiter."

"Mr. Polk, of course." Ada nodded vigorously.

Bertha clutched her dog as she addressed Emmeline. "Mr. Polk does wonderful work. He will be very put out. It will cost a great deal. But I'm afraid there's no other choice."

The ladies settled deeper into their seats. They folded their hands and lifted their chins.

"Thank goodness I found you." Emmeline forced a smile and hoped that her embarrassment didn't show too much. She tried her best to appear like an earnest student, grateful to receive the lessons of a master. "I have so much to learn from all of you!"

"You do, darling, but don't worry. We all must learn somehow." Bertha smiled magnanimously. "I will send Mr. Polk a note of introduction myself this afternoon. Do not wait till tomorrow."

"Of course not. Thank you. Thank you so very—" She broke off when she saw the figure hovering out in the hall. Fiona—good, constant Fiona. Emmeline gazed at her friend, tilting her head slightly in the direction of the other girls, with the thought that Fiona would quickly understand what a trial this all was, and give her a reassuring nod in return.

But Fiona must have interpreted Emmeline's gesture a different way. Must have thought Emmeline was summoning her. For in the next moment, she entered the parlor in a hurry.

Ten elaborate coiffures turned in the direction of the intruder, just in time to see Fiona almost stumble on an enormous potted fern in her haste to cross the floor. Too late, Emmeline remembered what she had told her friend yesterday—*"Go to Anders, and when you have news about him, find me, right away, wherever I am."* Though she willed Fiona to turn around, to disappear, she kept coming, all the way to the wing chair, where she knelt and began to whisper in Emmeline's ear.

"I've talked to him. He already knew about the engagement, because it was in the papers. So you don't have to worry, it's all right with him."

Bertha and her friends watched, their faces frozen in surprise at this interruption. Only Cora made an expression. She appeared quite happy, which was how Emmeline knew what a bad blunder it was. In the ensuing silence, Emmeline felt her stomach drop, and drop again. This afternoon had gone so wrong so fast, and she felt shocked, and rather snubbed, by Anders's indifference to her message. Who was he, anyway, to turn *her* down?

Meanwhile, Fiona's face bore a pleased, expectant look, as though she were waiting to be told what a good job she had done.

"Fiona Byrne," Emmeline said with a dismissive wave of her hand. "This is quite inappropriate. Mrs. Palmer has not invited you in. When I am ready to leave I will call for you from the lobby."

It took all of Emmeline's power to turn away, toward the small gold side table where she had placed her teacup, and, with a show of casualness, pick it up. She took a sip, feigning that none of this had disturbed her much, and gave the party a rueful smile.

"What was I just saying? Oh yes, how much I need your help. I *do* apologize. And you see it is not just me but my maid who will be needing lessons from you in style and grace. She begs your pardons."

To her relief, the company twittered with amusement.

Fiona was on the other side of the room by then, and Emmeline was glad she did not have to look at her. It pained her to speak sharply to her old friend, as though ordering her about, and she hoped Fiona understood. For Emmeline was only doing what she had to do. Only keeping up appearances, after this disaster of an afternoon.

Later that night, lying unable to sleep in the darkness of her bedroom, Emmeline clasped Anders's claddagh as though it might tell her what to do. She wished someone, or something, would. Since she had moved to Dearborn, she had conducted every day with a single purpose, which was to transform herself into what she was finally on the verge of becoming—a young lady of fashion and position—but now, propped up against goose-down pillows, with her hair brushed and bound in braids, she felt directionless.

Throughout her education in walking, talking, etiquette, and dress, Fiona had been her loyal companion. In fact, Fiona had always been better at understanding what was and wasn't allowed in polite society, and who was who. Sometimes, when Emmeline's interest in the interminable rules slipped, she would keep on just because she could sense that it pleased Fiona, sense that Fiona was charmed by all the decorum, all the million little ways a lady crafted her persona. But that afternoon, when it really mattered, Emmeline had failed as a specimen of fine manners, and

Fiona had made the scene worse. On the ride home from Field & Leiter they had not spoken, and after dinner Emmeline had claimed headache, and said she would draw her own bath.

And so she had been left alone, with no one to talk to, trying in vain to understand Anders's message. Perhaps the ring had no meaning. Perhaps Anders hadn't cared for her anymore already, when she left the neighborhood. It was only a childish romance between them anyway, a fairy tale they'd told to entertain each other. What else could he have meant when he told Fiona it was all right with him that Emmeline was engaged? Anyway, it *should* be all right. Freddy was the ideal fiancé, and her life was exactly as she'd worked so hard to make it. Acting as though Anders had never existed should be easy. She twisted in the sheets, pulling the covers over her head, and wished that he never had. But that was when she saw the faces of Bertha Palmer's "best girls," lined up in judgment of her, smirking at the wedding gown she'd dreamed of since she was a little girl.

She threw herself to the other side of the bed, but she found that she was still holding tight to the ring, and that her fist was unwilling to let it go. She thought that if she only went to sleep, her palm would open, she would lose it in the sheets, one of the maids would shake it out in the morning, and she would be done with that part of her life. But the more she tried to sleep, the more relentless memories of Anders became: the sensation of his lips after he put the ring on her finger, the sweet promises they used to make to each other, that first taste of love. What a rush it had been to suspect and then know that he loved her, and to feel her own heart seeking him at all hours of the day. She had seen her own beauty for the first time reflected in Anders's face, and she felt sad thinking he might never look at her like that again.

It had been love—maybe it wasn't now, but it had been. That was the only explanation for why her mind wouldn't drift to sleep, why her feet were carrying her across the floor, why she struck a match to ignite the gas lamp in her dressing room, the better to choose what to wear. She chose the cerise blouse with the loose sleeves and the fitted neck and wrists, which showed all the ways her figure had changed since last she saw Anders, and the long, dark skirt that skimmed her body like a mermaid's tail. Her hair looked lovely already in its careless pile, so she pinned a few strands and then went down the servants' stairs, holding her boots so that they wouldn't clack. She was lacing them, perched on the edge of the narrow bed in Fiona's small room, when Fiona stirred and woke.

There was a question in her eyes, so Emmeline spoke in a rush: "Remember those summer nights when no one cared very much what we did? We'd go wandering with Anders, down alleys and over rooftops? Shouldn't we have a night like that—now, before everything changes forever?"

Emmeline could see that Fiona remembered those nights, for she shuddered a little at the memory—how Anders would lay down a board between buildings and they would dash from one to another, thrilled by their own fear. But Fiona must still have felt sore over the way Emmeline had spoken about her that afternoon at Bertha's, because she seemed determined to tell her friend no.

"Come on, it will be fun," Emmeline pleaded.

Fiona shook her head, and gestured at the walls as though they might be listening. "We couldn't possibly," she whispered. "Anyway, Anders is boxing tonight."

Perhaps, on another night, Fiona's reluctance would have held Emmeline back. Would have seemed sensible, and provoked her own fears. But she was already dressed up in such a way that she would have felt quite sorry for herself if she had to go back upstairs to bed, and she was determined to find Anders, to see his face and understand what he had meant to her life. It seemed suddenly like the only thing of any importance.

"Well that's even better," Emmeline replied, not bothering to lower her voice. "We can go cheer him on," she explained with a grin, and Fiona didn't have an answer for that.

After all the years of rule learning, and rule following, and perfect dressing, and perfect walking, Emmeline couldn't help but be a little proud of herself for doing a very unlady-like thing, and going to a saloon. The skin of her face tingled and her heartbeat was jumpy with the notion that she was really here, inside Jem's—which was the kind of place a girl who gets engaged to Frederick Arles Tree was absolutely, without a doubt, not supposed to be.

The long, narrow barroom was frenetic with color and noise. Every corner was full of men, their shouting and their smells. They had fearsome faces, ruddy with drink in the low light, and they were not afraid to stare and cluck. They probably weren't afraid of anything. They sprawled against the bar, shoving at one another in a way that was half play, half not. A current of fear went up and down her spine. She hadn't felt so awake in days.

"Aren't they all so very interesting-looking?" Emmeline whispered excitedly, as she held tight to Fiona and returned the bald stares of the patrons.

Fiona did not seem quite so sure. At the entrance to Jem's, she had held back once again, saying they wouldn't be permitted inside. "Come on," she had whispered, grasp-ing for Emmeline's shirtsleeve. "We shouldn't have come. The cab's still waiting for us. We can go home now and nobody will notice we've gone. They'll never let us in, any-way."

But Emmeline, alive with the energy of the old neigh-borhood at night, had given the big bear of a man who guarded the door her most persuasive smile along with a ludicrous story about how they were Anders Magnuson's long-lost sisters, and a moment later they were ushered inside.

As they moved down the bar, Emmeline whispered, "I can't believe that worked!" And when she heard no response, added: "I feel a little brave, don't you?" and gave Fiona her brightest eyes. She knew Fiona would see how fun this all was, if only Emmeline could show her.

"A little," Fiona allowed.

"Thank you," Emmeline whispered. "Thank you for coming with me even though I know you'd rather be sleeping. I had a terrible afternoon and if I didn't do something absolutely bad I might have gone crazy, and I'd never have had the courage if you hadn't agreed to come along, too. Someday, when I am Mrs. Frederick Tree and do nothing but host afternoons, this will make such a funny story, and we'll laugh remembering it. Won't we? Do you forgive me?"

"Yes." Fiona sighed. "It's all right, I forgive you."

"About earlier, too?"

"Yes, it's all right about earlier, too."

Emmeline smiled, and knew they were on the same side again, the way they had been since they were little girls.

The energy of the place was wild, and it carried them back, back, through one long corridor and another, past small rooms in which men played cards on bare tables. They moved in the direction of a thundering crowd, until they arrived in a cavernous space. It was like a great barn, although much larger than any barn Emmeline had ever seen. Men perched in the rafters, the better to watch the frenzy below. The shouting was so savage it seemed to clamor from within her own skull.

A cheer went up, and everyone pressed in toward the center.

"Get up, Mag!" someone cried out.

"Kill him!" called another.

"Come on," Emmeline urged, putting her shoulders against the thick of bodies. Hundreds were jockeying for position by the raised platform, which was crudely built of unpainted wood, and cordoned with ropes.

Then, suddenly, she caught a glimpse of him.

If she had passed him on the street, she might not have known him, for he was broader, and his features had toughened since last she saw him. But in the ring, it was obvious that this was the first boy to whisper she was pretty and hold her hand with a tenderness that still made her heart light when she remembered it. He moved in the same spirited way he had then. He was as handsome as before, and he seemed even more himself in the ring—darting, compact, and fierce. His chest was bare above the waist, and he circled his opponent with fists hovering close to his face. Once she saw him, Emmeline had a strong notion never to take her eyes off him again.

The other fighter was almost a giant. Much larger, and older, too. He had a drum for a chest and a great scarred melon of a head, and he bellowed when he swung.

Emmeline elbowed the man next to her. "Who's winning?" she asked.

The man clucked at the sight of a girl amid that rugged company, and his eyes narrowed lasciviously. But his interest slipped when another roar went up. Not glancing away from the fight again, he replied, "Crowd favors the young Swede. Anders Mag, he's the house's boy. Kid Curley will win, though. He's old, but he knows how to finish a fight."

"You must be mistaken," Fiona, at her elbow, replied hotly, and Emmeline was glad to see her as fiery and protective of her friends as she used to be. "See how fast Anders moves!"

The man didn't acknowledge the outburst, but it was plain that Anders was the more energetic of the two. The older fighter seemed to tire with every lunge. He'd grunt and a shower of sweat would catch the gaslight. Even if his fists did find Anders, they lost their force by the time they reached his body. All the while, Anders's eyes were bright as mirrors, his torso glistening from exertion, his concentration absolute. How lovely, Emmeline thought, to be the object of such concentration.

Another round passed in the same way. And then for a moment Anders's attention seemed to drift. He slowed, gazed into the distance. He seemed almost to offer himself. Kid Curley seized the opportunity, and threw a hard punch that sent Anders staggering backward until he fell against the ropes. His body was listless—that taut, focused quality gone in an instant. He slid to the floor, blood mixing with sweat on his forehead. Emmeline blinked, not believing her own eyes. A moment before, he had seemed capable of anything.

The way the crowd shouted and booed, they must have thought he was finished. His opponent raised his arms in the air, bellowing and strutting for the onlookers. Anders had been so fleet, and now . . . Emmeline's heart shrank when she saw him brought low. He was still as the dead.

Fiona was at her ear, whispering to Emmeline they should go. But Emmeline barely heard her. She couldn't let this be the last she saw of him, bloodied and beaten. She lunged forward, grasping the rope with both hands. "Get up, Anders!" she cried. "Get up!"

Time became slow. He wiped sweat away with the back of his arm, lifted his head, and squinted into the crowd. Someone shouted "Maggot!" but it was unlikely Anders heard. He was staring at Emmeline, transfixed, as if wondering if it were really her, or if he'd been hit hard enough to have visions. Emmeline leaned into the ring, her gaze seeking his, the rope scratchy in her palms, her chest rising and falling. She knew then what it was to be looked at, really looked at, by a man. After a few seconds—it could not have been longer, though it seemed forever—Anders got back on his feet, and beckoned to Kid Curley.

The crowd roared when they saw him dancing again, light and taunting. Emmeline smiled and cheered, never looking away from Anders—she supposed Fiona must have felt the same as she did, delighted to see him in the fight once again, but she didn't want to stop watching him for even a second.

Now Anders seemed amused by his opponent's swings, and they rarely met even his fists. His face was bloody, but it did not trouble him. Once, he appeared to glance in Emmeline's direction with a grin and a wink. Watching his quick, sure movements, the way he ducked and swayed, she felt she was seeing life at last. His lean, forceful body and playful prancing made her think that the world of drawing rooms and balls and the right dressmaker and the wrong part of town was just a silly game. Only he seemed real.

In a few rounds, Anders had his opponent. He was too fast, and finally Kid Curley could only cower behind his gloves and be pummeled at his belly and his ribs. He attempted another charge, but his strength was spent, and he only made himself an easier target. Anders hit him five times in rapid succession, at the jaw and either side of the head.

A brief, stunned silence hung over Jem's as the big man crashed, like a great tree succumbing to the ax, and sprawled across the floor of the ring. Anders hovered above him, watchful while his opponent tried and failed to get up. The crowd erupted in agitation, howling and swaying. Everywhere people were shouting Anders's name, and Emmeline was one of them. She was trying to get Anders to look at her again, but the crush of bodies was stronger now. A fight broke out between two groups nearby—Emmeline caught a glimpse of Fiona's horrified face, before she was pushed in the other direction.

Emmeline felt the warmth of Anders's gaze, and she turned to find his eyes. They were as fierce and blue and focused as they had been in the fight. But he was closer now, having slipped through the ropes, and into the crowd. Her breath stuck and her lips parted, and she knew for certain that Father's carefully laid plan for her life was in trouble.

SIX

Why do the young men of this city submit to backroom contests,
where for scant prize money they may be near beaten to death?
When asked, they grin and say it is an ancient honor. I think it is
because only in the fight game do they learn their own might.
Only when they labor against a worthy opponent do they
finally find their true selves.
—*"The Sport,"* Chicago Crier, *October 5, 1871*

That moment, when Anders looked into the crowd and recognized Emmeline and seemed to come back to life, had rendered Fiona frozen, immobile. Although in reality it must have passed quickly, it had seemed to go on forever and ever, and Fiona felt that she was standing outside a glass case, hearing nothing yet forced to watch as Anders and Emmeline gazed at each other like the only two people in the world. Now the room was full of sound and fury, but Fiona was still cold, and having trouble making sense of what was happening around her. They were fighting, she knew. All around her, men were fighting, but she was oddly disconnected from the goings on, and she watched with detachment as Emmeline was pushed backward into the tumult and then knocked out of sight.

A mean part of Fiona flickered and rejoiced. Then she dropped the feeling, like a pan hot off the range that would otherwise scorch her. She could not really wish any harm to Emmeline—they had been friends too long. And anyway, she had no choice but to help her, and get them out of there as quickly as possible.

All afternoon Fiona had felt small and unsure of her place in the world, reliving that incident at the Palmer, feeling by turns ashamed of what she had done and indignant at being scolded for only doing what she had been told to do. It had been all silence between the girls on their return trip to Dearborn, and afterward they had gone to their separate realms. To be publicly humiliated in that way had smarted, but Fiona couldn't allow herself to be angry. Being angry with Emmeline never helped anything. Whenever Emmeline treated her like a servant, she was brought back to the reality of things: how precarious her situation was, how much she depended on the Carters' largesse. If Emmeline was bruised on the floor of Jem's, or somehow marked in any way, it was Fiona who would be in trouble.

She pushed through the bodies, and saw the hem of Emmeline's skirt pinned to the floor by a man's shoe. None of the men shouting and shoving seemed to notice the girl trapped underfoot. The realization that Emmeline would be crushed if Fiona did not get to her soon brought some sensation back to her limbs, and she yelled for the crowd to part. But before she could reach her friend, a man with a sly, punch-colored face had grabbed Emmeline by the shoulder joint and pulled her to her feet.

"Hello, pretty," the man growled as he pawed at her blouse.

Fiona, hot with sudden fury, threw herself between them and put her arm around Emmeline's waist to get her away. "Hurry," Fiona said.

They held hands as they rushed through the warren of rooms, not stopping to notice the disturbances swirling in every corner of the saloon. When they emerged, short of breath, onto the dark street, it was as though they'd stepped out of a forge and into winter. The cabbie was waiting, just as they had told him to, standing beside his vehicle and straining to make out the news from the crowd spilling through the front door.

"How'd it end?" he asked the girls as they approached.

For a moment, Fiona wasn't sure what he was asking. She could only wonder how the story of Fiona and Anders and Emmeline would end. But Emmeline, quick as ever, understood what he had meant.

"Anders Magnuson just knocked out Kid Curley," Emmeline replied. A moment before, she had been scared silent, but now she seemed quite proud of being able to deliver a line like that.

"Are they celebrating?" he asked.

"They must be!"

Fiona glanced over her shoulder. She would have thought anyone with eyes would have favored Anders—he feinted and jabbed so beautifully—but if that was so, they had a funny way of rejoicing. There were no embraces, only shoving, cursing, drinking. The patrons on the street were causing such a commotion that the driver had to hold his horses by the reins.

"Come on." Fiona climbed into the cab, gesturing for Emmeline to follow.

"But what about Anders?" Emmeline asked.

Fiona leaned through the cab's open door, reaching for her friend. "If we don't leave now," she said, "we might not get another chance."

She was right. Emmeline must know she was right. A riot was brewing and might soon block the streets, and then they'd never escape this place.

And yet Emmeline drifted, staring off in the direction from which they had come. The night was full of coal fires and braying drunks, and other things that had no place in the fantastical life that she—that they both—had worked so hard to make come true.

"Emmy," Fiona urged.

She sensed her friend's hesitation, but knew that in another minute logic would win her over and they would be in the carriage, and Anders would be left behind for now. Maybe Emmeline would never see him again. She'd be married in a few days, after all, and her life would be very different forever after. And so it might have been, if Anders hadn't appeared just then. He was wedged into a narrow space between two houses, a few buildings down from Jem's. An oversize coat was thrown over his shoulders, and a hat was tipped to his brow. None of that mattered; she would have known him anywhere, at any distance.

So, too, did Emmeline.

Fiona watched her friend dart in his direction, as though watching something precious she had dropped down a well disappear from her grasp forever.

As Emmeline approached, Anders withdrew into the shadow. Once again, there seemed to be a pane of glass between Fiona and her friends, and she watched with wide, fixed eyes as they spoke to each other for the first time in years. They were too far for Fiona to hear, really, but she had gooseflesh and her senses became extraordinarily acute and every word they said was somehow gratingly loud.

"I only wanted to see if it really was you," said the boy who Fiona had longed for for months, who had been her companion since she was a little girl. But his words were not for her.

"It is," Emmeline replied. "You know it is. How did you get in there? Come out." She was offering her hand, and Fiona felt some small relief that he did not take it. "We'll go for a walk and you can tell me everything."

"I can't."

"Why?" Her eyes sparkled. "You have a girl to meet?"

"No, but—if I'm seen on this street tonight, I'm dead."

Emmeline smiled as though he was joking, but then her smile fell away. Their heads bent in collusion, and Fiona could no longer hear, although she felt desperate to know what was passing between them. She couldn't feel her face and for all she knew the blood stopped moving in her veins. Then, suddenly, Emmeline turned and came rushing back.

"Can you drive those horses hard?" she asked the cabbie as she scrambled onto the bench seat beside Fiona.

"Sure," he replied proudly.

"Do it," she said. "Now."

Fiona searched her friend's face for an explanation of this strange and dramatic order, but Emmeline was looking away, to the place where Anders was hiding in shadow. "Hold on," she said. When the cab rolled into motion, she flung the door open again. Anders was already running.

Running as though his life depended on it. And when he caught up with them he grabbed the roof of the cab, and swung himself inside.

"Hey, Mag!" someone back at Jem's yelled, and Emmeline and Fiona twisted toward the back window. The mass of patrons began to break apart and chase after their cab.

"That was him!" said another.

A group of men had separated from the crowd. There were five of them, running in a line as though into battle. The one in the middle wore a long, flapping leather coat from which he drew a pistol. Emmeline covered her ears and closed her eyes, but when he fired into the air, the shot was so loud it probably didn't matter. Fiona felt its reverberation through her entire body. The cab turned a corner and hurtled north at a breakneck pace.

They passed several blocks, and the men could not keep up. It must have been close to midnight, and they turned again onto an empty street. Fiona said, "I don't think they can catch us now."

Anders had his face in his hands. At the sound of Fiona's voice, he lifted his head and put his elbows on his knees, but his gaze remained vacant. As if realizing that he was in the company of ladies, he hastily removed his hat, and they saw what had happened to his face. He was still bleeding at the temple, one of his eyes was swollen, and a purple streak was visible on his cheek. Fiona crumbled inside to see him like that. None of them spoke for a while, and the cab rocked and rushed on.

"Emmeline, Emmeline what have you done to me?" he murmured finally.

When she heard Anders say Emmeline's name that way, Fiona wondered how much more of this she could take. She fixated on her hands, which she saw had gone ahead and made tight fists without her knowledge.

"Have I done something?"

"No. Nothing. I suppose you didn't mean to."

"I didn't mean to what? I'm sorry if—"

"You came. Even though you're such a lady now, you came to the old neighborhood to see me fight. . . ." He shook his head, and lowered it back into the cradle of his hands.

"Anders," Fiona interrupted. She was desperate for him to cease that kind of talk. If he kept on, she felt that not only her heart but her whole body would cease to function. "Who were those men?"

"Gamblers. They bet against me, and they're angry I won."

"But aren't you supposed to try to win?" Emmeline blurted.

"They had a reason to think I'd lose." Anders raised his head again but he still wouldn't look precisely at either of them, and he had difficulty getting out what he said next.

"They paid me to lose. To throw the fight. I promised a man named Gil Bryce I'd be knocked out, and how, and he bet who knows how much on Kid Curley. Only, when you cheered for me—I hadn't seen you in so long, and I couldn't stand the idea of you watching me go down."

"Oh, Anders." Emmeline's eyes had darkened to mysterious pools. "I'm so sorry, I—I didn't mean to . . ." The cab had slowed, approaching the State Street Bridge. Soon they would be in the North Division again, and Fiona knew she should be glad that they were here, glad that Anders was safe. But she wished that he were not so close to Emmeline when she did that particular trick with her eyes. "You'll have to come home with us and stay the night. Fiona, you'll help, won't you? There must be someplace in that big house where we can hide him."

A sound like a lament escaped Fiona, and she covered her mouth.

Nobody spoke as they rolled over the river. "Fiona?" Emmeline prompted.

A few moments passed and Fiona murmured in assent, although she couldn't be sure of the exact words, for Anders met her gaze finally, and she saw his injuries, and she forgot to feel sorry for herself. She loved him still, and only wanted him to be safe. No matter how he spoke of Emmeline, Fiona had to do everything in her power to help him, help him no matter what it cost her.

★ ★ ★

It was a night of restless sleep and strange noises in the Carter household. No rainfall had been reported that week, and the thermometer at three p.m. had shown 83 degrees. Winds from the southwest were recorded at twenty miles an hour, and it cried under the eaves, waking Georgie, the newest and youngest of Mrs. Pelham the cook's assistants. She found that she could not fall back asleep, and that her mind kept returning to the remaining third of the yellow cake with lemon icing that had been served at the Wednesday luncheon for Miss Carter and her betrothed, and which she knew was still in the cold pantry, covered with a thin cloth. The cake had been decorated with clementine supremes—Georgie had been the one who supremed all those clementines, so it was only natural the dessert would live in her thoughts. The hour was late, and she could hear Mrs. Pelham snoring through the thin wall, and she figured it was now or never.

Having cut herself a modest slice, Georgie perched on the tiled counter, and paused to savor the cake's pretty color and elaborate decoration. Her mouth curved in happiness imaging how it would taste on her tongue. Then a less happy thought occurred to her, which was Cook's wrath if she should be discovered. Georgie set down the plate, figuring she could contemplate matters a moment, but could certainly not un-eat the cake. Cook might tell Miss Lupin, the housekeeper, and Miss Lupin might tell Mr. Carter or his daughter, Miss Carter. In the second case, Georgie thought she would come out all right—for Emmeline was generally kind to the servants, and was liked by them, for she had a flair for the delightful, and always appreciated their attempts to please her. Then Georgie remembered Miss Carter's lady's maid, who was unpopular with the rest of the staff, for though she was no better than the rest of them, she sometimes ate fine meals with the young miss in her quarters. *She* probably had cake all the time. Georgie picked up her plate, thinking how unfair it was that Fiona should be given so much, and set it down, remembering that she was not afforded the same privileges, and had had difficulty securing even this position.

It was strange that Fiona should have entered Georgie's musings just then, for only a few minutes before, Fiona had passed directly by where she was sitting, carrying a bowl of warm water and a set of clean men's clothes, feeling on the contrary that she was never given very much at all.

In the greenhouse, which had seemed the only logical place on the property to hide a fugitive, the atmosphere was tense and warm and melancholy. Overgrown plants crawled the walls, their tendrils spreading against the glass roof, while others had gone brown and dusty for lack of water. Emmeline stood by the entrance, her hand resting on a wilted potted palm.

"Anders." Fiona's voice quavered over the name, even though she had meant to sound so steady. They both appeared slightly startled, as though they'd forgotten she had gone to fetch clothes for Anders and a cloth to clean his cuts. "Does it hurt?"

In the dimness, motionless and washed by shadow, his bruises did not show so much. He appeared peaceful, like the Anders she remembered, resting until some mischief occurred to him, something fun that they must all do together, right away, before any more time got wasted. But he shifted forward, and she saw how puffy and purple his eye was, how his strong torso hunched over his knees in moody contemplation, how wrecked he was by everything.

"I'm fine."

"You look awful," she said.

"Don't you go sparing my feelings, now, Fiona," he replied, and she couldn't help but laugh at that. He, too, made a sound like a laugh and said, "Anyway, I've been hit worse. Is everything quiet inside? I suppose it'd be big trouble if Mr. Carter found out his daughter went to a prizefight, wouldn't it?"

Fiona stepped away from the entrance, and put the bowl of warm water down on the worktable, trying not to feel wounded by his worrying over Emmeline instead of her. She focused on arranging the clothes—she had found them in the laundry, and guessed they were Malcolm's—in a neat pile. "They didn't notice we were gone—they must not have, or Mr. Carter would've raised the hue and cry." *And I'd be out of a job*, Fiona wanted to say. *I'd be on the street, and letting my whole family down*. But she didn't say that. She took the clean cloth she'd brought from the house and dipped it in the bowl. "There are so many strangers here this week, I don't think you'll be noticed" was what she said instead. Nobody had been in the greenhouse since Mr. Carter put in a standing daily order with Harold's, the fashionable downtown florist. "So many builders and cooks and waiters, I mean. For the wedding." She hated herself for saying it that way—harsh, as though trying to make a point—and her eyes swung to Emmeline and then back in Anders's direction.

"Oh." His blue gaze rose to meet hers. In the moonlight, he had the aspect of a statue in a garden coming to life. He smiled in the old way, off to one side, and his stomach contracted with a mirthless chuckle. She liked looking at his face, even as it was now, and she wanted to go on looking at it until she'd memorized how all his features fit together. "Yes, the wedding."

"It's this Sunday . . ." she began.

"But who can think about that now," Emmeline cut in, and came to the worktable, and took the cloth out of Fiona's hands. "After tonight. Everything that happened tonight.

Anders . . . what *did* happen tonight?"

In the silence that followed they could hear the wind rattling the panes of the walls. "You saved my life tonight."

For a moment, Fiona thought he meant her, but then she realized that "you" was probably both her and Emmeline. Or maybe just Emmeline. After all, it was Emmeline who had been brave, Emmeline's quick thinking that got him out of the neighborhood. She felt embarrassed for caring—when all that really mattered was that he was safe—and wiped her damp palms on her skirt.

"I don't know how you go out there, knowing someone could hit you and hit you and hit you until . . ." Emmeline was saying as she squeezed the water from the rag, crossed the room to where he sat, and pressed it against his temple. "How can you stand the pain?"

"Oh, it doesn't hurt the way you'd think it would. There's so much fury. You feel it, all right. But every time you get hit, you want to hit back. You feel what you'll do to the other man, almost more than what he's done to you."

"Does it hurt now?" Fiona asked.

He gave a rueful smile. "Yes," he allowed. "But don't be wise, you'll make me smile, and it hurts worse when I smile."

Emmeline glanced over her shoulder at Fiona—a warning look. "Are they rough men?" she asked, her attention fixing itself once again on Anders. "The gamblers, I mean."

"Yeah." Anders shifted. "Pretty rough. They'll keep searching for me. When they find me, they'll . . ."

None of them wanted to hear how that sentence ended. "Do you need money so bad?" Emmeline prodded.

"The money was so I could leave."

"Leave?" Emmeline's voice rose in shock, but Fiona was surprised she could say anything at all. She herself could not have managed any sound. She felt as though she'd been hit, hit like Anders hit his opponent at Jem's, and for several seconds it was impossible to get air into her lungs. "Leave and go where?"

"Anywhere, as long as it isn't here. I can't stand it here anymore."

"You *can't* go!" Emmeline exclaimed with sudden passion.

"No? How could I stay? Everyone is gone, now. My mother, and then Father walked off one day, and my brother is drunk so often he might as well not be here. I'd rather be anywhere . . . New York, San Francisco, New Orleans, anywhere with fights. Once I heard about the wedding, there was no reason for me to be here anymore. Even Fiona began to act as though I were already gone, as though I were nothing."

"But—" The pain in Fiona's throat was such that it was hard to form words. Was that all he had wanted to tell her? That he was leaving, and it was all because he couldn't stand to be in the same city where Emmeline was marrying someone else? "But I didn't want you to leave."

"Now, after what I've done—now I have to. It's dangerous for you, too, if I stay here. Both of you."

Fiona wasn't entirely sure what Anders had just said, because after he spoke he flung off his coat and the short pants he'd worn in the ring, and stepped into the trousers Fiona had brought for him. The thought that for a moment he had been almost naked made her mind fuzzy, her body light. She concentrated on keeping herself steady, while he plucked the shirt from the table, and, with nimble fingers, buttoned it from the collar down, and tucked it into the trousers. When he was dressed, he folded up his coat and put it on the table.

"Will you get rid of that? I can't take it with me—I've worn it all over the neighborhood, someone might recognize me."

Fiona's mind was a jumble—Anders, so close, yet threatening to leave; the way he'd spoken of Emmeline, the sorrowful way he hung his head. It was too much to make sense of.

"Go on," Emmeline, on the other side of Anders, said.

"What?" Fiona replied stupidly.

"Didn't you hear Anders? Please take the coat away."

The imperious tone snapped Fiona to attention. "If your father should wake now—" she began.

"Fiona Byrne, you are not here to serve Father," Emmeline interrupted, stepping between Fiona and Anders. "If you are my true friend, you will let me have a moment with Anders. He says he is going away forever, and if he is going away forever, I must be able to talk to him, just a little while, alone."

Fiona nodded mechanically, and stepped past Emmeline and wrapped her arms around Anders's middle. Her body heaved with the effort not to cry, although he felt solid as a mountain. Her head was noisy with a thousand contradictory thoughts, but a clear voice in her ear whispered, *Tell him, you will not get another chance.* His arms and torso were so strong and real, she couldn't believe he would go. That he would not always be here. But soon he would be gone, and there was no stopping him. He was right about there being no other way. Nothing good would come of his staying here.

Here his life was in danger.

Here he'd always belong to Emmeline.

The circle of his arms tightened, pulling her against his chest. "Goodbye, Fiona," he said, and released his hold.

"Good night," Emmeline said pointedly.

Fiona felt awkward, thick of tongue and dense of body. She knew she was supposed to leave now but seemed to have forgotten how to go about it. Inside Fiona was a chaos that frightened her. She feared that if she didn't get control of this riot of emotion, it would be plain on her face how she really felt, and the last little shards of her dignity, the few things she had left to be proud of, would all be taken from her, too.

Emmeline blinked.

Anders put his hand on his hip.

Fiona dug her fingernail into the soft flesh of her palm to distract from the painful tightness in her throat. Finally, she realized that if she hesitated another moment, she would begin to sob, and it would be obvious why. With that thought, and a forceful directive to her feet to move fast, she withdrew.

In the kitchen, Georgie had finished her cake, and it was just as cool and sweet and lemony as she had hoped. She was licking her fork when she heard the door slam, and her heart leapt with the fear that she had been discovered. But her fear became relief when she recognized Fiona, and then changed again into a kind of cruel satisfaction, for Fiona was crying. Or at least trying very hard not to. Georgie did not wonder over the reason for the silent, gulping sobs, but assumed they were likely well-deserved. Then she had another notion—that she had been given a gift of sorts, if only she could discover how to use it. For the information that Fiona was going around at night acting strange was surely worth something, to somebody.

Fiona, for her part, did not notice the girl sitting in the kitchen, too consumed was she with her own sorrow. She had lost so much, so quickly, that she hardly knew herself, and only hoped that she could manage to keep her sobs quiet enough that none of the other staff would hear her. That no one would guess what had passed in the night, and thus cause her to lose her job, her dignity, along with her best friend and her love—to lose everything at once.

SEVEN

Emmeline Magnuson. Emmeline Carter Magnuson.
Mrs. Anders Magnuson.
—Diary of Emmeline Carter, May 16, 1869

Through the smudged glass, Emmeline watched Fiona close the back door that led into the kitchen of the big house. She felt relieved that her friend was gone, although she wasn't entirely sure why. The night had been wonderful and terrible, but she couldn't figure why *Fiona* should be taking it so hard. She wasn't the one who'd caught a glimpse of her first love, on the day before being married to one of the most eligible men in the city. It wasn't she who was driven witless with memories, she who was suddenly presented with impossible choices.

"You shouldn't talk to her that way," Anders said.

Emmeline turned around. The coat, which Emmeline had told Fiona to take away, was still lying on the table. His face was half his own, and half botched with the punches he had taken. Although the swelling and bruising was almost monstrous, the overall effect made him appear somehow more handsome.

Before she could think what to say, Anders had bowed his head, picked up her hand, and brushed his lips across her skin. "Goodbye, my Emmeline," he said, and went through the corridor of browning plants, through the door, and away without once looking back.

Emmeline felt that her breath had been taken from her. How could he go, like that, after all these years, with so few words? Didn't he want to know who she was now, and what she had been through? Didn't he want to tell her the same? She knew that she had caused the trouble he was in, and hated herself for it. But he had said all manner of contradictory things, seemed to adore her and be glad of her visit at one moment, and angry about it the next, and why had he said that about Fiona? He of all people should know that they were true friends, no matter the protocols of mistress and maid that they now observed.

Let him go, she instructed herself, with a stern inner finger wag. *He is the past and Freddy is the future.*

But Anders had only been gone a few moments, and she already felt stifled to find herself once again alone, richly dressed, waiting around to be married. She wanted the exhilaration of watching him in the ring, the mad longing she'd felt when she saw him across the alley in the old neighborhood, the rush of his eyes steady upon her. She wanted the thrill of realizing that his boyish crush had become something far more significant, all those years ago.

Stay, she admonished. But no thoughts about what she should do could match the wild, helpless feeling that rose whenever she realized that every second carried Anders farther away from her. Her hand still tingled where his lips had brushed the skin, and the sensation ferried her into the past, straight to the era when his every glance told her she was the most beautiful girl in the world. She grabbed his coat, pulling it over her shoulders to cover the bright blouse she had chosen earlier, and hurried out past the garden shed, the stables, the backhouses where the male servants lived, and onto Clark Street.

Murky darkness spread between the mansions, wherever the flickering gas streetlamps did not reach. Those circles of light she tried to avoid. Although the windows she passed were dark, she knew one sleepless neighbor lighting a candle might glance out their window and see the most talked-about bride of the season on the streets, wearing a strange man's coat. She tried to move in a casual, inconspicuous way, but when she saw no sign of Anders she began to panic.

She ran four more blocks before she saw his silhouette,

and opened her mouth to shout his name.

As it happened, she didn't have to. Perhaps he heard her, or otherwise he knew all along that she would follow. At the corner he stopped, turned, lifted his chin—as though gauging an adversary—and fixed her under his gaze. After that she slowed her pace, pulled the coat tight around her body. By the time she reached him she had managed to summon a little of the ladylike dignity she had tried so hard to acquire. If she could only find a way for them to begin again somehow, she thought he would remember all the sweetness that had once been between them, and stay still with her a little while. Stay with her long enough to know what was, what ought to be, between them now.

"Well, if it isn't Anders Magnuson," she said—gaily, as though they were meeting now by chance—"it seems you've become quite the boxer."

Despite everything, a smile flickered at the corners of his mouth. "I suppose you're an expert, Miss Emmeline," he replied. "In boxing."

"Oh, yes," she answered, walking toward him with a slow, rocking gait. "Any given evening you might find me in the saloons."

"Then it's all a fantasy to sell newspapers?" Anders went on, picking up her joking tone. She was relieved to hear the lightness in his voice again, relieved that the spell of seriousness that had hung over them in the greenhouse was broken. "That you're a lady of fashion now, soon to be married in style."

"You'll find the truth is rather more sordid." Emmeline paused and posed, arching a brow. "I've become quite tough, really."

Anders laughed and sighed and pulled his hand over his mouth, and looked at her again with an expression that was half wonderment and half despair. "Why did you come? Why tonight? I almost forgot you, you know."

"Did you want to forget me?" Emmeline frowned. "That would be sad. I couldn't, you know. Forget you. That's why I went tonight. Because I couldn't forget."

"Oh."

"Would you rather I hadn't?"

His answer was a long time coming, and his eyes flashed with some unspoken memory. "I'd rather you didn't act like I never was. I'd rather I didn't learn you were getting married from a four-days-old newspaper somebody left around when I was in the country training. I wish I hadn't busted my hand punching a wall that night. I wish you'd visited sooner. I wish . . . I wish you weren't more beautiful now. I didn't think that could be. But indeed you are."

"Oh, Anders." Emmeline was a little frightened by this speech, but she didn't want it to end, either. "We were children, you know, when we promised each other."

He looked away. "That we were."

A bird hooted, and the leaves of the big trees shimmered and chimed. He took a step toward her, and she was better able to make out his face. The swollen mouth, the bruised cheek; his low forehead and ardent gaze and full mouth. Her fiancé was handsome too, but in such a different way. Frederick had a regal brow and a prominent nose, like he'd inherited his features from a long line of dukes. Anders was younger than Freddy, but didn't look it. He had never been to Europe, and yet somehow he had traveled farther.

"We aren't now."

Suddenly she didn't care that they were standing on the walk in front of the Dawson family's block. She didn't care that the Dawsons' servants might be up early to begin the chores for the day, catch a glimpse of her, and spread rumors. "Would it have made a difference if I told you myself?" she replied, not bothering to whisper. "You would have been angry then, too, wouldn't you?"

"At least it would have meant you cared." He spoke with such force she felt the impact of the words as though they were physical things. Even so she longed for him to close the distance between them, to touch her for real.

"Of course, but I . . ." She furrowed her brow, and tried to think of all the reasons that wasn't possible. But she couldn't. A stubbornness in her belly dissolved. "I was wrong. I am sorry. I am sorry I didn't tell you. I suppose I knew that if I came to see you, I wouldn't be able to do it."

"Well, it's done now. And for the best. Now you've seen me; you can get married in good conscience. I'm leaving Chicago on the next train, wherever it goes, and then you can forget I ever was . . ." A moment ago, she was sure they'd be leaving this corner together. But with a simple shake of the head he turned and began walking south.

"Please don't." Emmeline hurried to keep up with him. "You can't leave. Not now. We've only barely gotten to know each other again."

"Should we have tea, then?" he replied without slowing. The broad line of his shoulders was sharp as a rebuke. "We can go to one of those fancy hotels, and I'll tell you all that has happened over the past two years, and then you'll be able to speak eloquently at my funeral."

"Oh." The wind off the river roughed Emmeline's hair, and a chill shuddered down her spine. She could feel Anders's absence already, and it made her cold in a way she wasn't sure would ever go away. But he was moving so fast. She kept pace with him another block, until the river was in view, its surface a deep and oily green. They had passed through the section of stately mansions, into a place of warehouses. She could see the towering grain elevator on the lake's shore and hear men shouting, even over the groan and scream of the swing bridge as it closed. It had made way for a boat that was now moving past the river's mouth, sails spread to take advantage of a strong wind. When the boat was gone, the chase went out of her. Anders's strides were long and strong, and she was wearing heeled shoes that were not made for walking. She could not keep up with him all the way to the train station. Anyway, he was determined to leave her behind.

But the sight of the river must have affected him, too, because he paused, a few paces ahead of her, and stood staring south. His neck tensed under the line of close-cropped hair, and the blades of his shoulders moved apart and together. She opened her mouth to implore him to stay, but did not get a chance.

"Shhhh . . ." Without another sound, almost before she knew what had happened, he turned, picked her up around the middle, and carried her into the stone doorway of a shipping concern. "Don't look," he whispered.

As if he had just commanded her to do so, Emmeline poked her head out. The bridge was swinging back into place. The only man waiting was tall, and he wore a long leather coat. His back was to them, but he glanced to either side, and the way he twitched and shifted, it was plain he was looking for something. When she last saw this man, through the rear window of the cab, everything had been happening too quickly to be afraid.

She was afraid now.

Gil Bryce, she mouthed.

Anders nodded. Neither moved for a long time after that.

They stood pressed together in the darkness of the door-way, trying not to breathe. Her heart was a hammer, and so was Anders's—she could feel how it pumped through the thin shirt he wore. His grip around her was firm yet light, and she wasn't sure if it was that, or the man with the gun, that more disturbed her stomach. Finally the bridge clanged back into place. The bridgemaster was shouting that it was safe to cross. "He's gone," she whispered.

Very gently, Anders pushed her back. "Then it's time I was on my way."

"Wherever you're going," she said, removing the clad-dagh from her ring finger and placing it in his hand, "you'll want this."

His posture was reluctant, but his palm still touched her palm.

A sad smile passed over his face. "Do you remember the day we brought her flowers?" he asked.

Emmeline had not thought about that day in a long time, but she remembered it well enough. It was during his mother's final illness. They had gone to all the flower stalls in the city, playing the same trick—Fiona would distract the proprietor with a lot of questions, and Emmeline would run by and snatch one stem, hiding it until she found Anders down the block, his arms laden with their haul. They had several canning jars full by the time they returned to his mother's sickbed, and she had laughed, to see the room full of flowers, and said, "Well, aren't you three the dar-lingest ever." Then Anders and Fiona had disappeared to do some household task that needed doing, and Mrs. Mag-nuson had touched Emmeline's cheek. "My boy loves you, doesn't he?" she had said. Emmeline had been too surprised to reply. "Well," she went on, "you never know who'll take the coal off your foot, when it's burning you." It was one of her homely phrases from the old country. "What does *that* mean?" Emmeline had demanded. "Ah, don't take it hard, lovely," she replied after a fit of coughs. "I only meant life is hard to predict and love is a peculiar thing, and everyone knows your father has other plans for you."

Emmeline hoped that Anders didn't remember that part. She hoped he remembered only the fun they'd had, run-ning through the city with all those flowers, or how quick she had been, plucking a stem.

In the darkness, in the doorway, he seemed neither to want to leave nor to want to stay. He was watching her, but his eyes were shiny with fear. She looked up at him, with an expression she hoped would remind him of a different day, the day he'd gone down on one knee on that roof in the old neighborhood and given her the ring. He had wanted to kiss her more that day, she knew, had wanted to caress her face and neck and the narrow of her waist. She had wanted that too, but neither of them had been brave enough.

Her heart pounded and she lifted onto her toes to kiss

him, and heard his heart again, its beat becoming as ragged as her own. His lips were soft, but they did not return the kiss. When she pulled away, she saw eyes moody with emotion, and wondered if she had finally been too reckless. If she had gone too far. The way he searched her face she thought she might disintegrate into a thousand particles and be swept out over the lake.

Then she felt his lips, and knew she was still in one piece.

His kiss was stronger the second time, but after a moment he drew back from it, as though frightened by what he had done. They heard a foghorn across the water, but it sounded like the echo of another world. To show him it was all right, she put her nose close to his, and he brought his mouth to hers again and again, so that the kiss went on, like a dance.

"Don't go," she whispered when it was over.

"Haven't you heard?" He exhaled and she felt his breath on the tip of her nose. "I have to."

"Then go tomorrow." She laid her head on his chest, and he put his fingers through her hair, cradling her head. "You can't go now—Gil Bryce is across the river hunting you. You'll be safe at our house through the night, and tomorrow we'll figure out how to get you to the station."

This was a lie, Emmeline knew—a sweet lie, but a lie nonetheless. Tomorrow she would try to make him stay again. She couldn't have him, of course. But neither could she stand to let him go.

EIGHT

Strike it before it gets the start of you.
That is the only secret to putting out fires.
—*Chicago Fire Marshal Williams, interviewed in the*
Chicago Crier, *October 6, 1871*

"Fiona, what do you think?"

The traffic was noisy five floors down on State Street. The morning light streaming through the high arched windows of Field & Leiter bestowed a special grace upon everything and everyone it touched. Mostly it touched Emmeline, encased in ivory silk and reflected three ways in the full-length, ormolu-framed trifold mirror. Mr. Polk, slender and of a nervous disposition, stood motionless at her side, briefly overcome with appreciation for his work. Miss Fay, the head seamstress, tugged at the corset and smiled encouragingly. In the far mahogany reaches of the dressing room, two attendants waited, one with the veil of Belgian lace spread across her outstretched arms, the other with a cushioned case of jewels. And Fiona, kneeling on the floor to examine one of the hundreds of little silk bows that adorned the great cascade of skirt, glanced upward to the sound of her name.

"Fiona, did you hear what I said?"

She had not heard. "I'm sorry." She blinked. "What was it?"

Emmeline's face was troubled as she studied her reflection. "I said: Do you think it's all right?"

If Fiona were to reply honestly—which she had no intention of doing—she would have said that her mind was elsewhere, that she was exhausted after a restless night, having been ordered away by Emmeline for a second time in one day and saying goodbye to Anders forever. That she did not care about the dress at all. That her heart was broken beyond repair. Or she might have answered that such an extravagant dress, and such an enormous to-do at the very last moment, seemed curious to her when the bride was so obviously determined to upend her own wedding.

Instead, she gazed at the mirror, as though seeing her friend for the first time. The bodice was cinched around Emmeline's slender waist and the skirt was fitted over the hips and bustle, fanning outward into a train that overflowed the Persian carpet. The sleeves were lace and the neck was high enough to graze Emmeline's delicate earlobes. Fiona tilted her head, considering.

Fiona rose to her feet. The dress was beautiful, but she hated it. If she had so many yards of exquisite fabric to work with, she would not have spoiled it with all those ridiculous bows. Somehow the effect was utterly serious and totally absurd at the same time. Posing in it, Emmeline looked haughty and remote as a queen. They had been friends since childhood, but this was the first time Fiona knew what it would be like to despise Emmeline. Despise her face and her voice and everything she said and everything she thought. "I—"

"Oh dear." Emmeline's nose twitched, as it did when she was trying not to cry. "You don't think it's right."

"A thousand pardons." Mr. Polk stepped back, and drew a hand over his lacquered hair. "Who is this . . . person?"

"My lady's maid, Fiona Byrne." He seemed unappeased by this explanation, so she went on. "My maid knows me, as you do not."

"I am the best dressmaker in Chicago. The most fashionable women in this town come to me to find out how they should look. I have never heard of such a thing."

"But you've heard of my father." Emmeline's eyes flashed. "Haven't you?"

An impatient exclamation, at once a laugh and a yelp,

escaped Mr. Polk's lips. He crossed his arms and showed Emmeline his back. Miss Fay murmured and began fidgeting with her belt. The two attendants became even more still. Fiona's eyes darted around the room. She wanted to run away, but her feet were stuck to the ground. With a sudden instinct, she knew how to fix the situation, and did.

"It's perfect," she said. "The dress is just perfect."

Emmeline's worried eyes found Fiona's in the mirror. "You don't think it's all wrong?"

Fiona shook her head. "No. It's lovely."

"All right." Emmeline sighed. "If you think so, I think so too."

No one spoke much after that, which seemed to suit Emmeline, and certainly suited Fiona. She withdrew to the margins, while Mr. Polk finished fitting Emmeline, and wished she could magically leave this place and go back to yesterday.

The others had gone and taken the enormous wedding gown with them before Emmeline addressed her again. "What is wrong with you?"

Fiona had been helping Emmeline into her day dress, a ruffled, fawn-colored silk with a hundred tiny pearl buttons up the spine. She glanced at the mirror. "Nothing," she replied, startled from her task.

"Liar. You have been strange all day."

Fiona put the last button through its hole and dropped

her hands to her sides. "Me?"

"Yes. *You*." Emmeline stared at her in the reflection. "You've been strange since yesterday."

"I'm just tired. I couldn't sleep last night for worrying." Fiona had only meant to explain herself, but as soon as she said the phrase "last night," she was furious again.

"But what do *you* have to worry about? I am the one whose life has been turned upside down!"

Fiona couldn't quite believe what Emmeline had just said, and before she could hold back she was shouting. "What do you know about worry? I was worried that we'd be caught leaving, worried that we'd be spotted in the wrong part of town, worried that you'd be seen with a man not your fiancé, worried that I'd lose my job. My family would be out of their home, you know. Not that you ever think of such things. Mostly, I couldn't sleep for worrying about Anders. Wondering where he is, if he's alone and frightened, wishing there were a way to know that he's all right, to tell him I am thinking of him. He could be killed, because of us. Because of us, he may never see his home again."

The words came in such a furious rush that she was sure Emmeline would reply in kind. But Emmeline simply twirled toward Fiona, eyes wide and shining. "I think I love him."

Fiona couldn't breathe. She had to put her hand on her belly for steadiness. "You think?" was all she could manage.

"Yes. No. I don't know. Isn't he just so—"

"Emmeline!" There could be no hiding her anger now, and no going back. Fiona didn't care if Mr. Polk was listening in the next room, didn't care if she were dismissed and forced to live on the streets. She didn't care if the whole world came to a sudden end. "You've always been selfish, but this is something else. You *think* you are in love with Anders? He left his city forever because you had to have one last little bite of him before you became Mrs. Frederick Tree, and now he's gone, and you can't even say for certain whether you love him. Do you ever think beyond your petty desires? Do the consequences of your actions matter at all? Perhaps a hundred people are working already for your wedding, but for you there is only Emmeline."

Emmeline flinched and stepped back. Her bottom lip quivered and her little upturned nose twitched and she appeared more slight than usual. "I see," she said, wiping some wetness off her face. "So that's how you think of me. Well, you're right, I suppose. I am selfish, and I do want a great many contradictory things. I ought to be able to say plainly that I love Anders. It frightens me to! But I do. Oh, Fiona, you're right, you're always right. I do." Tears were rolling from the corners of her eyes now. Although Fiona was too shocked to feel anything, she could see that Emmeline had reached for and gotten hold of her own wrist. "And, Fiona, he hasn't gone. He's still here."

"Here?" Fiona wanted to feel happy over this news, but after last night hope seemed like a very foolish thing to give in to. "He's still in Chicago?"

"He is planning to leave Chicago, but I convinced him to stay one more night. He slept in the greenhouse. But you're right, he has to go." She paused, took in a deep breath, and searched Fiona's eyes for approval. Fiona didn't want to return that look but there was nowhere for her to hide. "And if I love him, I have to go, too."

Fiona wasn't angry anymore. The floor beneath her feet felt unreliable, and she imagined falling through all the floors of the department store, through the basement with its gasworks, beneath the earth's surface, down and down until she reached someplace too dark for dreams. "You can't do that" were the only words she could summon.

"No. Of course not. Not right away. We'll need a plan, and money, of course. But if I can only make him stay another day . . . I think I can raise enough money for us to go to New York."

"But what will I—?"

"What will you say to Father?" Emmeline nodded and frowned. She turned, took several paces away from Fiona, then came back with even greater urgency. Her eyes had brightened, and she spoke in a hurry, as though she were forming the plan and speaking it at the same time. "Here's what. I will write Father a letter explaining everything.

How you tried to stop me and I wouldn't listen. I'll tell him he must keep you on here. If he doesn't, I will write the newspapers myself to tell them that I've run off with a lowlife boxer. He'd just *hate* that. But he does like you, you know. You're the only member of the staff he truly trusts. He only ever had one objection to you, which was that he was afraid it would be obvious we were friends, and that would make us seem common. But he always says we're lucky to have you, because you're the only one who really understands what all these fancy people want."

"Oh." Fiona's voice had shrunk to almost nothing. Her chin quivered when she said, "He'll find you, you know."

"Yes. Eventually. But by then Anders and I will be married, and he'll have no choice but to set Anders up in business. Stop crying. I'll miss you, too." Emmeline wrapped her arms around Fiona's middle and held her close. The notion of Emmeline and Anders married, after all Fiona had dared to want, was too painful to even think of, and she tried to make herself numb, tried to have no thoughts, just so she could stand the next few seconds. "But we'll all be together again soon, and you can run our household. You can hire your brothers and sister, too. Thank you, Fiona, thank you so much. We'd never be able to elope without you."

Afternoon had ripened, and in the wide front rooms of the Carters' home, the furniture was being rearranged. New pieces had been brought in and less fashionable objects removed. Another party was coming, and time was short, and every member of the household was busy with some task or another. Servants passed through the kitchen at such a rapid clip that no one stopped to question Fiona, preparing a plate of pork beans and fried eggs. When the food was ready, she carried it and a jug of water down the back steps as though this were quite normal. She found it easy to pretend. Her heart was empty, her head clear. Let them try to question her.

Yesterday, the idea of stealing across the backyard carrying a plate of food for a fugitive would have made her sick and anxious. The notion of Anders Magnuson close by would have set off many happy sensations. But the morning had crashed down, changing what she expected from her life. She had given up almost everything. She should probably never have hoped for so much. The next weeks would be hard, but after that she would be able to take care of her family better than she could now, for Emmeline had promised to give her an even better position, and to bring on Kate and Brian, too. That prospect steadied her hands.

The sight of Anders lying under his coat on a wooden bench, his arms folded beneath his head for a pillow, did somewhat test her resolve. He had been staring at the clouds passing over the glass ceiling, but his gaze swung to Fiona when she entered the greenhouse. His feet dropped to the floor and he rose to his full height. The promise she had made to Emmeline was still fresh, but even so Fiona had to glance away and remind herself this was all for the best. No one had ever known how she felt about Anders, anyway. There was some comfort in the thought that she'd always been such a loyal friend to Emmeline; it was one of the things that made her Fiona.

"I thought you forgot me," he said.

"We wouldn't."

"Course. I know that. It's only that you were gone a long time, so I had a lot of hours to think how I had better be going. I kept thinking, 'If I leave now, I'll make the next train.'"

Fiona felt him staring, and raised her eyes to meet his. If he had gone, she wondered, would it mean he didn't want Emmeline at all? "Why didn't you?"

"I don't know," he said after a pause, and she did not press him.

"You must be starving." She placed the plate and the water at the foot of the bed.

"Thank you." He picked up the plate, but seemed unsure what to do with it.

"I have a message. From Emmeline."

"Oh?"

Her breath surged at his indifferent reply, but she bullied that hopeful part of herself, which would only make it harder to do what had to be done. "She says that she is going to leave Chicago with you. She has a plan, but it may take a few days. She knows how to get some money, and you'll need money to get away. In the meantime, she says to wait here. You'll be safe—who would think to look for you on the North Side? I'll bring you food when I can. And whatever else you need. She'll find a way to visit soon, but it'll be harder for her than it is for me. She's having tea with her father now, and attending a party at her fi—at Mr. Tree's home this evening."

"What about the wedding?"

"She won't go through with it. She says she can't. She says . . ." Fiona's brows crushed together, trying to say for Emmeline the thing she'd always wanted to say herself. If only she had said it last night, if only she had said it in the days when she and Anders went on long walks, just the two of them. The words came easily, sweet and thick on her tongue: "'I love you.'"

"Oh." Anders sank back down to the bed, resting the plate of food on his knees. "Then why is she seeing him tonight?"

"She says that everything must seem perfectly normal until the exact moment when you leave."

Anders nodded, but his face was troubled.

"Rest. Eat. You must be half dead."

He lifted a forkful of beans to his mouth, and a few

moments later, the plate was clean. He wiped it with the hunk of bread, and swallowed that, too. He laughed, and said, "I'm like a big beast to you, huh?"

"No." Fiona couldn't quite laugh, although the corners of her mouth darted seeing how fast he ate. It pleased her, to feed him in any way. "I won't be so long again."

"Thank you."

She took the plate from his hands. "Are you all right?" she whispered.

His eyes searched hers. He opened his mouth, but did not speak. He reached for her hand, and when she did not offer it, he took it in his anyway. "I'm scared," he said.

With his hand touching hers, she felt dizzy again, warm and confused, and she had to remind herself what she had promised to do. Every time she remembered she was not to have him—that he was Emmeline's, that he always had been—she felt a sharp pain, like the twist of a knife in her side. She figured this would lessen, in time, and eventually go away entirely. Later, after the fire, she saw people who were too shocked by what had happened to know their own emotions, and she realized that she had been a little like that—a stranger to herself—on the day she promised to help Emmeline and Anders leave Chicago. "I'm scared too," she said. "But you're Anders Mag. They should be afraid of you."

"That's all talk," he said.

"No." She let go of his hand and stepped away. "It's not."

A shudder seemed to pass through his body when she began to retreat, but she probably imagined it. She was probably just hoping. She had almost reached the doorway before he called, "Come back soon?"

Fiona paused on the threshold, yearning for a final glance from him. A delivery of red roses had just arrived—Malcolm and Jeremy, who ran the stables, were carrying them up the back steps in steel buckets. The sun was low, reflected like a great blaze in all the windows of the west wall of the house. The grass in the neighbor's yard was brown, blanketed with fallen leaves from the parched trees, some of which had been raked together like big heaps of gold. A few fluttered upward on the warm wind. She ought to have returned already, to help Emmeline dress for her evening. If Mr. Carter noticed her absence, he would guess she was up to something. Anders was waiting for her to reassure him that he was doing the right thing—she could sense him waiting for a sign—but she knew that looking at him would be too much. If she did, her resolve would fail. So she made of her heart a mean little cinder, and willed away another flood of tears.

NINE

Please join the Tree family
for an evening
that we may better introduce
Miss Emmeline Carter
to all our friends
Tree Residence, Rush Street
October 6, 1871

By nightfall Emmeline was half crazed with strata-
gems and rather impressed with her own artful duplicity.
She dressed with even greater care than if she really
were going to a function with Chicago's best people—
in a dress of midnight blue that slipped off her pale
shoulders—thinking all the while how it was Anders who

would admire the abundant silken skirt, the Chantilly lace at the neckline, the narrow of her corseted waist. Earlier, over tea with Father in the second-floor parlor, she had dropped hints, eating almost nothing and complaining of faintness. Which was even almost a little bit true. She had no appetite, and had been light-headed all day. But that was on account of Anders, and what she now planned to do.

"The pearls, or the garnets?" Fiona asked, approaching with a necklace hanging from each of her outstretched palms.

In the course of the past two years, Emmeline had grown so accustomed to jewels that she could be fairly accused of carelessness. But this finery no longer seemed her reward for molding herself into a lady of fashion, but a crucial part of the plan she was forming in her mind. They would sell it, thus ensuring her and Anders's safe and comfortable passage to New York. Now she knew that each piece of jewelry had a price, that each represented another week away with Anders, and she felt ashamed of the absentminded way she had sometimes taken off a bracelet or an earring, leaving them on tea trays and windowsills for the housekeepers to put away, or maybe pocket. Emmeline drew her fingers across the naked line of her clavicle and shook her head. "Neither. The dress is plenty ornamented as it is. Simplicity is best, don't you think? And anyway, it's not as though I'm really going out."

"No, of course not." Fiona tilted her head in graceful subservience, and went to the oak armoire where the jewelry box was kept. "I only thought it would be more convincing, if you dressed as you usually do."

When Fiona turned back, there was a shine on her forehead and her eyes were shadowy. She'd mentioned sleeping poorly the night before, and her face looked unrested. Emmeline felt the twinge of an old irritation. When they were children, and about to do something new and adventurous, Fiona would always think of all the reasons that they ought not to, and Emmeline and Anders would have to answer her many questions, and consider the various outcomes, before they went ahead and did the thing anyway. In the end, Emmeline knew Fiona would come around, but she wished that for once her friend would not be so precise and careful about the details, and would instead relish the very romantic turn life had just taken.

Emmeline's gaze swung back on her own reflection, on the loose arrangement of pale hair atop her forehead, the inky blackness of her lashes. "We ought to go down now," she said, drawing the skirt away from her feet as she rose.

Fiona nodded, and folded Emmeline's camel hair wrap over her forearm. At the door, Emmeline reminded herself what she must do—as soon as she saw Father, she would collapse against the wall and slide down the remaining stairs. She didn't think she would have to do more, but just in case, Fiona was ready to suggest that, if Emmeline wasn't feeling well, the wisest course was for her to rest up, so that she'd be in perfect health by Sunday. Once Father had gone off to the Trees' to beg her excuses, she would slip down to see Anders. Fiona would make sure nobody saw her going to the greenhouse, and then she would leave Emmeline alone with Anders so they could . . .

Emmeline's eyelids got heavy, imagining finally being alone with him again, and her upper teeth sank into her bottom lip.

This was her expression when she pulled back the door and encountered her father, hand raised and ready to knock. The elaborate plan of the previous moment evaporated from her thoughts, and her spine went stiff.

"Oh," she said, and closed her mouth.

Father's big fist hovered a moment, before he put it with his other hand, behind his back. A canny light shone in his eyes, same as in the old days, on the nights he played cards, making her wonder if he'd heard what she said about not really going out. Did he know about the secret she had hidden in the greenhouse?

But he made no accusations. He only asked, "Are you ready, my dear?"

"I'm not feeling well," Emmeline replied not very convincingly.

His put his palm on her forehead. "You don't seem sick."

"I don't think I ought to go to the party," she said without managing to meet his eye.

"But you have to go to the party," he replied blithely. "The party is in your honor. Here, I have something that will make you feel better."

His hidden hand emerged from behind his back, and from it dangled a clutch of liquid gold strands. Before she could get a word out, he had secured the clasp behind her neck. The gleaming yellow metal fell, heavy and smooth, against her chest. She glanced down, gasping at its bright beauty, marveling at its heft. She had never touched anything like it; surely it was worth more than all her other jewelry combined.

"It's . . ." Her fingers rested against the strands, feeling excited and confused to have something so exquisite and rare hanging from her neck.

". . . hardly as precious as you, my Emmeline. But it does complete your ensemble nicely. Come, everyone will want to see you, see how beautiful you are. And the carriage is waiting."

"I'll be down in a little," Emmeline said.

"We are already late."

Her eyes darted as she tried to think. "I forgot something."

"Fiona." Father assumed his commanding tone. "Make sure she doesn't dally."

"Yes, Mr. Carter."

Once Father had disappeared below the second-floor landing, Emmeline faced Fiona. Father had made her nervous, and feel she should do as he said—and the thought that the people of Chicago would see her for the last time wearing heaps of gold seemed like some reward for abstaining from Anders one more night. As she draped the wrap over her shoulders, she said, "Will you go to Anders and keep him company? Tell him I'm sorry. Make sure he isn't lonely, and tell him he is in my heart. Can you do that?"

Fiona nodded, gently arranging the wrap so that Father's gift was most on view.

Emmeline gave the necklace a guilty glance, and met Fiona's eyes. "Don't tell him why, but you understand I have to go now, don't you?" She meant that Father might take the necklace away if she didn't go to the party, and they wouldn't have it to sell—although she wasn't sure if Fiona believed this, or if she did herself.

After a pause, Fiona said that she understood, and Emmeline went down through the house to the waiting carriage.

Two footmen stood stoically at the entrance to the Tree residence, each holding a torch. The wind-licked flames illuminated a great spread of lawn, kept green even in the dry season, upon which stood several large topiaries shaped like brides and grooms. It was as though ladies and gentlemen made of bushes were taking an evening stroll around the property. Emmeline had never seen anything of the kind, and wanted to go examine them up close, but she knew such curiosity would make her seem gauche. She felt slight amid the grandeur and solemnity of the scene, and gulped, remembering her role on this occasion.

Emmeline leaned heavily upon her father for support as they ascended the stairs, wondering if her lie hadn't become a little bit true. She was not, in fact, feeling her best. Her breath was weak, her belly aflutter, her bones felt light as birds'. The skin of her face was hot, but her hands and feet were cold.

At the top they were taken in by a British butler, who announced their names in his fancy-sounding accent. A string ensemble was playing a lively waltz somewhere, and the sound of dress shoes against parquet, laughter and chitchat, resounded throughout the house. For a moment—standing beside her father in the empty marble entryway—Emmeline feared the announcement of their arrival would go unheard. That had happened often in the beginning of their social career, and for a long time she always feared that she would be announced and no one would notice. Not since her engagement had her confidence dipped in this way, but she now imagined that the butler's blank expression masked a private judgment of the Carters. That he knew they did not truly belong.

But then Mr. and Mrs. Hastings Tree appeared from the ballroom, arm in arm. Like Freddy, they were impressive-looking: he tall and shiny in tails; she bright-eyed and richly attired in tiered velvet.

"My dear," Freddy's mother said as she placed a warm kiss on Emmeline's cheek.

"How lovely she is," observed Freddy's father. Then he gripped her father's hand, welcoming him.

"Ada has been eagerly anticipating your arrival," said Freddy's mother.

"Mr. Carter," said Freddy's father, "would you join me in my library? There are some gentlemen you ought to know."

Emmeline found herself reluctant to release her father's arm. "Go on, Emmeline, have fun," he urged before following Mr. Tree up the carved oak stairs.

"Ada is in the Turkish drawing room," said Mrs. Tree, and then she, too, departed, drifting into a private consultation with the butler.

Emmeline wandered into the drawing room off the foyer, and saw that it had indeed been redone in a Turkish theme. Heavy, patterned carpets hung on the walls, and potted palms filled up the corners. The gaslight caught the brass buttons of the gentlemen drinking from goblets, and the diamonds of the women who lounged in divans. On a low dais, a man dressed as some sort of Anatolian king sat on a golden throne, while a woman in a diaphanous white gown lounged at his feet, and a small boy fanned them. The scene was so elaborate, and richly colored, that Emmeline wished she had brought along her diary.

"You've never seen one before, have you?"

Emmeline turned toward a tall gentleman in white tie with sleek dark hair. "Seen what?"

"A tableau vivant." His small, precise features twitched in amusement. "They're quite the thing in New York. Isn't it thrilling to have one in our little backwater?"

"You mean the . . ." Emmeline indicated the people posing on the dais, and tried to hide her surprise at hearing Chicago, which was all she'd ever known, referred to as a backwater.

"Yes, I mean the living picture. You're Miss Carter, aren't you? Do you drink champagne?"

A waiter with a tray of sparkling flutes was passing, and the man with the sleek dark hair took one, and put it in Emmeline's hand.

"Are you often in New York?" Emmeline asked, sipping from her glass. The champagne fizzed in her mouth, and relaxed her throat. She liked saying the city's name, and knowing that she'd soon be there with Anders, and thought perhaps she should inquire what hotel the gentleman preferred, and if there were any restaurants that he recommended in particular. With Anders, she would have to be the guide, and know how best to travel in style.

"Oh, at least twice a year. My preferred tailor is there, and . . ."

"Emmeline!" Ada burst into their conversation and took firm hold of Emmeline's elbow. In a calm, forceful tone one might use to admonish a naughty child, she said, "We really must be going, Mr. Fleming."

"Adieu, Mrs. Garrison," the gentleman replied with a flash of teeth.

As they passed from the Turkish drawing room and into a smaller parlor with flocked vermillion wallpaper, furnished with small sofas upholstered in a burgundy satin, and occupied chiefly by young women, Ada maintained a tight grip on Emmeline. "Do you know him?"

"Know who?"

"Jim Fleming, of course."

"Was that James Olcott Fleming? No—only from the social column."

"Good. Don't get to know him any better. He is quite a flirt, and will take advantage of every opportunity to exploit the feminine nature. If you are seen talking to him too long, there will be rumors."

"Oh." Emmeline winced, realizing that she had almost told Jim Fleming that she was planning on running away. She really *was* out of sorts. The red parlor was populated with more people whose names she knew from the social column of the *Tribune*. She saw Delia Rockingham and Lucy Rawlings, and the Alexander Oleanders, and Mrs. Charring Pine. She saw John Jacob Dawson, tête-à-tête with Marianne Otis, who had once snubbed Emmeline at a private musicale, but who now watched her passage through the room with an almost awestruck expression.

Emmeline lifted her chin, and allowed Ada to draw her through the warren of halls. She understood that Mr. Fleming's attentions were rather embarrassing, but she couldn't help but feel a little bit flattered by his interest at the same time. They came into a long dining room, where guests stood in small groups beneath enormous, ormolu-framed portraits of the Tree family's ancestors. A table was laden with heaps of grapes, croquettes, frosted cakes, and silver tureens of broth; when Emmeline saw the food, she remembered how little she'd eaten that day. A waiter passed with a platter of fried oysters, and Emmeline grabbed two and put both in her mouth at once. This steadied her, which was a good thing, because a few moments later they arrived at the ballroom and saw, beneath an enormous chandelier, four couples performing the quadrille, and one of them was Freddy—*her* Freddy—paired with Cora Russell.

"She has been cornering him all evening," whispered Ada.

"Does she think she's going to get him after all?" Emmeline asked, surprised that Cora would challenge her, after the engagement had been made official and with the wedding date approaching fast.

"Well"—Ada emitted an accusatory little cough—"*is* she?"

Emmeline lengthened her neck, and placed her hands patiently together. She was not about to give up her place in the world before her time. The dancers took notice, and when Freddy turned, their eyes met. He grinned, let go of Cora, and reached for his fiancée. Emmeline returned his smile, and allowed herself to be pulled farther onto the floor.

Earlier in her social career, Emmeline struggled to remember the precise steps, and had an unfortunate habit of looking down at her footwork, with the result that she stumbled often and was sometimes not asked for a second dance. Now she moved easily—the music was brisk and it told her what to do, and she went on smiling and gazing up at Freddy. Daisy Fleming and Ralph Finch were the next couple over, and whenever Daisy caught Emmeline's eye, it was as though they had a private joke between them. When they had traveled across the room and back again, and the song was coming to a close, she caught a glimpse of Ada, watching her and Freddy with pride. Just behind Ada stood Cora, wearing a gloomy face.

When the music stopped, the guests who had been sitting along the wall stood and the sound of their applause reached to the ceiling. Emmeline made a low curtsy to Freddy, and he responded with a courtly bow, and then offered his hand to help her up.

"Shall we catch our breath in the other room?" Freddy asked.

The other dancers and guests parted for them as they made their way toward the arched doorway. There were so many eyes upon them that she did not immediately notice Father among the crowd.

"Are you feeling better, my dear?" her father whispered into her ear.

"Oh yes," she replied, before remembering that she had claimed not to be feeling well earlier in the evening.

"I suspected it was only a case of nerves," he replied so that only she could hear. To Freddy, he said, "Take care of my Emmeline. Perhaps I will claim my fatherly privilege of a dance later on. Meantime, keep her happy."

Freddy made a deep and theatrical bow, and said, "Such is my life's quest."

As Father retreated back into the crowd, she briefly considered chasing him, to claim she was still not quite right, that she must be sick after all. But she knew she could not play the invalid with any conviction now. Her spirits were high, and she was excited to taste all of the delicious plates the Trees had prepared, to dance until late, to show off everything she had learned since leaving the old neighbor-hood.

Soon this world would be behind her, so she might as well enjoy it tonight.

TEN

Pride, envy, avarice are the three sparks/
that kindle in men's hearts and set them burning.
—*Dante's* Inferno,
Translation 1853
Library of Ochs Carter

"What do you think they're doing right now?"

Fiona focused on the playing cards in her hands. The jack of hearts was winking wolfishly, and waxy to the touch. Anders hadn't spoken in a while, and the sound of his voice surprised her, and she was unsure how to reply. Not because she didn't know the answer. By ten o'clock, which it very nearly was, the Trees' guests would be famished from so much dancing, and the butler would have summoned them onto the lawn where they would be served *consommé de boeuf* and catch their breath in the fresh air. Afterward, the sexes would separate for a time, so that the ladies could regain their strength and reapply their makeup and repin their hair. They would sit in a private parlor, comparing dance cards, trying to divine some meaning in the repetition of the gentlemen's names written there in pencil. Those little pencils, they came in gold and silver and turquoise and scarlet, and they were attached to the corresponding booklet with matching ribbon—Fiona had seen many versions, brought home by Emmeline and left near the bathtub to be picked up and neatly folded and placed in her keepsake chest. Tonight, Emmeline's dance card would likely be of little interest, for surely Freddy's name would be scrawled on every line, and perhaps there would have been no point in keeping a record of her other dance partners at all. She would be expected to be at Freddy's side when they went down for the formal supper, and at his side when the guests gathered once again in the ballroom for the waltz. Fiona had listened so often to the stories of these evenings, it was almost as though she had been there, and memorized their grand sweep, and all their small intrigues, too.

"Fiona?"

When he said her name she remembered herself, her place. She was in the greenhouse, sitting on the ground, keeping Anders company while Emmeline maintained appearances, playing a third game of cards to pass the time, under a blanket that they had hung over their heads so the light of candles would not draw attention to them in the darkness. The white collared shirt she had taken from the laundry was large on Anders, and he had rolled it to the elbows, and his feet were bare.

"I don't know," she lied.

Anders's face was serious. His body was very still.

She continued prattling in a nervous way: "These celebrations always go on and on. She's surely bored and probably thinking of you."

"You really think she is?"

"That was the last thing she said before she left," Fiona reported dutifully. "She said to tell you that you were in her heart."

Anders nodded and rearranged his cards. Fiona couldn't remember whose turn it was anymore, and she sensed he wasn't thinking very much about the game, anyway. They had always talked about everything when they were children, but now, with silences and secrets grown between them, he seemed mysterious and remote. After a while he asked, "Have you ever been to a party like that?"

"Yes. Well, no. I've accompanied Emmeline, to help her with her dress and so forth, but I've never . . ."

"Been a guest?"

"No. Nor will I ever." She had intended this in a flat, careless way, but the words were bitter on her tongue. "I wouldn't want to," she added. After she said it, she knew it was true.

Anders put his cards down and lay on his back. "Why not?"

"I don't know. I just wouldn't. Would you?"

His head rolled in her direction, and for the first time that night he smiled a little. "No, I guess I wouldn't, either. I can't see the point."

"Do you go to the neighborhood dances?"

"Sometimes, but I'm not much for dancing."

"Why not? In the ring, you—" Fiona cleared her throat, embarrassed to remember the admiring way she'd watched him in the fight. "I mean to say that I think it would be easy for you."

"Well, at first I just didn't have much to do at those dances. The boys were dancing because they wanted the girls to be sweet to them, and there weren't any girls I cared for." He propped himself up on an elbow, a faraway look in his eyes, and took the cards and shuffled them. Fiona became conscious of a warmth at her collarbone under her own stiff, white collared shirt, of the heaviness of her black skirt over her folded legs. Wherever he was, it was a place of Emmeline, and Fiona felt it would be too much to know the particulars in his mind. "Then I started boxing," he went on, glancing up at her, "and there was so much to learn. Boxing was the only place I wanted to be."

"Every night?"

"Every night I could." Anders had begun separating the face cards, laying them out neatly. "In the summer, Jem had me out on his farm, and we trained all day. The air is sweet out there, and nobody worries about money or girls, and if we play cards, it's just for fun."

The way his voice changed describing it, Fiona could smell the countryside, the clean air after a brisk walk down a dirt road that went all the way to the horizon line. "That sounds like a nice place. Are there wildflowers everywhere?"

"You like wildflowers, don't you?"

Fiona had to think a moment. "Maybe I've never seen a wildflower," she admitted.

Anders exhaled. "You're an easy one to talk to. What do you do, Miss Fiona, when Emmeline has gone off to her parties? You must have friends here."

"Not many. They don't like me much. I'm not like them—but I'm not like her, either."

His head bobbed in understanding. "Are you bored?"

"No. Mr. Carter has a library with all the new books, and I try to keep up my learning, so I can help my brothers and sister. And there is always a dress to mend, or sew some new detail on. I've made a few on my own. I don't mind being by myself, I always have plenty to do."

"Don't you get lonely?"

"No, I . . ." Fiona lowered her eyes and put her hands in her lap. The truth was that she had often filled her mind with memories of Anders, and considered herself in good company. She felt silly, remembering those nights now.

"There must be some boy around here, pining for you to give him a second glance."

Fiona was having a hard time finding a natural place to look that wasn't Anders. She could only manage to shake her head.

"Then you haven't been . . . kissed."

By now her blush was catching—it went all the way to her throat—and she was trying with all her might to avoid his gaze. But this was impossible. "Only that once," she whispered.

The candlelight cast shadows around his full lips and hooded eyes, his strong shoulders and rough hands. Everything became a little topsy-turvy, and his body seemed treacherously close to hers, especially with the blanket overhead, making the world small and full of only them. The atmosphere was noisy with the earth settling, the creak of the structure slowly sinking, insects, night things, her own pulse. Fiona had made a promise to Emmeline, and she knew she was betraying it by conjuring that time Anders kissed her. She shouldn't have brought it up at all. *If only*

Emmeline hadn't gone to the party, Fiona thought, *I would not have slipped up*. The whole arrangement of the evening struck her, suddenly, as quite unfair.

"That night?" he asked.

His acknowledgment frightened her, and she wished this conversation was over already. The threads of her shirt clung, damp and irritating, to the skin of her chest. She was Emmeline's best friend, so she was bound to help her do what she wished. And she was Anders's friend, and wanted only for him to be safe.

Anders shifted. "Whenever I saw you, after that, I wanted to tell you—"

Fiona stood up abruptly, into the blanket, as though she could escape the memory. For a moment she stood like a ghost with the cloth draped over her head. Then she felt its fibers brush her face, its soft tassels against her cheeks, as he pulled it, pulled it down and away from her body. The disturbance had put out the candles. She heard Anders laugh his low, earthbound chuckle, and she was relieved, and knew that none of it mattered much. He did not think she was a fool; they had done no great wrong. Her vision adjusted by the time he was on his feet, and she could make out his grin. When she saw the grin, she felt she could tell him anything.

"Anders," she began.

But in the next moment she forgot what she had been about to say.

A light had appeared out there in the darkness and it was moving in their direction. The person carrying the lamp was approaching from the house, and her first thought was that it must be Malcolm or Mr. Carter, and that they were all about to be in a lot of trouble. She took a breath, and moved in front of Anders, as though that might protect him. The swinging lantern approached, and Fiona's stomach dropped again with the thought that it might be the gamblers, come for Anders—come to take him away.

Fiona squinted into the murkiness outside, and her shoulders relaxed. The person held the lantern high above her head, so that she seemed taller than she was, but it illuminated the pretty, pliant face of Georgie, who the Carters had taken on a month ago to help in the kitchen, and who could be easily bribed with a sweet treat.

Fiona moved fast, through the door and into the yard so that she could cut Georgie off before the girl noticed Anders. "What are you up to," she demanded. "Going about so late?"

Georgie lowered the lantern and glared at Fiona. "Could ask you the same," came her retort. She was trying to peer around her, through the glass and the wall of half-dead plants.

"Yes, but . . ." Fiona was a little surprised by Georgie's impertinent reply, and for a moment couldn't think what to say. "I take my orders from Miss Carter."

"Oh yes? She told you to be out here, this late at night, with—?"

Before Georgie could acknowledge Anders's presence, Fiona interrupted her. "Never you mind what I'm doing here." She was still angry at the girl for the fright she'd caused, and her outrage grew when she saw how stubbornly and stupidly she stood her ground. Once or twice the girl had slipped up, and Fiona had heard the Irish in her voice, and realized she was not who she pretended to be. There was something odd about Georgie, as though she did not quite understand that she was a servant, and was meant to murmur and bow, that she should not appear to hold opinions or want things. This quality had not bothered Fiona until now. "If you would like to speak to Miss Carter about how she chooses to manage her household, by all means, knock on her door. In the meantime, I suggest you return to your bed, or I'll report you to Cook for being out odd hours, and she'll finally have an answer as to why you're so slow peeling potatoes in the morning."

Fiona had hoped her harsh tone would send the girl scurrying. But she must not have been forceful enough, for Georgie's reply was a slight, defiant tilt of the head.

Meanwhile Anders kept silent within the greenhouse, but Fiona sensed him there, watching.

She squared her shoulders, lifted her chin, held Georgie's gaze, and said, "You go run along now." To her relief, the girl, after a long moment, pulled her skirt back from her feet and did as she was told.

As Georgie retreated to the house, her long woolen skirt swept over the fallen leaves, making a whooshing sound that was, to Fiona, excruciatingly loud. She would have liked to tell Anders that everything was all right now, but she knew it wasn't. Her blood was hot and quick and she felt furious with Emmeline for having put him in danger, but mostly with herself for letting herself relax, and enjoy being with Anders, when she should have been ever vigilant.

Emmeline's plan was dangerous, and this was no time for Fiona to be distracted, to let herself feel at ease. She would have to stay alert, lest they all be burned. After Georgie went back into the house, she made it clear that she was not open to familiar talk, and gestured to Anders that he ought to be quiet, and keep low to the ground, where the wall of plants shielded them from view.

ELEVEN

Careful of envy in your midst, for though you may not personally suffer from this fever, still you will be scorched by its proximity in the end.
—*Beatrice Parnell,* Aphorisms for Girlhood, *1868*

The evening had picked Emmeline up off her feet, twirled her around, and placed her down in quite a different mood. Upon returning from the Trees', she felt pleasantly exhausted, and leaned on her father's arm as they went up the stone steps and into the Dearborn house, which had over the past two years become her home. The carriage proceeded around the house to the stables, and they all said their good nights, and she walked through the rooms a little nostalgically, thinking of the many things that had transpired there.

In the full-length mirror in the front parlor, she caught a glimpse of herself in her impressive gown, which fit her body like a glove, and changed colors when it moved. She thought how she'd always have that vision of herself, at this precise moment: richly dressed, a little flushed in the face, at a very precarious juncture in her life. Midnight had come and gone, and it was now early morning of the day before her supposed wedding day, but all the things she'd assumed over the past two years had been thrown into question. The house was silent, and yet it seemed alive, and she had the sense that she was the only one who was conscious enough to see the fine parquet, the oil paintings and velvet couches and polished mahogany tables and chairs, to gaze at them with the clear sight that can fix images in memory.

Yet, at roughly the same time, Jeremy was helping Malcolm lead the horses from the carriage into their stalls, and happened to glance at the main house, taking in its monumental silhouette against the moonlit sky, and think how he'd always remember the grandeur of the Carters with that picture in his mind. And Miss Lupin, the housekeeper, who had trouble sleeping, had risen and was repairing the edge of the tapestry that hung in the front hall, which had been damaged by a visiting lady's lapdog. The gold threads and mysterious green trees that it depicted were, to her, quite the most wonderful ever, and as she gazed at them and went about her mending, she found she didn't mind so much her tired, aching hands. Most wide-eyed of all was Georgie, who had taken Fiona at her word, and gone straight to Miss Carter's room, where she put down the lantern she had carried across the yard, and gaped at the opulent surroundings where Miss Carter lay her head.

"You go run along now," she had muttered as she climbed the stairs, repeating in righteous anger the words Fiona Byrne had said to her.

But once she arrived in Miss Carter's bedroom, she forgot her anger, and moved around, running her fingers along the smooth and polished curve of the headboard, examining the tasseled bedspread, the upholstered stool at the vanity, thinking how she herself could well enjoy a life such as this. She had drifted into the bathroom, and put her nose to the bottle of perfume—which smelled of orange blossoms and musk and transported her to a first-class train in France on the way to a seaside castle—when she heard the door from the hall close.

She went back to the threshold of the main bedroom, and saw the lady of the house crossing the ornate golden carpet, dragging her heaping skirt of darkly shimmering silk behind her, removing a jewelry box from the wardrobe, and placing it on the bed. The arrangement of her hair had begun to unravel in the night and Georgie wondered if drinks had been served at the party. With a wistful and contented gesture, Emmeline unhooked the brilliant necklace that she wore, and placed it in its black velvet nest beside a crown encrusted with rubies and diamonds; an engraved watch on a chain; piles of bracelets, rings, strands of pearls, jeweled pendants.

"Oh!" Miss Carter exclaimed when she noticed Georgie. And Georgie in a rush told her all about Fiona and the boy she was trying to hide in the greenhouse, and what a liar and a cheat Emmeline's lady's maid really was. For a moment her face became so contorted that Georgie thought Miss Carter angry enough to go and fire Fiona straightaway! But then her expression became calm again, and she thanked Georgie for being such a loyal friend, and said that she would personally see that Fiona was punished for her late-night indiscretions. "I just thought you should know," Georgie told her as she rose to go, although she would have preferred to linger in the sumptuous regions of the house.

"Thank you," Emmeline said once again. "I am so grateful to have your friendship, Georgie."

And so Georgie returned to the servants' quarters, satisfied with the notion that she was already ascending in the Carter household, and on her way to a position of consequence there.

After Georgie left, Emmeline blinked, for everything looked a little strange now. The rooms on the top floors were warm with the rising air, and the precious metals and gems and the woven bedspread and the polished wood and the flocked pink wallpaper spread out around her. Yet for a few moments none of it seemed as real as the cold, cramped room with the little cot where she had lived with Father when they first came to the old neighborhood. How freezing it was in the morning before Father lit the stove. That was before she became friends with Fiona, and Emmeline found herself wishing that Fiona would appear already, so that she could explain what had happened with Georgie and help her out of her dress.

She did not have to wish very long, for just then Fiona appeared, pushing the door open with her back, and revolving gingerly as she came into the room so as not to upset the tray of tea and late-night sandwiches she carried.

Before Emmeline could say anything, Fiona set down the tray and made her most serious face. "We have to move Anders off the property."

"But why?" Emmeline's chest rose and fell, for she did not want Anders to go anywhere.

"Georgie, the kitchen girl—she saw us. Saw him. She knows, and she may tell others."

"No, no," Emmeline waved her hand. "I handled her. She thinks we're friends, and will keep our secret."

Fiona lowered her eyes and fidgeted with her apron. "He's in danger, Em. We need to keep him hidden until you leave. If he's discovered before then, if I'm caught going around at night, if rumors spread among the staff of a fugitive hiding on the property . . ." She trailed off, shook her head. "We can't just wait around until it's too late. We need a plan."

Emmeline smiled and gestured grandly at the jewels that lay on the bed between them. "We'll sell my collection, and Anders and I can get away from here and live quite safely."

Fiona's face became distant with thought. "I'll sell them. It will have to be tomorrow."

Emmeline nodded—she hadn't thought of that, but it was so like Fiona to know the answer to a problem before the problem became obvious. "While I'm having the last dress fitting."

"Yes," Fiona agreed. "Exactly. And in the meantime, Anders . . ."

"Yes, Anders." Emmeline liked saying the name. She tasted it like some new dish of Cook's, enjoying how the sound played along the edges of her tongue. It brought up all of him—the boy he used to be, and the man she had only had a tiny glimpse of. What was he thinking now? Was he wondering about her? Had her absence encouraged doubts in his mind? She wanted to go to him, and assure him that she had none. "Do you remember that place? That place we went that summer when the war was bad? On the other side of the river, with the barn."

All the grown-ups were busy in those years, and nobody

cared where they went or what they did. Her father had picked up a few adjoining lots to settle a debt, and like much he acquired in those busy years, he said he'd hold on to them until they were worth something. On that side of the river, the structures were less crowded together, and the people kept animals. "This is all yours," Father had said proudly, and Emmeline was very impressed, because nobody in their neighborhood owned much of anything. When the noise and the stench of the neighborhood became too much, she told her friends about the place, and they went. Fiona had been doing mending for the tailor—his son was away with the army—and she had some money of her own, and they'd buy all sorts of treats for picnics and cross the bridge to DeKoven Street.

In the barn on DeKoven, it always smelled of hay and sunshine.

As the summer progressed they put on little theatrical productions, and told each other stories, and Anders taught them how to play baseball. Fiona had flinched whenever the ball hurtled toward her, but Emmeline fixed it in her sights, swung, and knocked it into the hayloft. A family of swallows erupted, filling the big space with their beating wings, and the ball was permanently lost.

"Fiona," Emmeline had said once they gave up searching for it, "what do you want to be when you grow up?"

"I'd like to run a big hotel, eight blocks wide, with

hot running water in every room and a staff of hundreds and a restaurant and a dress shop and its own zoological park." She'd stopped suddenly, self-conscious of her dream. "What about you?"

"I'd lead an exploratory mission into the great North-west, and collect furs, and make friends with all the inhabitants we encounter, and found a town called Emme-lineville, with a view of the Pacific Ocean."

They both turned toward Anders. He was standing, as usual, a bit apart, and listening to their conversation in his way, as though their girlish talk was a foreign language he did not quite understand. That summer, they were both taller than he was. But he carried himself as though he knew he'd be big and strong soon.

Fiona spoke for both girls—she always did, for Anders had been her friend first—asking: "What would you be?"

"I'd be married to Emmeline," he said.

They were struck dumb. He'd never said anything remotely romantic before. The silence was sharp—then Fiona giggled and singsonged, *"Anders loves Emmeline."*

"I do not," he said, and broke into a run.

The girls had chased him, out into the wooden walk, past the cottages that lined the street, all the way to the rail-road tracks. When he could go no farther, he turned around and said, "All right, I do," and Emmeline had curtsied and offered her hand like a lady, and he kissed her knuckles. So began the love song of Anders and Emmeline.

Later, when they were older, and it was well established that Anders and Emmeline were destined for each other, there was a day when he had danced her across the floor of that barn. She couldn't remember why exactly, but she well remembered how it had felt to sway against him, held in his blue gaze, and she was certain—as certain as she'd ever been of anything—that she ought to follow him wherever he went. In fact, now that she thought about it, eloping to New York sounded like a fantastic adventure. Perhaps, in a way, it had been their destiny all along. She couldn't wait.

The events of the day had come on hurly-burly, tossing her this way and that. But now her eyes shone, and her pulse became calm. "He'd be safe there—in the barn."

"All right."

"We'll take him now."

Fiona's gaze shifted over the ceiling moulding, the chandelier. "No," she replied slowly. "No, I will draw your bath, and you will stay here. It's a bigger risk if we both go."

Emmeline's insides settled. She need not worry while her friend was thinking things through, for everything would go smoothly until the moment of departure, so long as Fiona was in charge. Emmeline tried to show her how grateful she was, but Fiona was occupied with placing the tray on the bedside table, and pouring the steaming amber liquid into a gold-rimmed porcelain cup. "Oh, Fiona," she gasped. "What will I do without you?"

Fiona put the teapot down. "You'll be back soon enough."

"Yes," Emmeline said, remembering her promise. "But I wish you could be with us in New York. We'd be in trouble so much less if you came, too."

Fiona glanced up in such a way that Emmeline felt ashamed for speaking lightly of what they had planned. But her shame dissipated as Fiona approached, for there was no judgment in her eyes. "You must avoid trouble," she said, reaching for Emmeline's hands. "And take good care of each other. Understand?"

Emmeline nodded. Fiona nodded, as though sealing an agreement, and went to draw Emmeline's bath.

Sadness washed over Emmeline as she sipped her tea and listened to water falling against marble. The realization that she wouldn't be able to talk to her best friend for a long time, maybe months, took hold. With it came a nervous anticipation of the many new things she would do and see—things she was accustomed to understanding only after a long discussion with Fiona. With some difficulty, she pulled her engagement ring from her finger, and put it on the black velvet, beside the rope of gold Father had given her. The precious gems and metals were a great weight in her hands, and she wished that they were already sold, that she was no longer burdened by them. So she removed the watch on the long gold chain quickly, and closed the box with the rest of the jewelry inside, leaving it for Fiona to find later.

"Fiona," she said, coming into the bathroom and putting the watch into Fiona's palm. "I want you to have this."

Fiona stared at the gold circle engraved with a simple, handsome design. "I can't take this," she whispered. "It was your mother's."

"Please don't argue with me. I don't have another way to thank you for all you've done. Anyway, it suits you, don't you think? It's beautiful in a classic way, just like you, no need for anything extra or fancy."

It was not in Fiona's nature to take compliments, although it was plain on her face she agreed. Even so, she shook her head. "If anyone notices that I have it—"

"Then keep it with your personal things for later. You ought to have something, anyway. Something of value. Just in case . . ."

Emmeline trailed off, afraid Fiona would make her finish the sentence.

"Thank you," Fiona said, and put her arms around Emmeline. They stood that way for a while, as the tub filled.

"Come now." Emmeline drew back, afraid they might both begin to cry. "Tomorrow is too important. We can't get mushy."

Fiona managed a smile, closed the faucet, and took up the lantern that Georgie had left beside the chaise longue. Off she went to take Anders to safety, leaving Emmeline to step into the scalding bath by herself.

TWELVE

Fire that's closest kept burns most of all.
—Book of Shakespearean Quotations, *1867*
Collection of Ochs Carter

That night they walked a long way, an hour or more, crossing to the west at the Kinzie Street Bridge and proceeding through unfamiliar streets. Neither Fiona nor Anders spoke much, only the occasional word to agree on their route. He had said he should go by himself, but Fiona would not allow this. Her own future was now entirely based on her ability to ensure the safe passage of her friends from the city, and anyway she knew she would not sleep if she had sent Anders to make the journey alone. She clutched the lantern that Georgie had waved when she found them in the greenhouse, and Anders carried a canvas bag with supplies: a blanket, a jug of water, a loaf of bread, and a can of sardines.

Not so long ago, they used to walk together every week, in easy quiet, looking at the city at night. There had been something he had wanted to tell her in those days, and she had not permitted him to say it. She had hoped then, and not allowed herself to know how much she hoped, that the thing he wanted to tell her was that he longed for her as much as she longed for him. But that hadn't been it at all. He had only wanted to tell her that he was leaving the city, and that the reason was Emmeline. Because it was Emmeline he had always loved and always would. It was some comfort that this revelation came at the same time as so many other catastrophes, so that Fiona was too numb to feel the weight of her disappointment, and her mind was kept busy with other terrors.

As they passed block after block she thought how every shadow might obscure a lurking figure, how the alleys were full of men who might mean them harm—not only Gil Bryce and his people, though they were the ones she feared most. When the fear crept up her throat, she pictured the place with the barn, the afternoons they had spent there, and she found she had some courage, after all.

But when they arrived on DeKoven and entered the barn, she realized that she had remembered it wrong. Fiona had at first felt relieved by Emmeline's suggestion, imagining a return to a place they had gone as children, where they had all been equal in friendship. A place she frequented in that long ago time before she permitted herself the ruinous notion that she loved Anders Magnuson. But now—having stepped across the threshold, inhaling the crushed hay and distant smell of animal—she was met by a different memory of the place.

The last time they were here it was the summer before the Carters made their move, and Fiona and Anders and Emmeline had been running around at night, jumping between rooftops and peeking into the church on Clark to hear the midnight choir. Returning to the old neighborhood, they had stumbled upon Samuel the butcher passionately pressing Mrs. Halloran, the grocer's wife, against the wall of the alley behind his shop. Her skirt was pushed up, and her naked thigh looked long and white in the darkness. For a moment they had all been so shocked that they stood frozen with their mouths agape. Then Samuel had noticed them, and given chase. They never ran so fast as they did that night—they lost him in a crowd on Van Buren, but did not stop running until they were on the West Side.

When at last they reached the safety of the barn, they had been surprised a second time.

They had burst into the dark space, and were catching

their breath, when they heard a low exhalation. A rustling. Emmeline had charged in to see who was hiding, and was greeted by a loud and angry moan that rose to the rafters. She had screamed and bolted, making a mad dash straight for Anders's chest. Meanwhile, Fiona had struck a match, and they all saw what had really made the noise.

"It's only a cow," Anders had said, catching Emmeline in his arms.

"What?" she had gasped.

"Just a cow!"

Emmeline gave a little shriek, and her laughter cascaded uncontrollably. Anders laughed too, and twirled her under his arm, and led her in a galloping dance across the floor. They went back and forth in a half-crazed waltz until they were out of breath again, and Emmeline paused and gazed up into Anders's face as though it were the sun.

Her hair had fallen loose, and was curling and shining against her pale pink neck. She chewed her bottom lip, but Fiona could plainly see it was really Anders she wanted to eat up. Neither seemed to remember that Fiona was there at all.

As she watched the way her friends moved together, her stomach seized with agony, and she became certain a fever was rising in her body. Emmeline's and Anders's hands fluttered and darted, seeking each other's faces, wanting to touch. Only Fiona's meddlesome presence prevented them from doing what the butcher and Mrs. Halloran had been doing in the alley.

At that moment, Fiona had had only one wish, which was that she could simply and completely make herself disappear. Instead she had shaken the flame from the match head, so that she would see no more, and pretended the light had gone out by accident.

There was no cow now. No sign of life at all. But Fiona felt just as foolish tonight—it was the natural order of things that Anders belonged to Emmeline. Fiona stepped forward, pulling down a cobweb with her hand. "You should be safe," she said. "Nobody comes here now, it seems."

"I suppose I understand why Emmeline had to go to her party tonight," Anders mused. "But why is it you who took me here? You'd lose your job, if you were discovered. What would she lose?"

His sharp tone made Fiona wince—he didn't even want her here now, and was only annoyed, as he probably always was, that she was not Emmeline. Well, she could accommodate him—she would see him settled and depart quick as she could. "I can always say that I was at my family's house," Fiona replied, standing. "She would have no explanation, and her father would know that she had something planned."

Anders nodded but seemed unconvinced. "You don't

have to do everything she tells you to, you know."

"I do, actually." Her skin prickled with irritation, although she wasn't sure why. "Ochs Carter pays me money to do exactly what Emmeline tells me, and that's how I keep my family in house and home."

In the lantern light, she had a good view of the sideways smile Anders gave her then. "Ah, Fiona Byrne is quite sick of me, and ready to have me gone."

"No," Fiona replied more earnestly than she had meant to. "I never want you to leave."

Anders tilted his head, considering her. "I don't want to either," he said slowly. "But it will be best for all of us. Not just because of Gil Bryce. Because of him, sure. But then there's also . . . Well, there's the problem of Emmeline, and you, and me . . ." He seemed unsure how to finish, and went silent a time. Fiona's heart beat fast and she wished she could reach out and grab hold of what he had been about to say. "Do you remember what it was like, before Emmeline moved to the neighborhood?"

Fiona searched Anders's face for the meaning behind the question, but his expression didn't reveal much. He waited for her to remember, but she couldn't. They would have been about seven, she supposed, when Ochs Carter moved from his family farm to be closer to the opportunities of the business district. That was around when her father had his accident, and those were years she had difficulty recalling.

"You don't remember, do you?" Anders glanced away.

"I'm sorry," she murmured, wishing with her whole body that he would look at her again.

"Don't be. It doesn't matter now. All that matters . . . What matters is . . ." He frowned, and shook away some idea. "When we were little, it was like you and Emmeline . . . it was like you were one girl. But we are all too old for that now. I know you don't think I remember that night. The night I . . ."

"The night you *what*?"

"It was your idea, you know."

Fiona felt half crazed and wished she could somehow have a written report of everything he thought. "*What was?*"

"Me and Emmeline. It pleased you, to think we'd be married and Emmeline would always be your friend, and of course I always did what Fiona told me."

"Oh" was all Fiona had managed to say. She hadn't known he thought of her that way, as the one who made the rules.

"You knew it would always be interesting as long as Emmeline was around, and thought if she were in love with me, she always would be. So I tried to make her love me, and fell in love with her, too, and by the time I saw how she really was, it was too late to take those feelings back. I had it bad for her, and nothing seemed to matter. But you—you could never see how she really was."

"How was she . . ." Fiona whispered. "How was she really?"

Anders made a dismissive gesture, turned, and walked toward the loft. "Emmeline Carter loves herself most of all."

"That's not true!" Fiona, sick of riddles, exclaimed.

"Oh no? Then why is it you who's here tonight? Why are you risking your job, why am I risking my life? We'll never get out of this city together. My only chance is to hop a freight car, and she's too fine a girl to travel like that. I'll be trapped here, and she'll have her fine wedding, and always keep the sweet, sad story of the tragic boy who died of love for her."

"No, you're wrong," Fiona shot back. She wasn't sure why, for she had thought something similar just that morning. Yet her loyalty to Emmeline was hard to shake, and no matter what had transpired these past days, she couldn't forget how much her best friend had given her. "Emmeline has a plan for how to get you out of here, and it depends on her acting exactly as though nothing is happening until the moment she leaves."

"And what, exactly," Anders, sounding very tired, asked, "is her plan?"

"Tomorrow, Emmeline will have several engagements, including a final fitting for the wedding dress, so it won't be easy to get away; you must not expect to see her. She'll be the center of attention, and so much to-do. If I can, I will bring you news. But I shouldn't be seen doing anything out of the ordinary, either. And that is of course when I will have to take care of the jewelry."

"The jewelry?"

"We're going to sell it. So you will have something to live on while you're away."

"Sell it?"

"Yes, sell it. Mr. Carter only gives Emmeline a little pocket money. On most days I have more money than she does." The cruel irony of this had never occurred to Fiona before. "So of course we will have to sell what Emmeline does have."

"But where?"

"That place they always speak of in the old neighborhood—Gorley's."

Anders exhaled sharply. "Have you been there?"

"No, but if it's so famous, it can't be hard to find."

"Gorley the pawn man." Anders shook his head. "Women don't go in there. You'd be robbed before you got to the door."

"It can't be the first time a lady has had reason to sell her jewels."

"He'd cheat you. He wouldn't give you a fair price. . . ."

"He'll want what we're selling," Fiona said.

Anders nodded, but seemed unconvinced. "I'll go," he said.

"You can't," Fiona broke in. "They'll be looking for you. You know they will. If it's as tough a place as you say, surely Gil Bryce and his men have eyes there."

"Gorley is his own king. He doesn't care what Gil Bryce says, he doesn't talk about who's come to him."

"Good." Fiona made her words firm and insistent. The feelings that had roiled within her subsided, and she saw clearly what she must do. All the broken bits of her that had threatened to come apart drew together instead, solid and steady. "Then he won't say he has seen me. You forget, we didn't grow up on the North Side, didn't grow up with fine manners. We grew up fighting for every scrap we got. I'll go. I'll go, and I don't want to hear of you going again. Emmeline is giving up her whole life and everything she's worked for to be with you, and you want to risk it with foolish heroics?" Fiona strode toward Anders, making her eyes blaze with determination. The trouble hadn't left his face, but he didn't argue. "I know what Emmeline's pieces are worth—they won't cheat me."

His eyes shimmered, sunshine on frozen water. "I don't think they'd dare," he said after a pause.

"Good," she said, "it's settled, then," and nodded in affirmation, until he nodded back. They might have been fellow soldiers, or wary adversaries, regarding each other over some unspeakable choice. She wanted badly to know what he thought—if he was frightened or hopeful; if he had any advice about how she ought to conduct herself; or if he truly thought she seemed fearsome. But she knew that she couldn't keep up her tough facade for long. "Well, then," she said, turning to go. "You have everything you need."

By himself, in the middle of the dark barn, Anders cut a lonesome figure. The air was full of dust and hay, too murky with darkness and floating particles for her to be sure if his eyes were really searching for hers. "Will I see you again?"

Fiona wasn't sure if he would, but she couldn't bear to say so. Instead she watched him as she moved in silence toward the door.

"Goodbye, then," Anders called after her.

"We'll say our goodbyes later." Fiona pulled back the weathered old door. "Now put out the lantern so you won't draw attention to yourself."

Although she didn't mean to, she looked back at him once before leaving the barn. He was gazing at her with an expression that made her think of him as a child of five or six, the boy she had known before Emmeline came to the neighborhood. Was that what he had wanted her to remember? How he had always insisted on knowing Fiona's opinion about everything, so he could do what pleased her? After Emmeline arrived—already curling her hair and wearing dresses ornamented with lace and shiny buttons—Fiona's opinion was that they must make the new girl their friend, and Anders had accommodated with all manner of ridiculous strategies. Her heart tore a little at the thought of what might have been, if only she had not told Anders to put the charm on Emmeline all those years ago, if only it had remained just the two of them.

Even now, he did not hesitate to do as Fiona said. He put out the light, and then she had no choice but to go on into the street.

THIRTEEN

And remember: A woman never reveals her whole self;
rather she allows different parts of herself to shine,
depending on who is watching.
—*Anabelle Carrington,* A Lady's Private Book,
O.P. Herring & Sons Publishers, 1869

Emmeline sat alone in her father's carriage, watching the only city she had ever known pass her by. She was trying to decide on the simple clothes, the few items, she would be taking with her when she left. A shawl, a coat, two pairs of shoes, two pairs of gloves, a set of silk handkerchiefs embroidered with her initials, her bristle brush with the silver handle. They would need to get Anders new clothes too, but she supposed they would have to wait until New York. Tomorrow would come on soon, and tomorrow meant they'd be on the train, and the train meant traveling fast into their bright future. She knew it would be bright, although she still couldn't quite picture it.

"Miss Emmeline."

Startled by the sound of Malcolm's voice, Emmeline came down from the cloud of her thoughts and saw that they were at the busy corner of State and Randolph. Field & Leiter hulked above them, a great marble monument, and horse traffic careened on either side. "Oh, I . . . I was away with the fairies, I guess."

The rest of her father's people—the builders and messenger boys, the accountants and advisers, the housekeepers and the decorators—were all kindly and inquisitive when it came to Ochs Carter's daughter, concerned with her preoccupations, gladdened when they could please her. But Malcolm, big Malcolm with his long, flat face, only offered his arm, neither averting his eyes nor inviting an explanation. As she floated through the busy first floor, as she ascended to the private fitting rooms, she reminded herself that she had not left yet, and that in the hours to come she must be very careful to seem like nothing more or less than a nervous bride. She must seem almost bursting with excitement.

Yesterday, she had disliked the officious and vain Mr. Polk, and thought Miss Fay's needlework mediocre. But today she was kind to them. She smiled and cooed as they wrapped her in white silk and lace. She murmured enthusiastically and twisted on her little platform to appreciate their handiwork. When they clasped their hands, delighting at Emmeline ensconced in nuptial glory, she let a happy tear escape the corner of her eye. Perhaps that was a bit much, but she thought Anders would have admired her flair.

"What a vision!"

In the standing mirror, Emmeline saw Ada entering the dressing room. Behind her was Daisy Fleming, and behind Daisy was Cora Russell. The skin at the back of Emmeline's neck prickled when she saw Cora.

"I see you didn't bring along your maid for consultation this time," said Cora as her eyes roamed the room for something to dislike.

Mr. Polk made an awkward, jerking movement, rising so as to keep his back to Emmeline, and Emmeline realized that he had gossiped about her behavior at the first fitting. Her mouth puckered in anger, thinking of him and Cora saying unkind things about that upstart Emmeline Carter. For a moment Emmeline felt very satisfied that she had won Freddy, and that Cora would remain forever envious. But then she reminded herself that after tomorrow she would not have to think about Cora Russell ever again, and relaxed her face.

"No, she didn't," Daisy replied with a little snort. "And if you caught on to the way of things as quickly as she picks up the rules of decorum, you might be engaged now instead of attending a wedding by yourself."

Ada gave a rich laugh and crossed the room, her full-length tartan skirt swaying. She arrived at Emmeline's side, ushering in a spell of hushed admiration during which Emmeline brightened her eyes to share in Ada's joy. "Are you almost done, Mr. Polk?" Ada asked presently. "We have a surprise for Emmeline."

"Yes, Mrs. Garrison," said the chastened Mr. Polk, and he began the laborious process of removing the dress from Emmeline.

As they descended the grand stairs of the department store, the entourage of stylish and high-born girls surrounded the bride-to-be with an air of giddy protectiveness, and Emmeline couldn't help whispering in Ada's ear.

"Why did she come?"

"You mean Cora?" Emmeline nodded. Instead of replying, Ada linked arms with Daisy and walked ahead. "Go on, Miss Russell," she called over her shoulder.

They had arrived on the second-floor landing, and Emmeline faced Cora warily. But if Cora's expression were any indication, *she* was the one with a bad case of nerves. "Miss Carter," Cora began. Her gaze was fixed upon the marble floor as she pulled at the hem of her jacket. "I've been rather unkind to you, and I am . . ." Her words disappeared into a murmur.

"What?"

"I'm sorry."

"Oh."

"And I was wondering—"

"Yes?"

"After you're married, if you could sort of—I don't know—throw me the bouquet?"

"Oh!"

"Well, you see, because, if a girl catches the bouquet, they say it means . . ."

"Yes." Emmeline gave Cora a reassuring pat, and took her by the arm. She pressed her lips together to keep from laughing at this sudden turnabout—she was rather charmed by Cora's request, and almost wished that she would be able to oblige. But she was happy to do the next best thing, and agree to what she asked. "Of course," she whispered conspiratorially. "You just get as close to me as you can, and I'll toss it right to you."

They took the Garrisons' open-topped barouche downtown. Malcolm was nowhere to be seen, and Ada ushered them onward with authority. Once they were all seated, their skirts overflowed the facing double seats, so that the carriage floor was entirely invisible, and their vehicle proceeded at a slow speed, as though they were taking part in a royal parade. Emmeline did not ask where they were going, but she could see that the other girls knew. They practically hummed with their secret. Their eagerness pleased her, but she felt no need to press for explanations. She had her own secret, after all, and it softened her smile and glazed her eyes. The sky hung above them like a curtain of perfect blue.

As they turned from Van Buren onto Michigan Avenue, she heard the clack and pant of the Illinois Central, and had a presentiment of their destination. They were going to Terrace Row. Her father used to take her this way, when she was a girl, to see the mansions. They had been new then—ten grand houses, a continuous edifice of limestone, stern, and fine—and had caused something of a scandal in the newspapers, on account of their ostentatious expense. But her father had not been scandalized—he had taken her only to assure her that she would one day have a house just as remarkable.

A Terrace Row address was not something he'd managed to acquire, yet there was Father's polished burgundy phaeton—not at all like the little cart they'd had during the war—and Malcolm standing beside it, with that impassive face of his.

"Well," said Daisy, her eyes darting and bright. "Congratulations."

"Tomorrow will be so much fun," said Cora, sounding

almost genuine. She was smiling—Emmeline didn't think she'd ever seen Cora smile before. She was almost unrecognizable when she smiled.

"Here," said Daisy. "From us."

"For tomorrow," Cora explained, and she pinned a small lapis brooch on Emmeline's dress. "You know—something blue."

The driver had already helped Ada down to the street. Now she made an impatient gesture. "Come along."

"We'll say goodbye here, then," Daisy went on, remaining in the barouche, although it was clear that she wanted to follow Ada and Emmeline where they were going. She wanted to see what was inside the house on Terrace Row.

Emmeline bowed her head. She was a little touched, in spite of herself, and rather wished that they really could be her friends. If she were to stay in Chicago, she knew they would be, and thought what a formidable group they'd make. "What a lovely day you've given me."

"Thank you!" called Cora as Ada and Emmeline made their way up the steps of a house in the middle of the block, the one closest to where Malcolm waited.

They crossed the threshold, and encountered a grand still life. There was Freddy, his hands clasped behind his back, his expression frozen. There was Freddy's butler, offering a tray of champagne flutes. Another servant stood off to the side, holding an ornate candelabra. Instead of the usual dozen roses he brought when he took her for a drive, there were maybe a hundred stems, all frilly white, filling several enamel vases. And there was Father, leaning against the balustrade, beaming.

"My darling," Freddy said when he saw her, and made a deep bow. "Welcome home."

"Home?" Emmeline stepped farther into the foyer and glanced around at the carved oak ceiling, from which dangled a chandelier of crystal droplets.

"Do you like it? This was where my grandmother, Genevieve Gage Arles, entertained Chicago's best people. Of course, I've had everything redone for you. This marble—you'll never see any better, I can promise that." He indicated the pink-streaked tile underfoot. "I've had it brought from Italy. And the carpets were all originally made for the Mughal emperors. The furniture is rosewood rococo, shipped from New York, the latest style. I chose the pieces myself on my last visit. Let me show you—"

He was interrupted by three sharp coughs, and turned with sudden energy toward the sound. The servant holding the candle shrank from Freddy, his face contracting fearfully, as though bracing for a blow.

"Morris, you idiot—" he began but broke off when he saw that Morris had stepped backward into the drapes that partially covered the entry into the parlor, forgetting entirely about the lit candles he held, so that the fabric peeled upward into pale yellow flame.

"Oh dear," Ada murmured.

"Damn you!" Freddy exclaimed, his voice reaching a high pitch.

"It's all right," Father said, pulling a bunch of flowers from a vase and throwing the remaining contents at the little blaze. "They're only drapes."

They stood in silence, smelling the damp burnt odor.

"I wanted everything to be perfect." Freddy's voice was still angry, but when he revolved toward Emmeline, his expression was so crestfallen that she almost pitied him, and wanted to make it better.

"Everything *is* perfect," she said, moving close, resting her hand on his cheek, and giving him her most incandescent smile.

For a moment he appeared mollified. But when he drew her hand down away from his face to examine her finger, anger seized his features once more. "Where is my ring?" he asked.

"Oh! Well, it's . . ." Emmeline, in a panic, urged herself to say nothing stupid, but the words were coming fast and beyond her control. "It's being polished. For tomorrow. It didn't need it, not really. I just wanted everything to be—"

"Perfect." Freddy's whole being seemed to settle with the

thought. "That's why I love you, my Emmeline, you see the world as I do, and will not settle for anything short of perfection."

With a firm grip on her hand, he drew her up the stairs and from room to room. Ada and her father followed, keeping quiet so Freddy could explain the provenance of every vase and painting, every settee and end table, assuring her that it was the best, the very best a man could buy. They went up the stairs and down, as Freddy imagined the dinner parties they would host here, the people they'd invite, what sort of music they'd listen to, how they would dress.

The tour ended in the front parlor with the big picture window, through which she could see the small skiffs on the lagoon, and beyond the train tracks, the little whitecaps on the lake as it spread toward the eastern states. Throughout the weeks of her engagement, she had never quite been able to picture how she and Freddy would live. Now, strangely, she knew precisely where and how their days as a married couple would be spent, only after realizing they'd never be.

"Aren't you going to say something?" said Freddy.

"It's beautiful." Emmeline turned back from the view, toward the three people waiting breathlessly for her opinion. "Everything is beautiful."

"You will be happy here," Ada said with a confident smile.

"Yes." Emmeline forced the words out of her mouth. "Very happy."

"Well," said Ada. "It's bad luck if we linger. You must be a surprise to each other on your wedding day."

Freddy advanced, as though to take hold of his bride, but his sister held him back.

"None of that yet!" she giggled.

Freddy glanced at his sister irritably, but did as he was told. For a brief moment he gazed at Emmeline as though he couldn't believe she was real. This was not exactly the way Anders looked at her, but it had something in common with his innocent adoration, and she wondered that she had not noticed it before, that she had noticed only his worldly manner and fine dress.

"Sleep well, my Emmeline," he said. His eyes welled with such yearning and hopefulness that she almost forgot he was wealthy and powerful, and saw only a young man eager to earn her affection. "I hope I will please you as a groom."

Emmeline curtsied, and tried to maintain her happy expression until Freddy and his sister departed. Father was watching her. He must have been watching her the whole time. She knew what he was going to say—she had not shown enough enthusiasm, she had not been perfect—and she was angry with herself for not better concealing her private worries. On long, brusque strides, he crossed the room to her.

"Do you remember when we used to go far out of our way to see this block?" he whispered. "We had only one horse, and you had only one dress."

Emmeline shivered. "Yes."

For a while he was unable to speak. Only slowly did it occur to her that the difficulty was not on account of his displeasure with her. In fact, he was trying not to cry. When she saw his tears, hers came, too, and they were not the fake tears she'd produced for the dressmakers. "We've come a great distance, haven't we?" he asked at last.

"Yes," she said, and nodded. She wasn't sure she'd ever seen her father cry, and her heart swelled, seeing him pink in the face and sentimental, and she couldn't help but throw herself into his arms.

"Emmy," he said, calling her by the nickname he'd banished when they moved to the North Side, and holding her tight. "You're a real lady now. I can't begin to tell you how proud I am."

Guilt stung in her throat. She wanted Father to have his Terrace Row house, and like all her wants, it came on abruptly, and demanded to be fulfilled in a hurry. "I'm sorry," she whispered.

"Whatever for?"

"I don't know, I just . . ." She trailed off, wishing she could tell him everything, all the wild turns her life had taken. She wished she could say a proper goodbye, and explain why she had to leave. And she wished she could leave and somehow also stay, so that she would not have to give anything up.

"I've been hard on you, haven't I?" he said. "It was only that I wanted you to have all this, everything I couldn't give you as a little girl. Well, I shall be easier now. Let's get you home, so you can rest. Tomorrow will be a tiring day."

FOURTEEN

Do not be fooled by velvet and lace, silk and tulle, crinoline and fur.
A woman's dress is her suit of armor, tough as any metal.
—Anabelle Carrington, A Lady's Private Book,
O.P. Herring & Sons Publishers, 1869

"There goes a fine bit of stuff."

The man was leaning against a wall, his shoulders high and rigid, the rest of him relaxed as water. His eyes were a murky green amid bloodshot white, and his jaw was black with stubble.

"Shut up," sneered the man next to him. "Or she'll scare."

For her trip to Gorley the broker's, Fiona had chosen a ruffled plum skirt and little matching jacket. She had plaited her hair in an elaborate arrangement, and blackened her eyelashes. Fiona had tried on clothing of Emmeline's before, but she had never gone into the world in fashionable dress. All the boning and corseting, the stiff embroidery and standing collars, made sense to her in a new way, now that she was the one conspicuously put together. Not because her elegant facade saved her from fearing the men of Gorley's block. No, they could stir menace with the slightest tilt of the head, and inside she quivered. But she sensed they were a little intimidated by her appearance, too.

"Where's Gorley's?" she asked impatiently, as though it was not so much their leering that perturbed her as their slowness to be of assistance.

Leisurely—as though weighing what it would gain him to help her—the man pointed to an unmarked storefront across the street.

"Thank you," she said, and tossed him a coin. "Go to the baths," she added as she lifted her skirts to cross the dusty street. "I can smell you from here."

This strip of Market was just east of the south branch of the river, a place where stolen things could be bought and sold. Its denizens watched her from shadowy doorways and second-story windows. They glared from their perches on carts and coaches, or as they passed—too close—on the sidewalk. She heard whistles and grumbles, laughter and profane hisses. A cool whisper traveled up and down her backbone, but she kept her gaze steady and went on, neither fast nor slow. She was alert to the jewelry box she carried, wrapped in burlap, although she was careful not to grip it too tight, or draw attention to her precious cargo in any other way. The only time she startled was when she thought she saw a familiar phaeton go by. She twirled and strained to see if it was Malcolm in the driver's seat. But the vehicle was gone too quickly, and the door to Gorley's was before her. She gave herself a little nod of encouragement, and pushed inside.

The walls were covered in oil paintings and hunting trophies, and furniture was stacked in the corners. Shotguns were piled behind a glass-case counter, which was full of bracelets and necklaces, cuff links and tie-pins. There were so many clocks in that room, ticking from all sides. A large man stood just inside the door—she wasn't sure if he was keeping people in or out, for the men who loitered by the cases and waited in the doorways had a twitchy manner, like prisoners.

"Gorley," called the hulking person by the door. "You'll want to see this one."

A few moments passed in which Fiona would very much have liked to pretend to be absorbed in studying the brush-strokes used to conjure clouds in the maritime scene hanging by the door. But she did not give in to this temptation. She stood still, and did her best to seem annoyed at being made to wait. Presently, a man emerged from behind a curtain.

He was short and stout, with a shiny bald head and small, plump hands, which he wiped against his shirt, as though to absolve them of sweat or grease. She was surprised by his diminutive stature, but only for a few moments. He had the sharp black eyes of a bird of prey.

"What can I do for you, little lady?"

"You're Gorley?"

"What do you think?"

She blushed at this reply, but came forward anyway and put the box on the counter. "I won't do business with anyone but the proprietor."

He grinned at her, as one does an amusing child. "No, I suppose you wouldn't," he replied, and began to undo the burlap wrapping. "Dolled up as you are."

The other men in the store approached, breathing coarsely and jockeying for a good view of what was inside. Fiona put her hand on the box, to prevent Gorley's opening it. "It's awfully stuffy in here," she said. "I may have to go elsewhere."

"Step back," Gorley barked, and the others did as he said.

Fiona removed her hand and waited. He took his time, turning over every piece, examining each pearl on the long strand to make sure a fake had not been strung up with the real ones, holding the gems to the light, examining the work of each engraving. He examined the diadem and placed it rakishly on his bald head. There was a stretch of quiet minutes for Fiona to think, which was unfortunate. She had been avoiding thinking. Since that long walk to the barn with Anders, she had been able to carry herself with nobility on account of her selfless dedication to her friends and family. She was able to do all she did with the thought that it would at least keep Anders safe. But here, as she waited for Gorley to name a price, as she held still and kept an eyebrow cocked to show she would not be cheated, the thoughts came, and she could not stop them. Emmeline would have been better at this task, and braver—she would not have been so chilled by the ogling; she would not have felt the danger. The unfairness of the whole arrangement struck Fiona, struck her like a closed fist, and afterward the ache wouldn't go away.

Gorley sniffed. "I'll give you five hundred for the lot."

The amount made Fiona light in the head. Her family could live on that much for two years, maybe four. She shut the lid, and gripped the box. "That's kind," she said. "But it's worth at least a thousand to you."

As she drew back the box, Gorley put his hand out, stopping her. "Six hundred," he said.

"Seven."

A man, tucked into one of the corners, giggled at a high pitch. "All right," Gorley said, and grinned, and she knew he was satisfied that he'd made the better bargain.

"It's too little," she said proudly. "But I'm in a hurry."

"Ladies in your situation always are."

Fiona's eyes grew large with anger. In *what* situation? she wanted to demand. She, who had only done for others, being accused of low morality! The suggestion enraged her, and she longed to tell him what she was made of and how very wrong he was. But an outburst would do her no good. This man's opinion did not matter, she reminded herself. She would never see him again. Emmeline and Anders could live comfortably on seven hundred a long time. She should think only of leaving, as quickly and quietly as possible.

"Well, then." She held out her hand, so that he could see the fine weave of her glove.

He laid the bills out on the counter, and she nodded that it was the correct amount, and then he wrapped them in brown paper.

But she could not stand to simply go, and be remembered as a desperate woman. "I'll take a receipt, thank you."

"A receipt?" His eyebrows shot up theatrically. "If you come back for 'em, you'll pay double."

She gave him a blank stare. "By next week, it will be a small amount to me."

"As you wish, mademoiselle."

He placed the packet in an envelope, and scrawled his name across its white expanse: *Gorley's, of 101 Market Street*, as though he were a fancy jeweler, and then on the other side the name of each item and how much he had paid.

"I look forward to seeing you again," he said, and pushed the envelope in her direction.

Quick as she could, she dropped the envelope into her pocket. She leaned into the counter to conceal how her fingers darted, with the ready needle and thread, sealing the payment within her skirt. A few seconds and it was done, without anyone noticing.

"Thank you, miss," Gorley said. "Good luck to you," he added. He seemed to be saying that she would need it.

"Goodbye." Fiona pronounced the word with what she hoped was haughty finality.

Outside, the sky was blindingly bright. The bills in her pocket were heavy, they seemed hot there against her leg, and she knew that she was not safe until she was clear of Water Street, until she was back on the North Side. She must not relax yet. Such was the muddle of her thoughts as she moved in the direction of the Carters', and perhaps it was for this reason that, when she felt a hand grabbing a fistful of her bustle, her mind went first to the seven hundred dollars in her pocket.

It took another few seconds to realize that it was she who was in danger.

The hand belonged to the man with the black stubble and the bloodshot eyes. She struggled, but in an instant he had dragged her into a doorway, and trapped her in his arms. She fumbled, adjusting her skirt and pushing the money away from him, but he didn't notice, or care. His hands were huge and sweaty, smearing across her neck, her chest.

"Hoping I'd wait for you?" His breath stung her face, so swollen was his tongue with gin, and his rough fingers tugged at her braids.

Her pulse raced and her body shrank. "No," she managed through her terror.

"No?" He grinned, and held her tighter. "Feisty. I've always liked a feisty gal."

She tried to wriggle free, but this only allowed his body to push against hers, pungent with its awful lust.

"That's a dear," he laughed. "Come close."

The blow came from nowhere, sudden as a brick hurled from the sky, and it met the man's face with as much force. She heard his nose crack, his teeth break, the wind whoosh as it left his body. She herself was free, the money she had come for safely sealed within her pocket, and now it was her assailant who was smashed back into the doorway, pummeled and pummeled until he bled from the nostrils and cried out for mercy.

"Anders," Fiona whispered. "He's already beaten."

Anders glanced over his shoulder at Fiona. He blinked at her and seemed to remember his purpose. He threw the man to the ground, and gave him a final kick in the head, before turning to her, still panting in exertion. Although they stood a foot apart, she could hear the crazy beating of his heart. "Are you all right?" he asked. "I'll kill him if—if he hurt you."

The man made a pitiable sound, like he wished he were dead already.

"I'm all right." Anders was still frenzied from attacking the man, and Fiona wished she could calm him somehow. "I'm fine, really," she added.

"I told you not to . . ." he mumbled. "I wish you hadn't . . ."

"But I did," she said.

He drew his fingers over her hair, smoothing the places where the man had yanked at her braids. With worried eyes, he examined her ripped-open jacket, and her ruffled shirt. He carefully brought the shirt and jacket back into place. She averted her gaze instinctively, not wanting to invite more attention from a boy who was—who would soon be—entirely Emmeline's.

The gentleness of his touch, especially after the fury with which he'd beaten the man with the murky eyes, made her chest rise in a way she couldn't disguise. The old want was there, before she could stuff it away. She wanted him to do exactly what he had done that spring night: press her against the wall and put his mouth to her mouth. To distract herself, she asked, "Did anyone see you come this way?"

"I was careful."

"Good. You had better be careful, and get back soon."

"First I'll see you as far as Water Street."

This seemed unwise, and she was about to tell him so. But he came forward and clasped her hand.

"You can tell me not to, but I'll still follow you. I've been following you all day. Didn't mean for you to know. I was trying to keep a safe distance, or this man never would've gotten so close to you."

"You should go back to the barn," she said.

He pressed her hand, and released it. She raised her eyes to his to show she meant it, but he only stared back in a way that made her stomach weak. His hand floated to her face, tucking strands of hair into place, and—afraid of what he might do next—she stepped out of the doorway and onto the sidewalk.

Although she had told him not to, he followed her all the way to the river. She sensed him like her own shadow—always a quarter block behind—and walked tall knowing she was safe.

FIFTEEN

We are beside ourselves with anticipation for the wedding of
Miss Emmeline Carter to Mr. Frederick Tree tomorrow afternoon.
We all agree she is very lovely, and we all acknowledge she is
very new. How will she bear up under the pressure of being a
society bride with all eyes upon her?
—*"Leisure Life" column,* Chicago Crier, *October 7, 1871*

From the plush chaise by the picture window in her bedroom, Emmeline watched a parade of deliveries enter the
Carter residence. The flowers and tables and chairs, the
arches and tents, the crates of lemons and oranges, a gold-
foil box the size of a person, which she supposed contained
her wedding dress, as well as a smaller box for the veil, and
another for accessories. Father's new suit was among these
deliveries, too, and it was the image of Father in white tie

and black tails—proud to see hundreds of the city's most prominent people assembled on his lawn, gathered to watch him escort his only daughter to the altar—that she found most difficult to part with. She did not see Fiona among the busy traffic on the lawn. It was Fiona she was watching for. But her friend must have come in the back way to avoid notice, and gone up the servants' stairs.

"Oh, there you are," Emmeline said. "I was worried."

"I'm all right," Fiona said.

"You wore the burgundy," Emmeline went on, gazing wistfully at her friend. "You look beautiful in burgundy."

"You were right. If I'd gone in my maid's clothing, we would have gotten less." Fiona was bent over, examining the skirt. She yanked the fabric suddenly, ripping a seam open.

"Oh!" Emmeline jumped from her seat. "What are you doing?"

"Here." Fiona pulled out a few errant strands of thread, and handed a stack of bills wrapped in brown paper. "Seven hundred."

"Oh." Emmeline took the money, and went back to her chair, to the twilight view of the property where the Carters had built their reputation. The trees were orange, the lawn purple. She had never found it quite so lovely as now. "Seven hundred."

Fiona was unbuttoning her jacket, stepping out of the

full-length skirt with its tiered ruffles. "You'll be able to live in hotels for half a year if need be on that."

"Yes, I suppose."

"Eat well, dress well."

How many days had passed since she had decided to leave? Not many, especially when she counted up all the days she'd lived in the North Side, all the days of her engagement, all the days she'd planned to be a bride. Of course, she had imagined the hotels she and Anders would stay in, the first-class train tickets, the fine suits she would buy him so that they could go to elegant restaurants without anyone questioning their presence. What a good story it would be—Emmeline Carter, who had in a few seasons won the attention of top-drawer Chicago, on the run with a lowlife boxer. Fiona had just handed her enough money to make it all come true—and yet those dreams seemed more elusive now. It wasn't so much that she wasn't curious for her life with Anders—it was that she couldn't wish this world, with its lawns and parties and fineries, away. "I suppose."

"What's wrong? I thought you'd be happy."

Emmeline rolled over on the chaise, and regarded her friend in petticoat and corset. "I am," she replied not very convincingly. "Very, very happy."

Ever since she had left the house on Terrace Row, Emmeline had yearned for Fiona. To tell Fiona everything, and have Fiona listen, and agree that it was an impossible predicament. They would go over every detail, and consider every outcome, until it was perfectly clear what Emmeline should do. Until there was no doubt. But there was something stiff and uninviting about Fiona, even though she had stripped to her white underthings. She stepped forward, regarding Emmeline with those knowing green eyes.

"What happened?"

Although the question lacked the usual Fiona openness, Emmeline couldn't help herself. The whole afternoon, with its agonies and indecisions, its revelations and desperate desires for contradictory things, came in a rush. She told her of the amusing episode with Cora, and the dressmaker, and the impressive house on Terrace Row. "The house," she said, after saying a lot of other not-quite-sensible things, "the house is so perfect, and Father was so proud. I can't *stand* the notion that I'll never have him over for a supper in the grand dining room."

All the time Emmeline had babbled, Fiona had been still and impassive. When Emmeline stopped speaking, Fiona gave a slow nod, and went into the closet. A few moments passed before she returned, with the plain, worn clothes that made up her maid's uniform.

"Well?" Emmeline asked a little desperately. Fiona was never so slow to reply. "Aren't you going to say something?"

Fiona was buttoning her plain white collared shirt, and she didn't answer until she had reached the top button. "Have you ever known anything for sure?"

Emmeline didn't understand what this had to do with the house on Terrace Row or disappointing her father or Cora Russell wanting the bouquet. "What do you mean?"

"Known something was true with such certainty that your whole body got quiet and told you so?"

"Well, I've known a lot of things. . . ." Emmeline felt confused and wished Fiona would stop acting strange. "You mean, like, that blue is your best color? Or that you truly dislike someone and always will? Or that you've said the wrong thing, said it out loud, and you'll never be able to take it back?"

"Not exactly." Fiona had pulled her skirt over her hips, contorting to do the buttons at the small of her back.

"Then what do you mean?" Emmeline asked impatiently.

"You love Anders, don't you?"

"Yes."

"Do you love Freddy?"

Was that what Fiona had been going on about? Emmeline had never asked herself this question, not really. But now, with Fiona giving her that serious face, she was certain that she did not. And just in the way Fiona had described:

her insides got very quiet, and she knew the truth as though a clear, strong voice had spoken it directly into her ear. "No. . . ." she whispered.

"In that case, you can't go through with the wedding. Of course you'll be giving up a lot; I know that will be hard. But you may get most of it back, and in the end, it will have been worth the risk. When you know for sure what is good and right, what is true for you, you must act on that, and not convince yourself of something else. We must all be true to our own hearts."

Emmeline felt cold, and small, and she wished Fiona would make her tea and tell her a silly story, so that they could both laugh until their bellies hurt. But Fiona's attention was fixed on buttoning the cuffs of her shirt. Emmeline sighed, and threw herself back against the silk pillow of the chaise, clinging to it as though it might comfort her. The formality with which Fiona waited, fully dressed and attentive as any servant, seemed some sort of rebuke.

"You should have seen the view from the parlor," she said, not quite to Fiona. "The lake, the whole view was the lake, going on and on forever. . . ."

Fiona had crossed the room by then. If she heard what Emmeline said, she gave no sign. "There is a lot of work to do, and they'll be wanting all the help they can get downstairs. Do you need anything?"

Emmeline put her fingers against the windowpane, and shook her head.

"I know you'll do what's right, Emmy. Get some rest tonight. You'll need it." Emmeline thought Fiona had already left, when she spoke again. Her voice had gone down an octave as if in warning. "I couldn't stand by and watch otherwise," she said. "If you went ahead with something that wasn't true to your heart."

SIXTEEN

'Tis the last rose of summer
Left blooming alone;
All her lovely companions
Are faded and gone;
No flower of her kindred,
No rosebud is nigh,
To reflect back her blushes,
To give sigh for sigh.
—*Thomas Moore, "The Last Rose of Summer" (1805)*

When there was no more work to do, Fiona entered her own narrow bedroom, rested her shoulders against the door, and shut her tired eyes.

For once, the Carter household staff did not resent her.

Everyone was run off their feet, but Fiona had worked as hard as any of them, carrying the long tables into the backyard under the white tent that had gone up that afternoon, arranging flowers, kneading bread, steaming tablecloths, sorting silver. Emmeline's bell did not ring, and so there had been no reason for Fiona to leave the general hubbub that filled the lower areas of the house. Now she was weary to the core. But it did not matter. She already knew she could not sleep peacefully here tonight.

Instead of preparing for bed, she lit the candle on the little wooden table. The candle's flame flickered, and Fiona gazed into its light, wondering what on earth to do. She'd had to force herself to abandon Emmeline, helpless and needful of advice as her friend had been. Fiona knew that look on Emmeline's face, and was accustomed to rushing to her aid when she was in distress.

Yet tonight some stubborn part of Fiona had refused to go along with Emmeline's wishes.

Certain facts that she had tried to bury had become impossible to deny. After seeing Anders, after sensing him behind her as she walked the long blocks back to the North Side, after hearing the beat of his heart . . . she loved him. And that meant more than it had before. It was not only that she wanted to watch the way his smile broke open when he made himself laugh, to listen when he talked about anything, to make him happy, and keep him warm. She wanted him to treat her as he had today, as though she required watching out for, too.

Upstairs, when Emmeline had made those wide, inconsolable eyes, Fiona could have told her it was all right.

"Marry Freddy," she could have said. "Move into the elegant house on Terrace Row with the lovely view of the lake and make your father proud. No one will ever know you planned to run away with a boxer from the old neighborhood, for I will never tell."

Then Anders would be free. But he would be wounded, and it was Fiona who would have delivered the final blow. He might be hers in the end, but only because she'd told lies and played cruel tricks. Anyway, he wasn't safe here—that was the mean, final fact she kept coming back around to. The best thing for him was if he and Emmeline escaped, with their considerable funds, and were far away from here as long as possible.

Through the thin walls of the servants' quarters she heard murmurs and snoring, the restless turning over of old bones against stiff sheets. Fiona had trained herself long ago to do what she did not want to do. She was used to unpleasant tasks, and not afraid to suffer. But tonight, on the eve of the wedding of the season, as the household drifted into anxious sleep, there was no right thing for her to do. So she blew out the candle, and left her little room.

The Carter residence had been transformed for tomorrow's festivities, but it felt ghostly without any music or voices to enliven the nuptial decorations. As Fiona went through the backyard, the dry grass crunched underfoot. The tent rippled. She half expected an alarm to ring when she left the property, but there was nothing. No dog barking, no light from an upstairs window. She was free to go, and always had been.

In the past few days, she had done a great deal of sneaking around at night. But the streets did not frighten her now. She crossed the river without a tremor. She had the strange conviction that as long as she did the right thing, no harm would come to her.

As Fiona crossed the river, she heard the courthouse bell ringing the fire alarm, but did not make much of it. Since October began, bringing with it a dry blast of late summer, the fire bell had rung every night.

Even in the midnight dark, the tar still bubbled and hissed from the baking it had received during the day. But to see any of this, one had to be above the skyline— as were the editor working the night desk at the *Tribune*, the men filling the six-story grain elevator, and Gabriel, Anders's cousin, who had been awakened by the smell of smoke and crawled out his window and up to the Dorrans' roof to see what was burning. From that high vantage in the old neighborhood, a bright orange haze was indeed visible, due west—past the ship masts that rose from the docks, across the south branch of the river. Gabriel hurried to fasten the shiny new brass buttons of his uniform's vest, which he loved, don his brimmed cap, and then ran all the way to the Van Buren Street Bridge.

A policeman was holding back the crowd of curious gawkers on the eastern side, but Gabriel's uniform allowed him passage to the west side, where the rumors were general—the trouble had begun in the planing mill on Canal, and the culprit was either the boiler or some mischief-maker, though it didn't matter much in a place like that. It was all wood and scraps. Any little spark would do the job. Everyone agreed that they were lucky it was a windless night, although no one felt lucky. There were several lumberyards in the surrounding blocks, where the great trees of the Wisconsin woods, having been turned into planks and posts and boards, were stored before being shipped south and east.

Gabriel had never been this close to a real fire, and it humbled him to stand beneath the brilliant spectacle, awful and beautiful at once. The buildings that the flames had spread to emanated heat like the gate of hell, and their former shape disintegrated and transformed so that what loomed above them seemed some terrifying beast from another world—it screamed, clawed the night sky, and devoured everything it came across. At least three engine companies had arrived at the scene by then, and their canvas hoses crisscrossed the street. A dozen or so men aimed their weak streams of water at the old mill. Gabriel stared helplessly at the structure, at the smoke that billowed from its roof, the flames that gusted from its upper windows.

Yesterday, Gabriel had just been a watchman, and a novice at that. But a man on horseback whipped the men into formation, like soldiers coming into battle. They soon acquired an awful aspect—singed beards, swollen eyes, their clothes in disarray, their faces blackened.

They needed every able and willing body. Like that, Gabriel became one of them. He understood this abruptly and thoroughly. No one asked what company he was with, or doubted that he belonged. They were an army, fighting a common enemy, and their individual names and where they had been earlier in the day no longer mattered. As long as the enemy continued its destruction of their city, they would move together, act together, doing all they could to halt its voracious path.

Meanwhile the whirl of bright particles was blown upward and away, over a sleeping city, blissfully unaware of the conflagration that spread and threatened their homes and ways of life. And even Fiona, awake past midnight, was so consumed with her own tortures that she did not consider what raged across the river.

"Fiona!" her mother exclaimed in happy surprise, and lowered her feet to the ground. They had been resting on Fiona's father's lap; Fiona had never seen her mother go barefoot before. She stepped into her slippers, put down her tin cup, and came to the door.

"Where is Jack?" Fiona asked, surveying the cozy scene. A beaten book of verse lay open in her father's lap, and her mother still held the crochet hook and yarn she'd been working. "Where are Kate and Brian?"

"They're asleep, love. Do you know how late it is?"

"Oh, yes—of course." Walking south from the Carters' Fiona had not known where she was heading, but now in the presence of her mother and father—assessing her with their kind, bright eyes, waiting for her to explain what she was up to—she knew she had come to the right place. She wanted to forget her life, and curl at their feet and listen to their stories of Ireland. "I should be, too."

"Oh," her mother laughed. "You're a grown girl now, with your own job, you can come and go as you please."

"Come, my Fiona, sit with us awhile," her father urged.

The windows were open, to clear out the cooking smells and let in the night air, and Fiona settled on a cushion by her father, resting her head on the sturdy wooden chair he'd built many years ago.

"Must be busy up at Ochs Carter's place these days," Father said after a spell of quiet. "The newspapers have been going on and on about the lavish to-do."

Fiona glanced up at him, and saw that he understood this was no ordinary visit. But her belly tightened and her eyes watered at the prospect of having to explain everything that had transpired.

"We're lucky to see Fiona, what with all her responsibilities at the Carter house," her mother interjected, giving her husband a warning look. It was plain that she, too, knew her daughter was in the midst of a crisis. "Let us not count our blessings."

"No," her father agreed. "We won't count our blessings when it comes to Fiona, we will only be grateful for her lovely presence."

Fiona smiled up at her parents, grateful that they seemed to comprehend what she needed without an explanation. "What were you reading, Pa? Can I hear it?"

He kissed her forehead, cleared his throat, and began: "'Tis the last rose of summer/left blooming alone/All her lovely companions/Are faded and gone. . . ."

Fiona closed her eyes and listened to her father recite the familiar words in his rich lilt. The chair's arm was smooth like stone from so many years of use. She inhaled the smell of that room, so that she could remember it always as it was that night. There were the usual scents—her mother's rose soap, and Father's tobacco—mixed with the odor of pine. The Byrnes had begun stockpiling firewood for winter, a fact that Fiona found reassuring. They were not so unprepared for changes as she sometimes worried, and would make do without her envelopes, if it came to that. In a neighboring house, someone was playing the fiddle, and farther away, the courthouse bells made their mournful tone. Winter would be a while coming, Fiona thought, if they were still ringing the fire alarm every night. When her father reached the final stanza, she glanced up, and saw that her parents had interlaced their fingers, and were gazing at each other in silent adoration.

"When true hearts lie withered," he concluded from memory. "And fond ones are flown/Oh! Who would inhabit this bleak world alone."

Fiona's heart was sad, but it settled with the sound of poetry. She worried too much over other people. Here, tonight, she could see that her family was all right. Here her loneliness did not feel quite so mean. After tomorrow, Anders and Emmeline would be on their journey. She would see them safely off, and—content with the notion that her friends had escaped present dangers—she herself would find a new way to be happy.

★ ★ ★

That was the hopeful thought with which Fiona drifted into sleep. By the time the night sky began to pale, so too did the terrible light of the mill fire, and the Frontier Engine Company left the scene to get some rest. With them was Gabriel, who could no longer remember the feeling of loneliness. They walked, a loose confederation of men who had done their duty—teary with relief, grinning with pride, heavy-footed from their effort. At the station house, beer was passed around and talk became easy, and many things were said.

"It was a perfect fire—the air so dry and hot, and so much to burn."

"We were lucky to have stopped it where we did."

"Could have been worse."

"Could have been bad."

"Could have been the end of everything."

"The city'll be on alert now. Whole city will be careful when they hear what happened tonight."

Gabriel lay on a cot and listened. One drink of beer made him sleepy, and his eyelids were heavy, so he closed them for a minute or two, listening as the men retold the story of tonight. The story of what, for one day only, would be known as the Great Fire. By the next night, the world as they knew it would be gone, and there would be no mistaking the Great Fire for any of the small conflagrations that came before.

SEVENTEEN

Last night more than half the firemen in this city were deployed to fight a West Side blaze. These brave men triumphed, but only after seventeen long hours, and the total destruction of four square blocks. There are fewer than two hundred firemen in this city, and they are worse for wear today on our behalf. We tip our hats to them.

—*Chicago Star*, October 8, 1871

The first light woke Fiona, and she left without saying goodbye to her family, who were all still dreaming. In the early-morning streets, the only activity was that of milk deliveries and newspaper boys, which was how she first heard the story of the big West Side fire. But she did not make much of it. The headlines were always melodramatic—she thought about it only long enough to

calculate that it was far enough from Anders, that he probably would not have known of the disaster from which he
had been spared. She was alert to any threat to the plan
that she must execute, and did not allow anything else to
cloud her thoughts. She kept her head down, and hoped
this day would be over soon.

Arriving back at the Carters, she saw that the staff was
already busy preparing for the day's festivities. The smell
of bread filled the big kitchen, and a fleet of hired help was
arriving to see that the wedding guests never wanted for
anything for even a single moment. Their uniforms were
piled under a makeshift tent, out behind the kitchen, and
Fiona took a spare maid's getup from the rest, and tucked
it under her arm as she went into the house, and down into
the servants' quarters. Here she washed her face, braided
her hair neat and tight for the day ahead, and put on a fresh
shirt and skirt from her drawer.

Then she went and prepared for the day as she always
would: she made a tray of tea and toast for Emmeline, and
went to wake her up. Before she climbed the stairs, she
checked the watch on the gold chain that was her reward for
giving up her best dream. It was now almost nine o'clock.
By eleven, it would all be over.

As she had walked home, as she had gone about her
morning ritual, she had been confident that she could execute her part of the plan out of love for Anders and love

of Emmeline, and that like every member of the Carter staff, she could do her duty with dignity. But when she entered the room with the flocked peach wallpaper and the magenta chaise, when she saw Emmeline awake already but still in bed, she felt the agony take hold of her belly, and knew that she would have to say little and perform what needed doing in as perfunctory a manner as possible, lest she lose control and ruin everything with her own poorly contained misery.

"Oh!" Emmeline cried wistfully when she saw Fiona's face. "Don't be sore with me."

"I'm not." Fiona sighed, and put down the tray as she had so many times before. "But I feel a little serious this morning, don't you?"

"Yes," Emmeline acknowledged. "Quite serious."

"Did you pack your bag?"

"I started to . . . but then I couldn't decide whether I wanted the black patent-leather boots or the white doeskin ones, and—"

"The black," Fiona said, and turned away, and went to draw Emmeline's last bath. So that Emmeline could dress herself to go off and make Anders hers forever. To distract herself from this fact, Fiona checked the temperature obsessively, and measured out just the right amount of jasmine perfume for the water. When she returned, she saw that Emmeline was still lying under the covers, and staring vaguely in the direction of the window. So she picked up the hairbrush from the vanity, went to the bed, and sat beside her old friend to help her undo the tangles she'd acquired in the night. "I know you're scared," she said. Speaking these reassuring words caused an ache in her throat, and they tasted bitter on her tongue, but she made herself go on. "Don't worry, though. You'll have each other."

"I know," Emmeline said.

"You will be all right with one pair of boots."

"You're right, Fiona, you're always right."

Fiona, wishing that were true, finished brushing her friend's hair, and then said: "You remember the plan, don't you?"

Emmeline nodded. "I will dress in the maid's uniform, and slip down the servants' stairs, and meet you on Clark Street. . . ."

"You will have to do it by eleven. Remember, that's just two hours from now. That way, there will be a lot of servants that nobody recognizes around the house, but none of the guests will have arrived yet. I'll help you pack the rest of your things, and then I'll go down to Water Street to find a cab. It'll be easier, anyway, for you to go unnoticed without me. All right?"

"All right," Emmeline replied, with the firm determination that had carried her so far, so quickly, into high society, that lifted her over any slight or setback, and radiated through the bones of which her lovely features were composed.

If Fiona had secretly hoped she might change her mind, the hope dwindled and died when she heard Emmeline answer in that way. They were busy awhile with Emmeline's dress and the final decisions about what would and would not go in the trunk, and so much time passed that Fiona worried she would not be able to return by the designated hour. She picked up the tea tray, and with a sore heart went back down through the house, so that she could walk a few blocks and find a cab, and thus initiate Emmeline's escape from her own wedding.

Although the ceremony was planned for one o'clock, the anticipation and general chatter surrounding the Carter-Tree nuptials was such that curiosity got the better of many of the wedding guests, and they began strolling onto the property at quarter past eleven. The band had still been warming up at that time, and Mr. Carter's man, Malcolm, had gone down and told them to hurry up and get into their places. The servants had still been laying out the silver and the crystal under the great white tent on the front lawn and had to rush to circulate glasses of lemonade to the thirsty early arrivals.

They were pink in the face, and wiping sweat from their brows, for the elements were already oppressive. Georgie was staring out the kitchen window, when she witnessed the arrival of Ada Garrison, in a dress of tiered grapefruit-colored chiffon, and thought how she'd happily trade her soul for one just like it. Upon Mrs. Garrison's head was a matching hat with the wingspan of a swan. Fiona Byrne came through the kitchen just then, asking absentmindedly if Georgie wouldn't mind washing Miss Carter's tea things, as she was in a hurry to find needle and thread for something amiss on the wedding gown. Georgie barely heard her, for she was thinking how, if she could find a window on the upper floors, she might get a better view of Mrs. Garrison's exquisite dress. She took the tray, quickly stored it under the stairwell, and went up the steps from which Fiona had come.

By then Fiona was in a panic. The fine people who would be curious and watchful for a first glimpse of the bride were arriving so much sooner than she had counted on, and the plan depended on Emmeline leaving when there was the most hired help and the fewest guests. She muttered angrily to herself, and did not consider that Georgie might be the one to notice something amiss.

EIGHTEEN

Mr. Ochs Carter
cordially invites you
to witness the marriage
of his daughter, Emmeline Carter,
to Frederick Arles Tree
at the Carter residence
October 8, 1871
One o'clock

By noon, the rented chairs of white and gold damask had been arranged in neat rows across the two front rooms of the Carter house, and people in their best seersucker and pastel had begun to occupy them, a full hour ahead of schedule, and Emmeline, who should have put on the stolen servant's uniform the moment Fiona had left, had instead found herself harassed by Georgie, who had popped her head in to see if the bride needed anything on her special day.

Emmeline had sent her away to find Fiona, but of course that had been the wrong tack. Emmeline well knew where Fiona had gone—she'd left with the single-minded purpose of securing a cab for Emmeline's own escape. And meanwhile, for some dimly understood reason, Emmeline's feet were still planted firmly in place.

"She's gone?" Emmeline asked when the girl soon reappeared.

"Nobody's seen her since she brought down the tray. But don't worry, I'll help you."

Emmeline's gaze flicked from Georgie, waiting expectantly to be told what to do, and back to her own reflection in the mirror. Her eyes looked puffy and purplish after a restless night. *I look like Anders after the fight*, she thought. The picture of his face hovered in her mind's eye, and her heart got jittery, and she wished that she had run away earlier, before the Carter residence had been transformed for a wedding. She wished they were already a hundred miles gone.

Georgie stepped a little farther into the room. "Are you all right?"

"I couldn't sleep last night."

"But you look as beautiful as always, Em—I mean, Miss Carter."

"Perhaps for a trip to the horse track." Emmeline gave a dismissive wave of her hand, feeling quite suddenly like an older girl, the kind who has already seen it all and become quite jaded about everything. "The sort of people you find there might be tricked into thinking *this* is beauty. But not for today." It was Anders she wanted to look beautiful for today, but neither could she quite let go of the vain desire to look beautiful for Chicago's best people, too. She knew how to transform, and an audience was already assembled to witness her performance. "Do we have any cucumbers? Go to the kitchen for me, and fetch some."

If Emmeline believed that Georgie's absence would allow her to finally creep away, she was mistaken. She only had time to wish again that she had not made Georgie think she was her friend. If not for that error, she would not have barged in, and Emmeline might have been able to slip out as easily as Fiona had. By now, they might have been across the river and in the West Division, and none of the Carter household need have been alerted to her doings.

But something held her back, and there was Georgie again, so quickly, with sliced cucumbers and a cold cloth press, nudging the giant gold-colored box through the doorway with her foot.

"May I help you get dressed?" Georgie asked. She was speaking in a very affected manner, which Emmeline supposed was how she imagined a lady's maid spoke to a lady.

"That's the delivery over there, from Field and Leiter."

Emmeline tried to think. They were already late to meet Anders. But if she started acting strange now, the household would become aware of something not quite right, and she might never be able to leave. No, he would understand that she might have difficulty leaving, guess that she could be delayed for a thousand reasons, and would wait for her. Anders always waited for her. The best course was to go along with Georgie, who would whisper to the other servants that Emmeline was taking great care with her toilette, just as expected, and the other servants would tell Malcolm, and Malcolm would tell Father. As long as Father believed that she was going to walk down the aisle, there would be time to make her escape.

But, oh—Father. He was probably reading his stack of Chicago newspapers just now—he had all of them delivered every morning—relishing the sight of his name printed in each one. How humiliated he would be. She felt as though she were on a merry-go-round operating at a wild speed with no sign of stopping. "Just put the cucumber slices on my eyes, would you?" she instructed. "Georgie, you will have to be my lady's maid today. Do you think you can do that for me?"

Georgie nodded eagerly, and Emmeline realized that she was lucky that it was Georgie who had intruded, and not one of the servants who had been with the Carters since the beginning. Any of the others would have been scandalized by Fiona's defection and tried to find out the reason why. But Georgie was easily distracted by the prize of taking her place. The cucumber slivers were cold and damp against Emmeline's eyelids, but even this did not soothe her agitated mind. In fact, it made it worse. In the cool darkness they provided, she was able to feel the creeping loneliness. Fiona had been her loyal shadow all these years. Tonight, Emmeline would be on a train far east of here, carrying her away from Fiona, and her father—away from all of this.

She was about to tell Georgie to give her just five minutes of peace, when she realized that Georgie was taking her assignment as lady's maid quite seriously.

"Where is the crown?"

"Oh, it's here somewhere," Emmeline replied carelessly.

"The one Mr. Tree gave you? The one with the rubies, the one that belonged to his grandmother?" Georgie's eyes were wide, almost reproachful, and Emmeline realized that she should not have been so cavalier. "I've looked everywhere. Surely you're going to wear it when you become Mrs. Frederick Tree? The whole house was abuzz about the crown, and . . ."

"Oh, I don't think . . ." Emmeline removed the cucumbers and frowned. This was not a possibility she had considered. When she had sold her jewelry, she had assumed this moment would never come. She had not thought of a gaggle of servants and rows upon rows of society people speculating on the absence of the Tree family heirloom—which had been reported on in several of the society columns—during the wedding ceremony, because she had not thought there would be a wedding.

But there wouldn't be. She had to keep her head on straight and not be washed away by every little ripple.

"Miss Carter . . . it's not . . . *lost* . . . is it?"

"Of course not, but a few of the stones were loose, and we had to send it in to a jeweler, and it's not ready yet."

Georgie's eyes sought the four corners of the room, and she let out a little yelp. "And where is your engagement ring?"

"Oh, Georgie, don't be so simple, nobody wears their engagement ring when they get *married*." Emmeline wasn't sure where that notion came from, and she certainly hadn't meant to sound so furious. But it seemed to work, for Georgie's eyes lowered, and her cheeks darkened.

A few moments passed, and Emmeline realized that she must not let Georgie sulk. The story she'd just concocted made little sense—everyone knew Freddy was too exacting a man to give jewels that needed fixing, and the claim about the ring would not be believed by anyone if repeated.

"Georgie," Emmeline said as she crossed to her wardrobe. She pulled her robe in tight to her body, and tried to move with the elegance and importance of her station in life. Using her body to shield Georgie's view of her actions, she pulled open a drawer, and removed most of the bills that Fiona had earned selling her old jewelry, except one, which she put back into the white envelope. "You'll be run off your feet today, and have to work much more than your usual wages compensate you for. Here. Let me give you this. For your trouble." She returned to Georgie and put the envelope in her hand. "Now, I need just a little time to calm my nerves, and you—go get a little lunch, who knows when you'll be able to eat again!"

Georgie gave a stubborn, solemn shake of her head. "There's no time for that, Miss Carter. It's ten past noon and your guests are already arriving. If we need to summon the tailor, if there's anything that needs fixing about your appearance, we'll want to know now."

Outside, Emmeline heard the string section of the band begin to practice a lively tune.

"Even so, I'd like a little . . ."

"Please," Georgie said, and before Emmeline could stop her, she had removed the wedding dress from its box—pulled it out by the stiff, adorned bodice so that the great sweep of the skirt spilled over the side of the bed like a mighty waterfall. "Please, try it on? For me."

"All right," Emmeline replied, hoping this would appease the girl. "But then I'd like just a few minutes alone."

Georgie gave a little squeal and advanced toward Emmeline with the great white dress.

For perhaps the sixth time, Emmeline sent Georgie away to fetch something, and Georgie began to wonder if being the friend and confidante of the lady of the house wasn't more trouble than it was worth. She had almost entirely missed the parade of finery as the guests arrived (which she had so been looking forward to, and was the only reason she'd come up to the third floor in the first place) and been generally run ragged since.

"How is the young lady of the house?" asked Cook, who had finally found time to put her feet up, and seemed somewhat amused to see Georgie rushing to make a pretty tray of lemonade. Georgie supposed that there would be some jealousy among the staff regarding her sudden elevation, and rationalized that Cook was only being mean out of spite.

"I think she's nervous."

"White as a sheet?" Cook chuckled. "Here, give her some of this," she said, filling an enamel coffee cup with the dark liquid she used when she made her famous baba au rhum.

"Thank you," said Georgie, and went off with the rum and the pitcher of lemonade.

As she came up the servants' stairs, the low rumble of voices from the parlor ceased. Even within that corridor,

Georgie could hear the heels of a pair of fine dress boots clack against the Carters' parquet. Then there was applause, and then she heard the servants down below, peeking out through doorframes, saying what a handsome groom Mr. Tree made, and what a lucky girl Miss Carter was to be his bride.

Mr. Tree had already arrived!

The nervousness this aroused in Georgie became something else when she reached the third-floor landing, and saw Mr. Carter leaning against the paneled wall.

"Where is Fiona?" he asked coldly.

"I . . . I don't know," she muttered, and Mr. Carter made a face as though he thought it was all poor Georgie's fault.

"You better hurry up and get Miss Carter ready, then," he said without moving. "The guests are beginning to talk."

If she'd had more time, she would have changed into the maid's uniform, and slipped down the back way. But she was out of time. She would have to take the servants' stairs, and if she encountered anyone, make up some ludicrous excuse—she was seemingly full of those today—and put them off long enough to leave the property. Georgie had kept pace with Emmeline as she made a thousand alterations to her appearance. On that score, she had not failed as a lady's maid. The mirror in the dressing room reflected the very picture of an immaculate bride.

Georgie returned, and said Mr. Carter was most eager that Emmeline should appear soon, as it was now half past one and the guests were becoming agitated on the first floor.

"Go tell him I'm ready," Emmeline said. Then she noticed the cup in Georgie's hands. "What's that?"

"Cook said it would help with your nerves."

Without a second's hesitation, Emmeline drained the rum. "Oh," she groaned, and shuddered in disgust at the way the liquid burned a trail from the back of her throat to her belly. Yet Cook must have had the right idea, for in the next moment she felt ready, and was on her feet, possessed with conviction. "Go, go now. Tell Father to meet me on the second-floor landing."

That way, she could escape down the servants' stairs, and be halfway to the river by the time he realized she was gone. Emmeline took the veil, so that at least when she reached the streets, nobody would know *which* bride was not where she was supposed to be. She closed the suitcase, and picked it up. When Georgie came back, to say that Mr. Carter was on the second-floor landing waiting, her eyes went straight to the suitcase, and Emmeline couldn't think of a good explanation, so she didn't bother with one.

"Thank you," she said instead. At the door, she glanced back once. "Georgie? I'll never forget what you did today. If they ask you, please just tell them I had to be true to my heart."

Georgie was strangely unable to meet her eye, but Emmeline couldn't worry about that now. She was worried, mostly, about figuring the quickest route to the West Side, and also about the alarming acceleration of her heartbeat.

But her heart nearly stopped when she stepped into the hall and saw Father. He was just outside the door, with his jaw tilted at the ceiling.

"I . . ." Her voice was so small, she barely managed to make a sound. "I told Georgie . . ."

"Yes, I know what you told Georgie. But I pay Georgie, not you, and whether you stay and marry Mr. Tree—or go, and don't—it will still be *I* who am responsible for her keep."

"Go?" Emmeline repeated stupidly. Then she remembered the suitcase in her hand, and tried to put it down, behind her skirt, as discreetly as possible.

"Yes, my darling Emmeline. I do not know what you have planned, but I know that your engagement ring is not being polished, and I know that you went to a boxing match in the old neighborhood the other night. I know, of course, that that boy who courted you before we left has made a name for himself at the fights. Do you think my interests do not require me to know such things? Did you forget I built our prospects on winnings from the card table? This—" He gestured at the the mouldings, the framed landscapes on the mahogany paneled walls. "All this is because I happen to know when someone is lying."

Emmeline's face was hot and she could not seem to lift her gaze up from the floorboards. "I don't love him," she said. "Freddy, I mean."

"But you will, in time. Enough. In a manner of speaking." He cleared his throat and shifted his weight from one foot to the other. "Emmeline, you are the thing I love most in the world, but if you betray me today—if you humiliate us, and ruin my name—you will not be welcome back here. I will be destroyed, you see. Not financially, perhaps, but in other ways. Do you understand? If you leave, you leave forever. It is up to you."

Emmeline found the courage to glance up, and winced when she saw the sad, steely quality in his eyes. His attire was smart and lustrous, but his face was tired.

"I will be on the second-floor landing, as you wished," he said, and walked away.

His footsteps echoed in the stairwell and the hall was chilly like a room after a spirit has passed through. All her hopes and fears and wants and schemes evaporated into the air: Her father would not come to understand, as she had hoped. He would not set up Anders in business. She would not be able to hire Fiona and her siblings, as she had promised. Now it was plain that she could not do as she had planned. They would have to give up too much, and they would have to live on too little, and her promise to Fiona would be a lie, and she would, in the end, let everyone down.

Anders! her heart cried, and she wished with the whole force of her small body that it was still that night, that they were in the doorway down by the river, that he would put his mouth to hers as he had before, that they had left then. But her father's voice in her head told her no, she could not have that, and must not think such things anymore.

She wanted Anders, still. To see the color of his eyes change when he tried to make her laugh, and know what would be between them now, these years later.

But she had just discovered that her father's chief lesson—that she could have anything she wanted—was a lie. The realization made her weak. Perhaps she should not have wanted so much. There was nothing to do now but go along with what Father said she could have. If she did now what her Father wished—well, there would be some nobility in that. She would make him happy, at least—him and Freddy. And maybe he was right, maybe in time she would learn to love Freddy, as he loved her.

She brought the veil down over her face, as though it were sharp enough to sever her from the sweet dream of eloping with her first love.

NINETEEN

"A lady keeps them waiting" *is a general principle*
that is never so effectively used as on the day she
becomes a married woman.
—Private diary of Mrs. Fletcher Fleming, 1863

By the time she reached the second-floor landing, Emmeline had become tough to her own wild heart. When she
reached Father, she saw that he was relieved and proud,
and she knew she could go through with it. She was as
steely as he was, and made for grand occasions such as this.
He took her by the arm, and down another flight they
went. He cleared his throat, and the band started to play.

Every inch of floor was taken up by chairs—Emmeline
had not known there were so many chairs in the whole city!
Only the aisle was left unoccupied, and this was covered by

a path of white rose petals. As the music swelled, the people in the chairs turned, and she saw expressions of impatience melt into appreciation. The rum had been for courage, but now it made her feel faint, and she was glad Father was holding her up.

The air was fragrant with the lilies erupting from the vases on the windowsills. Through the net of lace, Emmeline saw how the faces in the crowd smiled, nodding their approval. The music seemed to lift her up, as though she were floating on a gentle breeze. For a moment she was sure the hours she had stalled upstairs were a folly, and that the romantic notion that had disrupted her life over the last few days was a delusion. She was born for this. A destiny greater than herself was moving her onward through the crowd, past notable gentlemen and fashionable ladies, toward an altar made of apple branches. When they arrived there, her father kissed her cheek.

The music stopped, and the moment ended.

Emmeline stood alone, facing Freddy. His hair was slick for the occasion, and his black tailcoat had the high gloss of patent leather. Even through the veil, she could see that his face would always disappoint her. No matter how long she looked at that face, it would not be Anders looking back. Anders with his quick smile. Anders who knew her. Anders who she had always loved, and always would. Emmeline glanced in the direction from which she had come, but the room was too crowded; there was no route of escape. The priest had begun his droning ceremony. Emmeline's body went cold. The only thing she could feel was the bouquet, although she could not remember how it had arrived in her hands. She gripped the collection of lilac and hyacinth, trying to stay upright and appear as normal as possible.

The priest went on and on, but Emmeline heard only a few solitary words. The guests who watched fanned themselves to keep awake. Finally, Freddy's young cousin, Reginald Tree, appeared with the white satin cushion. Emmeline murmured along with Freddy as they slipped the rings onto each other's fingers. The brightness of the gold band caught her eye, and she almost laughed, for she knew that once the rings were put on, you were married. But in her heart, this did not feel like a marriage at all.

"I now pronounce you man and wife," said the priest. "You may . . ."

Freddy stepped forward, lifting the yards of lace away from Emmeline's face. The sunlight surprised her and she was afraid he would notice her insufficient happiness. But this fear was unwarranted; he noticed nothing at all. He had a grip on her shoulders, and his mouth was suddenly pressed to hers. This was not the way it had been with Anders—every kiss asking if there could be another kiss—but an awkward collision of lips. When it was over, Emmeline had to fight the instinct to dry her face with the back of her hand.

"Oh, Emmeline," Freddy murmured, and she wished she had the heart to say something sweet and happy in return.

Meanwhile the wedding guests had risen. They whooped and stomped their feet. Emmeline glanced back, trying to see her father, but Freddy was already pulling her down the aisle. The noise had become so loud it rattled her bones. When she saw Cora, smiling her garish red smile, Emmeline felt relieved by the opportunity to unburden herself of at least one thing, and simply handed her the bouquet as they passed on through the crowd.

Emmeline was too completely shocked by the very permanent thing she had just done, and had not meant to do at all, to notice as she passed into the hall that several members of the Carter household had gathered in the narrow passage that connected to the kitchen (the better to watch the bride return from the altar) or that Fiona was among them, in the back. Fiona, too, was numb with shock, although she had realized somewhat ahead of Emmeline that there had been a change of plans. This was after she had gone down to Water Street and hailed a passing hansom, after she had begged the driver to wait with her among the other carriages on Clark, after she had tipped him extra to stay just a little longer, and finally, at long last, admitted to him and to herself that Emmeline wasn't coming, after all.

A few days ago, all she wanted was for Emmeline to marry Freddy Tree. Once that happened, Fiona had believed, her own love story could begin. But now that it had come to pass, the news cast a shadow on her heart. Although Emmeline had seemed to vacillate yesterday, Fiona still could not believe that she had gone through with the marriage, after everything. After all Fiona had been through to secure the money for the elopement! After the hardening of her own heart through these awful days. After keeping Anders in a town where he was wanted by gamblers who meant him harm. For Emmeline to not even *say* anything, to either of them. For her to explain so little. Rage surged in Fiona, so fast and molten she was afraid it might sweep her away and melt her down to nothing, too.

In her little room, Fiona sank to her knees in prayer, as though that might help her stop the seething, airless anger. A floorboard sighed overhead, as someone went up the stairs, and a conversation floated by the door. Her gaze focused on the edge of the blanket, where the thread was loose. The stuffing was escaping in little wisps, and the stitching was all ragged. "Damn," she whispered, annoyed with herself for not noticing before, when she'd had her sewing tools out to repair the dinner napkins. And then it occurred to her that if she was gone—if she left now, regardless of Emmeline's choice—it would not matter if the blanket was coming undone. None of this mess would be her concern any longer.

Fiona scrambled to her feet in a hurry, before she lost her nerve. She took down the old duffel that she'd packed her clothes in when she moved to Dearborn. Into the duffel went Emmeline's old best boots, her winter coat, the books on etiquette and ladylike attire that she had been given to help Emmeline with her education, two sets of clothes, and her sewing kit. She would need that where she was going.

The pocket watch she turned over, considering. She wondered if Emmeline might come to regret losing her mother's prized piece. But—Fiona reasoned—Emmeline did not as a rule give away possessions she was not entirely willing to part with, and, anyway, as Emmeline herself had said, if Fiona ran into trouble she might need an item of value. In the meantime, just looking at the elegant design of the watch—so heavy and shiny—made Fiona feel that she could carry out the audacious plan that was only now taking shape in her head. She hoped she could keep the watch forever, and hold it in moments like this—moments when bravery and doubt warred within her—and know what she was capable of.

She, too, could buy a train ticket. After all, she had some savings. She, too, could travel to a new city. She was already an accomplished seamstress—everybody said so—surely she could get work somewhere else. Maybe, in time, she would become something even greater. A dressmaker of renown, her name carved in the lintel of her own shop. The only way to find out was to try.

In the third-floor hall, she found the suitcase that Emmeline had meant to take with her when she went to Anders. She picked it up, put it on the bed in the room with the flocked peach wallpaper, and placed her goodbye letter inside, where only Emmeline would find it.

The wedding of Emmeline Carter and Frederick Arles Tree was to be an all-day affair, as Emmeline knew, having had a say in the planning. Now she could only think of the long sequence of formal dances and activities as an interminable series of empty gestures. She stood dutifully in the reception line, as Chicago's best people came to congratulate her, and afterward, sat under the oak tree on the front lawn for the photographer.

Because the photographer told her so, she knew that she was the picture of happiness, the perfect bride. But her soul seemed to hover somewhere slightly above her body, looking down on a white dress, a posed family, which had nothing in particular to do with her.

Meanwhile, her heart was with Anders. The dusty barn where he had waited for her to arrive—might still be waiting, for all she knew—was more vivid than her own wedding. She hoped that he was still waiting, although she knew she shouldn't. That was a cruel thing to hope for. He must have realized, by now, that she was not coming. At the very least, it must have occurred to him that this was more than a small hitch in their plans. How long would he wait? And would he be full of sorrow, or full of rage, when he finally understood that she had abandoned their plan? She had not thought of that. He might wander the street; he might not be careful of his safety. Gil Bryce might find him, and . . .

"Please do smile, Mrs. Tree!" the photographer called from beneath his black cloth, and she responded with a mechanical uptick at the corners of her mouth, and held still until he appeared again. "Thank you, ladies, you may return to your dancing," he said, dismissing Ada and Daisy and Cora. They rose from the places where they had posed, and began to drag their long, citrus-colored skirts across the lawn.

"Is it my turn yet?" Freddy asked, approaching the photographer. Another gentleman, wearing a dun suit and bowler, had arrived with him.

"Oh, certainly, Mr. Tree, whenever you are ready."

"Emmeline." She heard Freddy's voice as though from a great distance. "My darling."

Emmeline lowered her gaze from a few distant clouds— she had been wondering if Anders could see those same clouds from wherever he was—and blinked at Freddy and his companion as they walked toward her.

Freddy pressed, "Mrs. Tree?"

"Yes?"

Her husband laughed through his nose. "You see, only a few hours of matrimony, and she only responds to her married name!" He appeared so pleased by this that she felt a little sorry she didn't think she'd ever be Mrs. Tree in her heart. But not as sorry as she was for having given up the chance to be Emmeline Magnuson.

The man in the bowler laughed, too. When he saw that Emmeline wasn't laughing, he stopped and offered her his hand. "May I congratulate you? I am Felix Dray of the *Evening Journal* . . ."

Emmeline nodded and removed her hand.

"Mr. Dray is here to write a little piece on our wedding," said Freddy.

"We plan to run it on the front page, actually. A few details of the lovely ceremony and exquisite décor, the bride's dress—"

"And the groom's," Freddy put in.

"Yes, of course, and the groom's."

"And he wanted a quote from you."

"From me?" Emmeline replied faintly. She was trying to remember when the *Evening Journal* arrived in the neighborhood, when the boys started shouting the headlines from the corners. She imagined Anders hearing the news from a corner barker, and beating his fists against brick walls in fury. She hated that. Her mind went quiet, and she felt the terrible permanence of what she'd done.

"Are you crying?" the reporter asked.

"No, of course not." Emmeline brushed away the tear. She could hear the seconds ticking by now, and she was finding it once again easy to pretend. "Only happy tears. You see, I've been overwhelmed with emotion all afternoon. It's the most important day of my life, and there's nothing about it I will ever forget. I don't think I've ever been so happy."

Mr. Dray scribbled on his small writing pad.

"Mr. Tree," she went on, lowering her chin and lifting her gaze flirtatiously. "Would you excuse me just a little while? The maid misplaced my engagement ring while I was getting ready, and we had already kept everyone waiting so long, but I am sure I can find it now, and of course it must be on my finger when we take *our* picture."

Freddy's face was all smug contentment. "Yes, my dearest, you are absolutely right."

"Pleasure to meet you," she said to the reporter. Then she crossed to the house, moving as fast as she could without drawing attention to herself.

The guests were dancing already. The shadow of the

house was becoming longer at that hour, but supper would not be served for some time. Emmeline should have taken off the enormous confection of white silk and lace, but she did not think she had the time. Instead she picked up the heavy skirts with bunched fists and half crept, half ran to the back side of the house, where the guests' carriages were blocking Clark Street.

"Fiona!" she cried, and all the chauffeurs who leaned against their vehicles in waiting glanced at her, and she could see that some of them were trying not to laugh. But Emmeline's whole being was trembling with the terrible mistake she'd made, and embarrassment seemed like the very least of her worries. "Fiona!"

"Fiona!" sang out one of the liveried drivers who waited along the street.

"Fiona, Fiona!" chorused another. "Where are you, Fiona?"

Emmeline's face went scarlet and she shifted on her feet, trying to see if Fiona was there, with the cab, waiting. But she wasn't. She was gone. The girl who had been Emmeline's faithful shadow all these years had disappeared into the unknown. A howling loneliness came over Emmeline, and threatened to knock her to the ground.

The band was still playing on the lawn—she could hear it even from the back corner of the property. Emmeline moved in the direction of the orchestra, the tent, the hub-bub of a fete in full swing. But all that looked strange now, as unreal as a dream.

Later that night she would have reason and time to again wonder over what might have been. How her life would have been different, if Freddy hadn't been standing there, at the edge of the lawn, a little apart from the party as though he had been there the whole time waiting for her to turn and see him. Would she have found her own way off the property? Or gone straight to her bath, and never been seen by anyone ever again?

But he *was* there, like the picture of everything she thought her life should be, dressed in his tails and tie, mak-ing a gracious little bow, and extending his hand for her to take.

"Don't worry about the ring," he said. "We'll hold hands in the picture, and no one will notice."

The sadness of Fiona's disappearance, of perhaps never seeing Anders again, was overwhelming, and the prospect of a hand to grab hold of, any hand, was too tempting. "I'm tired," she told her husband, sounding like a dull girl.

"It's been an exciting day, my dear. But we'll just stay a little longer. Our guests want to see you dance. We will give them a little more of a show, and then I will take you home."

TWENTY

Tree Family Scion Weds Society Newcomer in Lavish Ceremony!

—*Chicago Crier*, Special Late Edition, October 8, 1871

At Water Street a breeze touched her face, but the air it stirred was warm, and made Fiona's skin prickle and blush. The Illinois Central Depot was only a few blocks east, south of the river by the lake, but she had practically memorized the train schedule when she had helped Emmeline plan her escape, and knew that the next New York train was a midnight departure. That if Emmeline and Anders had missed the two o'clock, they could take the late train. Again, she checked her watch: It was not yet five o'clock. She had plenty of time to say one final goodbye.

★ ★ ★

On the West Side, folks had given up doing work. The heat had not mellowed with the slow sinking of the sun. On DeKoven, they had retreated to the shade of the porch, and the street felt abandoned. In daylight, she saw things she had not noticed before. The wooden sidewalk was farther from the dusty ground than she had realized, and the alley that separated the barn from the neighbors' shack narrower. Dry weeds crunched underfoot as she approached, but she glanced right and left, and saw no one who might be alarmed by her presence. At last she could not stand the racket in her own chest, and went inside.

"Hello?"

Bits of hay drifted in the fading daylight that shot through the roof in rays. Her blood was moving too fast; for a moment she was sure she'd faint.

"Ah," he said.

She tried to make her eyes adjust to the dimness. He was on the far side, up in the loft, lying on his stomach, his head propped up on his fist, like he had been watching the door a long time.

"Anders?" she asked, although she knew him by one syllable of his voice. She would have known him anywhere.

"So she sent you? Sent you to say she won't be leaving with me after all." He sounded so weary, she did not need to see his face to know what he had been through that afternoon.

"No," she murmured. She had not meant to keep quiet, but nerves cinched her throat.

"No?" The word contorted with irony, as though he had no hope left.

"No . . . she won't be leaving with you after all. But that isn't . . ." Fiona's thoughts were confused, and she had to shut her mouth and try to remember what she had wanted to say to him. In a moment or two, she had the words. After that she forgot to be nervous. "That isn't why I came."

"Oh?" He sat up, swinging his legs so that his feet hung over the loft's edge. "Why did you come, Miss Byrne?"

When he said her name like that, she sounded like a stranger, a stranger to both of them, and her heart tightened, and she wished that they were as familiar as before.

"Because I love you."

He exhaled as though by force. For a while he was silent, unable or unwilling to reply.

"I always have. I didn't come to try to convince you of anything, or tell you that I am better for you than Emmeline. But I've always loved you, and I'm leaving, maybe for a long time, and I couldn't live with myself if I didn't tell you the truth."

"That night, after the funeral, when I . . ." Anders's eyes

searched the ceiling. "Well, I worried I'd confused things for you."

She shook her head.

"I worried you didn't want me like that. Because you avoided me after. I thought I'd treated you wrong somehow. Thought you were insulted by me."

"I hope you see now. How it really was. I've felt this way a long time, I think. It was just that I realized it, that night. When you—" Her pulse slowed, and she was there again, on the street where she grew up, with the wall of the Madigans' place at her back and Anders's nose brushing against her nose and the smell of his skin up close.

But the Anders before her seemed far away. He gazed into the rafters, and the line of his mouth was tense. "But you always kept me off to the side. Since I can't remember when. I always wanted to be where you were, do what you did, but you always had something important to take care of, something that couldn't wait. Kate and Brian needed you, or you had a job to do. And then Emmeline came, and you said she looked like a princess, and I should be sweet on her so she'd be our friend, and you kept insisting on it, and insisting on it, until I was. Until I *was* sweet on her."

Fiona flinched, hearing herself described this way. She sounded like a cold little girl, the first one to disregard her own true feelings. Was that her? How it had been in the early days came back—slowly, and then in a rush. She had caught a glimpse of Ochs Carter's daughter—the fair Emmeline—who even in the lowness of the neighborhood walked like a person of royal lineage. And what did poor, plain Fiona have to make the exquisitely blond and dainty Emmeline her friend? What did she ever have, except Anders? "Anyway," she went on, wishing to forget all that. "I only wanted to tell you the truth. I am leaving. I couldn't be Emmeline's maid anymore, but I've learned some things, and I have it in me, now, to make my way in the world. I love you," she said again as she turned for the door. There was so much more she wanted to tell him, but she added only: "I hope you will be happy somehow."

She faced the door, and the door faced her back. In a matter of seconds, she had said out loud a thing she'd forced herself not to say for half a year, and in speaking it, she had become a new person. But she hardly knew what this person should say, what this person should do.

There was a whoosh of air, and a crunch of hay, and she imagined a stranger, lurking outside. That they were about to be discovered, that she'd be the old Fiona again, just like that.

But it was Anders, behind her. He had jumped from the loft and landed on the hay-blanketed ground. "Fiona, Fiona—I can't remember a time before you. It wouldn't be the world without you. It got all mixed up. But it was always you."

"I have a train to catch," she said stupidly.

He was closer when he spoke again. "When does it leave?"

"Midnight." Suddenly the hours of the clock seemed like a strange way to measure the contents of a day. She rested her fingertips on the weathered wooden door, as though she'd push it and go out to the street. The hay made a soft sighing sound as Anders approached. He lifted her braid, and lay it over the front side of her shoulder.

The next thing she knew was his lips on her spine, traveling upward to just below her hairline. "Where are we going?"

She didn't care anymore. "New York," she said. "But . . ."

"New York will do fine."

Her chest was ecstatic with breath as she revolved into him. When his bright blue gaze met hers she felt the smallest parts of herself begin to hum.

"I love you," he said, so simply and sweetly that she felt he had said so before, and this was only the first time he'd said it out loud.

She was smiling with her whole self when she said the words back. "I love you."

TWENTY-ONE

In the heat of the fire, the true nature of the soul is revealed.
—Reverend Swing's sermon, North Side Methodist Church,
Sunday, October 8, 1871

"Where am I?" Emmeline was being carried. Her arms tightened around Freddy's neck as she lifted her gaze to him.

"Home."

"Oh." He meant the place on Terrace Row. Behind them was the white landau with the red velvet cushions that he ordered especially for the day, and had decorated with bunches of white lilies. Her eyelids were heavy, and her tongue thick.

"After the dance, you fell asleep on the bench in the kitchen, and one of the servants came to tell me that you'd had enough for one day. I'm sorry, my dear, I realize today was a bit much excitement for such a young lady."

She peeked over his shoulder and saw the lake, vast and lurid in the fading light, on the other side of an empty avenue. To her surprise she also saw Georgie, following along with Emmeline's suitcase. Although Emmeline tried to catch the girl's eye, she remained steadfastly focused on her own shoes as they climbed the stoop.

A butler greeted them wordlessly at the door, and they continued up the main staircase.

"Wait here," Freddy told Georgie, when they reached the third floor, and took the suitcase from her hand. Then he continued carrying Emmeline all the way up to the top.

They crossed the threshold of the master suite, and he set her down. The sun had streamed through the windows when she saw this room for the first time, and the view had seemed to offer up all of Chicago for her pleasure. At nightfall, illuminated by the gas wall jets, the ice-blue wallpaper and the pale oak furnishings appeared stark, and she was afraid to go close to the windows, for fear of discovering how perilously far she was from the street.

"Shall I have your maid come and help you undress?"

The word "undress" sent a shivery shot of electricity up her spine. "No," she said instinctively. "Not tonight. She can help me in the morning."

"As you wish. I'll go tell her she can retire for the evening." He moved toward the hallway, tripping on the edge of the carpet as he went. He cursed, and stamped it back in place, as though it had been trying to humiliate him on purpose.

"Are you all right?" she whispered, but he didn't seem to hear.

At the threshold, he said her name, and she lifted her gaze slowly to meet his. "You love me, don't you?" he asked. "As a wife loves a husband."

Emmeline forced herself to nod. Neither spoke for a few moments, and she wondered if he was going to tell her that he loved her, too. *Look happy*, she admonished herself, but before she could summon a smile, he'd closed the carved oak door. Emmeline looked around the room, trying to remember how impressive it had all been only yesterday. But the magic was gone from the elegant furniture and extravagant decorations.

The only object she found reassuring was the suitcase, the old black leather one that she had planned to take with her when she and Anders left for New York. She drew her fingertips over its surface and fiddled with the brass latch. As though it had been waiting for her, the latch sprung open, and she saw the items that she had chosen for a different life. On top was a folded piece of white paper.

Dear Emmeline,

I'm sorry to say goodbye like this. After I saw you go through with it, with something you knew wasn't true, I knew that I couldn't serve you any longer. I have been false too in my own way and must try to be different. Thank you for all you have done for me.

~Fiona

Perhaps Emmeline had already known the reason for Fiona's defection, but she shuddered to have it put so plainly. Of all today's hard things, this was the worst: that Fiona should no longer be impressed by Emmeline, and was in fact so disappointed by her that she just walked off.

The matrimonial bedroom that was to be Emmeline and Freddy's looked as peculiar as a stage set. She could hear the seconds ticking by. How real Anders had looked in the ring! The memory surged in her mind's eye. She wanted that, wanted it so badly she ached.

She had gotten stuck comparing a life of prestige with Freddy to a life of adventure with Anders. But what she had lost was not really the adventure, but Anders himself— Anders who had loved her when she was just plain Emmy, and who she had loved with the same simple purity.

If she did what was true, her path would be easy, and she would not be noticed going down the stairs, out the front door. Some guardian angel would make sure of it. Wherever in the city Anders now was, she would find him.

★ ★ ★

"I love you," Anders said again, and then he and Fiona repeated it, back and forth, every time with greater wonder, until she lost count. Then he crouched, picked her up below the waist, and carried her toward the ladder. They seemed to move too slow, and halfway across the floor she stepped down, took him by the collar, and pulled him onward, her fingers nimble as they undid the buttons of his shirt. He stumbled a little and caught hold of her, so that they fell clumsily against the ladder, and his mouth breathed into her mouth. As they ascended, he stepped on her skirt, and—not wanting to untangle herself from him—she simply undid the sash. They reached the loft, each grasping for the other as though they couldn't stand being apart for even a second, and he laid her down upon the spread blanket. Through the thin cotton of her knickers, she could feel his thigh pushing open her thigh.

"Fiona?"

"Yes," she answered.

Under his shirt his skin was slick with a glistening sweat. Her hair had come loose, and her mouth sought his like she was hungry for him. He held her, pushing gently, and there was at first a pain that spread from deep down to behind her eyes; but it subsided and she felt only that Anders was so close within her that they'd always be together.

"Fiona?" he asked again.

"Don't stop," she said as he buried his face in her hair. "Please don't stop."

"I love you," he whispered, and did as she had told him.

When Emmeline last stood in front of the old barn, she had been happy and young. Now she felt sick over what she'd done, and had no one to blame but herself. If only she had been braver, earlier, then she might now be full of reckless joy, she might be with Anders already, and not doubtful of his devotion. Anyway, what did it matter, what she had already done? She could only listen to her own insistent pulse and move onward from now. She could be just as true and sure of purpose as Fiona.

Inside the barn, there was no light, but the air was thick and smelled of wood, earth, and straw. She heard a shifting of a body against the hay, and remembered the old cow, and felt afraid to call out. Anders must have been careful, over the days he hid here, not to be noticed by the neighbors, and she was hesitant to make any noise lest she, too, be discovered. As she moved cautiously onward she was startled by a distant murmur—it might have been a cooing bird in the rafter, but in her belly she knew the sound was human. Emmeline took an uncertain step backward, and her foot met with a metal object. She bent, heart-racing, suddenly afraid of who might be hiding in the dimness of the barn, and felt the lantern that Fiona had taken away a few nights before.

Her hands sought for the matches, found them, and worked quickly to get the thing lit. Once the wick was ablaze she stood and went forward triumphantly, as though warding off a ghost.

For a few seconds, she believed it was a ghost. The pale form hovered above her head, a being half flesh and half spirit floating in the middle of the barn. She blinked, and the being became two, and then her eyes began to see what was really there. Two figures asleep in the hayloft. The arm of one wrapped around the other as they lay partially undressed upon a blanket that Emmeline recognized perfectly well. It belonged to the Carter residence. The figure closer to the edge turned her face, revealing the dreamy smile of Fiona Byrne, not quite awake.

The mad rushing that carried her across town was gone. Emmeline felt as though she were a mile under the ocean, crushed by its weight and certain to drown.

No. Her mouth moved, but made no sound.

She wasn't sure if she could even make a sound.

Her best friend looked so happy there, in the arms of the boy Emmeline's heart had called for all afternoon, for days, and years before that. They were tangled up with each other, as though she—Emmeline—had never existed. As though Fiona had never been her friend, as though Anders had never proclaimed his eternal love and devotion for Emmeline.

No, she thought, *no*.

And no matter what she did her mind could not make sense of how this came to be.

But it was, it most certainly was. And Emmeline, her bones fragile with shame, her eyes stinging with hurt, dropped the lantern so she wouldn't have to see any more. She picked up her heavy skirts so that she could get away, as quickly as possible, from this terrible place.

AFTER

TWENTY-TWO

Let the Great Fire that destroyed four square blocks of the West Side and was still burning as of this morning be a warning to all Chicago.

—*Chicago Crier*, October 8, 1871

Anders was coughing.

Fiona, eyes closed, smiled at this wondrous notion. Any sound he made would have pleased her ears. As her mind awoke, she comprehended that it was Anders's arm thrown around her waist, it was Anders's chest pressed against her back. Anders Magnuson, the boxer, beloved of the neighborhood; Anders who, when they were children, had taught her to climb up to the rooftops where the air was fresh. Anders—for months she had yearned for any glance from him. Now she knew that she had been hoping for too little, and her lips curled with the memory of what they had done. Soon they would be on a train, with hours and hours together, and she could ask him when he had started falling in love with her. They would be passing through towns they hadn't known existed, and they could talk and talk until they were sleepy again.

The train! Earlier, she had been aware of every minute before its departure, but her sense of time had become funny since that miraculous crashing into Anders. She fumbled for the pocket watch with the gold chain, but she was dressed only in her underclothes, and could not immediately locate her skirt. When she sat up, she, too, began to cough, and tears stuck in her lashes.

The scene was purplish and hazy, and no matter how she squinted she couldn't make out any objects below. There was a distant roar, like the chaos of a downtown street jammed with traffic—wheels crunching over refuse, whips cracking in the air, horseshoes clattering on pavement. But they were far from any street that busy. She blinked, but nothing appeared out of the murk. Another cough seized her lungs, and she doubled over in a fit. Once she managed to take in a full breath, she hurried down the ladder, finding her skirt on one of its rungs.

The ground was glowing. A streak of vivid orange light reached from one side of the barn to the other. At first she thought her eyes were playing tricks, but then a knot formed in her belly. These were flames spreading from near the door—where the lantern was overturned—all the way to the far wall. It was strange—she couldn't remember igniting the lantern. But then, everything had happened so quickly.

"Anders!" she called as she stepped into her skirt and tied it at the waist.

He coughed, and leaned over the edge. His sideways smile played on his face only for a moment. "Oh no," he said, and the smile fell away.

The smoke was thicker than she'd thought, and it obscured her view of him. He pulled on his pants as he came down the ladder, dragging the blanket behind him.

"Is there any water left in that jug?" she asked.

"No," he managed through another fit of coughing. He moved past her, pushing her gently toward the rear of the barn, and began to swing the blanket down over the flames, snuffing them where he could. A gloss of sweat clung to his shirtless torso. The temperature inside the barn had not at first seemed peculiar—it had been so warm for so many days. But now she noticed how the heat rose up and warped her vision.

"Anders," she called.

He turned to her. She involuntarily covered her mouth with her hand, and felt a sudden panic that she would not be able to explain to him that it was not a little patchy fire after all, but rather a wall of intense heat that stretched from end to end, blocking their path to the door. The door itself was indistinct as a mirage, bent by the atmosphere. But he saw her panic in an instant, and revolved toward the flames.

The blanket was all burned at the edges already, and discolored by smoke, but Anders set about beating the flames with even greater force. He went at them angry, like he was fighting them in the ring, the muscles of his back and arms taut, his feet quick. In a few moments the spot he attacked was blackened, and the flames seemed to retreat. Hope shot through Fiona—they could beat a path to the door. But then she saw that he had fanned the flames to his right, and before she could cry out to him, they reached the hay bales stacked against the far wall. Fast, so that it seemed unreal, the bales caught, exploding with sparks and embers, engulfing a support beam of old fir. The flames traveled easily after that—in a matter of seconds they had reached the rafters.

Anders bolted backward, taking her by the waist as though to shield her from the heat with his body, and urging her toward the ladder. At the top rung she glanced back, terrified that they'd be trapped up there. The air close to the ceiling was so hot it singed the tip of her nose, and the smoke made her eyes run.

"Hurry." He was coming up behind, pushing her into the loft.

Everything beneath them was burning. She had the

sensation of staring into a large fireplace, which seemed, briefly, like a comfort. Then she realized that if they were looking down on a hearth, that meant they were cornered in its chimney. Her heart raced and she reached for Anders, wanting to convince him they must go back down immediately. But he was dragging the ladder up behind them.

"What are you—"

"We'll never make it out otherwise," he said.

"But . . ." Fiona could hardly breathe. The old beam had carried the fire to the roof, where flames engulfed the old planks.

The bottom of the ladder was smoldering. Anders threw it on the ground, and pounded the wooden ends with the sole of his shoe until they were out. Then he lifted it again and began to bash the outside wall with force. He blinked drops of sweat out of his eyes, and his hair became slick with effort, but he grimaced and kept on until a weak spot in the wood gave way, and he was able to bend back the surrounding boards.

"Go on," he said once he had managed to force the ladder through and down to the ground. She must have hesitated, because he added, "I'll be right behind you."

The air felt cool and delicious on her skin, although she knew it was a hot night. They had all been hot nights as of late. It was only refreshing compared to the inside of the barn. As she climbed down the ladder, her skirt snagged on a shard of wood. Her eyes—shiny with terror that she would not be able to untangle herself, that he would be trapped within—met his.

"Here." He held her gaze as he carefully freed her skirt. "Are you all right?"

She nodded and hurried down.

As soon as her feet touched the ground, she looked up, but there was no sign of Anders, only the gaping hole in the side of the barn. Now the sound was unmistakable, a roar like a furious, shrieking mob. She was too frightened to call for him, and didn't think he'd hear in any case. A few seconds passed and the pain of not knowing whether Anders was all right became too much to bear. She was halfway up the ladder when a shoe flew through the opening, hung in the air, and thudded on the dead grass below.

Another shoe followed, then two more, two shirts, her jacket, and finally, to her enormous relief, Anders. Anders moving nimbly down the rungs until he reached her, pulled her tight; Anders grabbing fistfuls of slip at her low back, and kissing her as though he needed her to teach him how to breathe again.

When they released each other, he brushed his hand over her hair, smoothing it with his fingers, as though in apology for the passion of the previous moment.

She asked, "I look a wreck, don't I?"

To her relief, he grinned. "No. Let's get out of here."

They dressed in a flurry. But by the time they reached the street, they had managed to affect the appearance of calm. Anders held her hand, and they walked in as unobtrusive a manner as possible away from the barn.

The street was full of gawkers, their heads tilted to assess the flaming roof of the barn. Everyone shouted contradictorily about what should be done. No one took particular notice of Fiona and Anders as they hurried along DeKoven toward the river.

"The firemen will be here soon." Anders squeezed her hand.

"You think everything will be all right?"

"As long as the fire doesn't jump to another roof. Don't worry, they'll get it," he said, though he didn't sound entirely sure. "Are we going to miss our train?"

To her surprise, the watch was still solid in her pocket. The face showed a quarter past nine. Her step was light with relief. Her life savings was still carefully sealed in her jacket pocket.

They might have perished, but instead they had escaped.

She might never have told Anders how she felt about him, but now they were together, on the verge of a great adventure. She thought how she must be the luckiest girl in the whole city tonight.

"We'll make it," she whispered, and they broke into a run toward Canal Street.

TWENTY-THREE

Once wed, a woman will tend to the feminine realm of house and home, where she naturally thrives, and let her husband see to the complicated and dangerous world outside their door.
—Cressida Marr, Advice for the Young Bride,
Ostrich Press Publishers, 1870

"My great-aunt was called away quite unexpectedly, and I thought it was only right that I see her to the station," Emmeline said as the hansom rattled along Van Buren. "Since she came all this way to see me married, and all."

The driver sat stoically on his perch and did not respond to Emmeline's obvious lie. She had flagged him on a street by the lumber docks, a good distance from any train station where a society lady might depart in a rush. And even in the unlikely event that a bride of the beau monde did personally attend to such a mission, at this advanced hour, she would have certainly been accompanied by her own personal chauffeur. But Emmeline's heart was strangely quiet and cold, and she was finding it easy to once again bend the truth to her own purposes.

"It was a rather sensitive matter, with my great-aunt," she went on some minutes later. They had arrived at the house she had wanted so much, and the driver stood waiting to help her descend from the cab. "I'd be grateful if you didn't mention my little excursion to anyone."

"Course not, miss," he replied too quickly to credit.

"Thank you." She smiled gloriously for his benefit, and handed him a ten-dollar note.

Once he was gone, she let the smile fall away. She gave the Terrace Row house, which she had not thought she would be coming back to, a wary glance.

As Emmeline contemplated the cold and impressive facade, Georgie went around the inside of the place, taking advantage of the mistress's absence to investigate every luxurious detail. Of course, Mr. Tree expected her to be looking for Emmeline, but he was distracted by his own frantic search for his bride. So Georgie, having concluded that he would not find her here, went into the dressing room on the top floor and sat at the vanity to examine her reflection.

She was pretty, truly pretty, with her dark eyes and long

lashes and small, upturned nose. Whenever she looked at herself, in a fine mirror in a well-appointed room, she was reminded of this fact, and thought how she might, by leveraging her fine face and figure and sharp mind, live a very different kind of life. She had been close in England. And though it had gone terribly wrong, and been the reason she had had to leave in haste, the whole episode had proven what she was capable of.

Such were Georgie's thoughts when Mr. Tree burst in, his face all comical with panic. For a second or two, Georgie thought he was handsome, and that if Emmeline did not come back, he might be the one to deliver her from her temporary poverty. But then he stumbled on a little stool, and Georgie realized that he was precisely the same type as the future Duke of Langham, who had loved her for a season and then been bullied by his family into giving her up. Americans were more naïve than in the old country, Georgie reflected, and were blind around anyone who dressed flashy and was known to have money. They were not as quick to recognize that Freddy, like the future duke, was a fool who would never be good at anything, and was laughed at behind his back, even by the staff, and would always be dependent upon his family's whims for status and money.

Oh well, Georgie thought, and felt a little sorry for

Emmeline for not realizing the kind of man she had married until after the fact.

Freddy—distraught over Emmeline but not yet able to admit that he had lost his bride—was blabbering incoherently. After a moment Georgie realized he was distracting himself by accusing little innocent Georgie of having stolen precious family heirlooms.

"The crown," he said, not for the first time, "the engagement ring—*you* took them."

Georgie sighed, and stood, and gave him her most penitent face. "I am very sorry. I should have told you sooner. I noticed that your grandmother's crown, and the engagement ring, and several other fine pieces, were missing this morning when I was helping Miss Carter—Mrs. Tree—get ready. I'm just a kitchen girl, you know, but her lady's maid, Fiona, was nowhere to be found. Isn't that strange? What with the jewelry missing?"

Georgie was relieved she didn't have to spell things out further. Mr. Tree's features twitched with rage. "Fiona?"

"Yes." Georgie nodded vigorously. "Fiona Something Irish. Byrne, I believe."

Freddy did a strange turn about the carpet, his shoulders flaring dramatically.

"There was a boy, too. She had him hiding in the greenhouse. I did tell Emmeline that part, because I thought she'd want to know, but she said she'd take care of it herself. She seemed like she knew already, to tell the truth, but I didn't want to go sticking my nose where it doesn't belong. . . ."

"A boy?" Mr. Tree's eyes were shadowy, and his features were drawn down as though he were in pain. "What kind of boy?"

"A man, really. Rough-looking. Handsome . . . if you like that sort of thing."

By then it was clear Mr. Tree's anger had found other people, and Georgie was able to have a private thought to herself, which was that it was a true shame that one never came across rich, seduceable young men who had a look like that boy of Fiona's.

That boy of Fiona's was what Emmeline was, at just that moment, doing her very best not to remember.

As she stood on the stoop of the Terrace Row house, unsure whether to go in or stay there, she focused instead on the hem of her wedding dress. The fact that it had gone a little brown at the edges did not truly bother her, but she had so little else to care about now. Earlier, light-headed with romantic hope, she made a mad dash across town, only to see her true love and her best friend in carnal repose. On the return trip, her fury had burned fast and bright, and when it flamed out there was nothing but emptiness. She was desperate for a distraction, and fretting over her gown seemed as good an occupation as any other.

Still, questions swarmed her: Had Fiona always coveted Anders for herself, or was that afternoon the first time she wanted him that way? Did she urge Anders to forget Emmeline—or, worse, did they grab for each other without once mentioning their former friend? "Former friend" stung, but what else could she be to them, now? The memory of Fiona's happy, sleeping face, the unseemly bareness of her arms, the familiar way she and Anders clung to one another, soured Emmeline's stomach with disgust. And yet she knew—in that clear, deep way Fiona had described—that everything might have been different if she had only woken up that morning and gone to Anders straightaway.

"Emmeline." The light from the front parlor illuminated one half of Freddy, standing in the front doorway, and left the other half in shadow. His tone sounded wary, yet he opened his arms to her, and she—very tired, and very sad—couldn't resist moving into his embrace.

"Did you miss me?" she asked weakly. She had frequently greeted Freddy in just this way, but she could not summon her usual flirtatious verve.

He did not reply, which was probably for the best. She knew she should be grateful that he didn't ask where she'd been. Instead he allowed her to throw her arms around his middle, resting his hands on her shoulder and at the small of her back. She hadn't known how much she needed somebody, anybody, to hold her as though she were too precious to let go. In his arms, she felt the awful loneliness of the past hours. Her body was sore with loss.

"I was worried," he said eventually.

"Oh." She pressed her face into his chest. A trace of tobacco and cologne clung to the fibers of his shirt—the smell was strange, although not unpleasant, and it occurred to her that she didn't really know Freddy at all. But perhaps, in time, she would forget the boy she'd tried so hard to be with today. Perhaps she'd come to know Freddy instead, and that would be good enough.

"Are you all right?"

She nodded vigorously, afraid that if she had to speak she might begin to sob.

"Emmeline?"

"A little tired," she managed.

"Won't you come inside, and tell me where you've been?"

With all the spirit she had left, Emmeline turned her lovely eyes upward. She gazed at her husband of a few hours as though she already adored him, as though she were about to give him everything, and trusted him to protect her in return.

The smoothness of Freddy's appearance had been some-what undone by half a day of intense heat, and his eyes were bloodshot. He regarded her for several minutes, during which it was impossible to even guess at what he was thinking. His eyes had a weird quality, as though he could not quite focus on her.

"Let's go in," she told him, hoping it would feel more right once she was inside.

"As you wish." He lifted her into his arms and they crossed the threshold of their home. As they continued up the stairs, Emmeline kept trying to think of it that way, but as they came once again into the bedroom, and as he stooped awkwardly to set her down, she found that it all seemed even stranger than before.

While she lingered on the grand carpet with its navy and silver crests, Freddy went to the door and turned the key in the deadbolt, which whined as it clicked into the jamb. She tried to find something to say, but could think of nothing.

Freddy seemed at a loss for words, too. He stood awhile with his back to her, giving Emmeline time to wonder if she had not permanently ruined her chance for happiness— if she would have to go on forever, in a room like this, without love.

"Can I go to sleep now?" she asked, her voice sounding pathetically like a little girl who has been naughty asking if her bad day can please be over now.

"Soon." Freddy revolved to face her. "But first I want to know where you've been."

TWENTY-FOUR

Try to always be at least a little in love. It is a much more effective beauty aid than rouges or lip stains.
—*Anabelle Carrington,* A Lady's Private Book,
O.P. Herring & Sons Publishers, 1869

The wind was warm and firm against their backs, pushing them northeast along the south branch of the river, ruffling the light fabric of their shirts. Fiona's hair was loose and a little messy, and though she had not seen her reflection in some time, she somehow knew that her disorderly appearance had a kind of loveliness. They had agreed they would cross at Lake Street, the better to avoid the old neighborhood, and head straight for the Great Central Station.

Neither Fiona nor Anders spoke much. Words seemed

inadequate to the change they'd been through, and a little silly, given everything.

The men who had searched for Anders through the city still worried her, but she had the impression that the world had been irreversibly altered. That was then, and life was sweeter now. They were watchful, and kept in the shadows of the buildings so as not to draw attention, but having escaped the burning barn, made it to the river, on their way to leave behind the city that had owned them all their lives, she suspected that some divine presence was watching from above, and that they would be safe as long as they stayed together.

"Fiona," he murmured as she walked ahead to make room for an old woman pushing a vegetable cart.

"Yes?" Her voice wasn't much more than a whisper, and as she twirled to face him her feet seemed to just skim the earth.

"I wanted to say it," he replied. "That's all."

"Say it again."

"Fiona."

"Anders." She shivered. "Have you ever heard anything so nice?"

He shook his head and grinned.

The sensation of being kissed by Anders, of touching his arms and the muscles of his back, of his fingers in her hair, and her legs wrapping around his legs, was still with her.

The memory was sweet in her limbs, and she didn't want to disturb that with any idle chatter—she wanted the traces of the time they'd spent in that loft to linger on her skin as long as possible.

The courthouse bell had not yet rung, and from their street-level vantage, Fiona and Anders had every reason to believe the fire in the barn had been contained. The city was going about its nightly business, and in the cupola, Gabriel was as content as they were, because he had drifted into a dream of victory parades and cheering crowds and a happy, sun-soaked day when he and his compatriots were celebrated like heroes.

The first sign that all was not happiness was Hiram, the telegraph operator, calling his name. At first Gabriel thought Hiram was merely waking him so that he could better keep the watch. For Hiram well knew that Gabriel had not slept at all the night before, what with the Great Fire, and had been prone to nodding off through the afternoon.

The city to the east rolled out, on and on, the barges on the water, the grain elevators taking in their stock even this late in the day. But when he looked west, he saw the wind lift the terrible trail of reddish light, and the smoke billowing above—black, except where it was illuminated like low clouds on the Fourth of July. In a panic, Gabriel shouted out the name of what he hoped was the right alarm box, so that the nearest engine company could be alerted, and get quickly to the scene.

By the time he realized he had called the wrong company, the courthouse bells had already tolled the alarm many times over, and Hiram said there was no point in correcting it, for at this point the firemen would surely see the source of the smoke.

Gabriel, who wanted only to do good in the world, regarded himself hatefully.

The wind was blowing to the northeast, at least. It would move the flames toward the natural barriers of the river and last night's fire, where there was nothing left to burn. Yet he was stricken with nauseous foreboding. All over town the wind cried against the top-floor windows, whipping flags, making the dogs crazy.

Tonight was a bad night for a fire.

By the time Fiona and Anders reached the far side of the bridge, they could hear the bell at the courthouse ring the alarm, and their mood shifted, too. A bank of smoke was now visible in the distance, rising over the West Side. They still didn't speak much, although now she reckoned it was for different reasons. Neither wanted to think too hard about the scene that they had rushed away from.

The train station was full of bustle. Despite the late

hour, periodicals and peanuts were being hawked from every corner, and there seemed to be almost as many arrivals and departures as at noon. But here, too, an anxious mood prevailed. Even the man who kept the flower stall was disagreeable. He seemed grimly determined to sell the rest of his stock and go.

"Come on, doesn't your sweetheart need a rose?" he called to Anders as they passed. "She looks like she needs a rose."

Anders's eyes darted to be sure that no one had noticed him, and then he quickly handed over a coin for one long-stemmed deep-red rose. Although there were other worries, Fiona couldn't help a little spasm of disappointment that Anders's first gift to her would come so unwillingly. But when he took her hand, drew her close so that he could kiss her cheek and put the rose just under her nose, her cheeks flushed with joy.

"That man said you're my sweetheart," he said.

"Am I?"

He grinned and rested his forehead against her forehead. The flow of passengers and porters, tour guides and cab drivers, continued on either side as they swayed together.

"Hey there," barked the flower salesmen. "The Grand Chicago Hotel is right around the corner, you can rent a room from the booth across the way."

Anders turned on his heel. He stalked toward the man,

and she saw the anger make a rigid line of his spine. He seemed larger—the span of his shoulders grew, and his fists nearly throbbed. The flower vendor stepped back, smiling a crooked smile and raising his hands in jest. "Anders," she whispered, grabbing for his hand. "Come on, let's go."

He allowed her to lead him, and they moved swiftly down the huge corridor toward the train shed.

"Forget it," she urged him.

She wished they could return to the silly sweetness of earlier, but she knew she couldn't rush that. He would come back to her when he was ready. Meanwhile, they reached the grand entryway onto the enormous room where the tracks came to their terminus. The machine exhaust rose up to the iron and glass ceiling, and uniformed personnel moved back and forth preparing for the midnight train's departure. Fiona thought how, as soon as they were sitting comfortably on the train, they would be safe. They would be almost as good as gone, and no gamblers would be able to find them where they were going.

They glanced up at the board that announced the track numbers.

"New York," Anders murmured, and she felt relieved that he was looking to the future.

On they went, past a group of farmers, close enough to overhear their urgent discussion.

"They say it's burning out of control," said the tallest one.

"But the harvest. We'll need you on the farm every day till November."

The tall one shook his head. "My wife is there, staying with her sister on the West Side until the baby comes. I have to go."

The other nodded in solemn agreement, and they shook hands.

Fiona turned to watch how swiftly the tall man left the train station. He had a great lumbering gait, and a patchwork coat, and she could see him even among the hordes of people as he made his way back through the gauntlet of shops on his way to the city street. Her jaw tightened, and her temples went cold. A boy ran by, shouting the latest news—it was as the farmer said, the fire on the West Side was out of control.

The farmer knew something she did not. And suddenly she knew it too: a bad thing was going to happen tonight.

"I have to go back," she whispered.

"What?" Anders's brow rippled with concern.

"My family, they . . ."

"Because of the fire? It's on the West Side, Fiona, it'll never get to the old neighborhood."

"But *if*. If it should . . . I just have to tell them to be careful, to be ready to leave, if . . ." She trailed off, frustrated with herself that she couldn't explain what she knew she must do. "Their place, they're always in those little rooms. And it's like where we were, in the barn, but worse. They'd be trapped."

Anders glanced at the train and stood quietly taking this in.

"Get on the train. I'll just go and warn them. They'll understand. I'll be back by midnight, before departure time. You'll be safe here, and my mind will be easier if I just . . ."

Anders grimaced. "If you go, I'm going with you."

"But Gil Bryce, if he or one of his people should . . ."

Anders raised his blue gaze to hers and gave her a sly smile. "I'd do the same if it were my family, Fiona Byrne. But if you think I'm going to let you go off into the city by yourself now, after everything, then you're crazy for sure."

When they left the train station, the wind was harsh in their faces, as though urging them to retreat. But Fiona was relieved that she'd be able to say a proper goodbye to her family, and see them safe one last time. And with Anders close by her side, she felt certain that everything would be all right in the end. Soon they'd be leaving, but with their minds at ease and their hearts full of nothing but each other.

TWENTY-FIVE

A girl's wedding day is the most glorious and treacherous of her life. She will be fawned over and feted for her beauty during the early hours, but at night she will have to face her wifely duties. My advice is that she puts out the lights and urges her husband to do his business quickly.
—*Cressida Marr,* Advice for the Young Bride, Ostrich Press Publishers, 1870

"Emmeline?"

That was her name, she well knew. Yet, spoken with gentle concern through the dressing room door, it sounded odd, and sad-making. She had always rather liked her name, but now she hadn't the slightest idea what it was supposed to mean. Who was Emmeline, anyway, if not the best friend of Fiona, the beloved of Anders? As she sat on the short fur-covered stool—still encased in her wedding gown, faced with her own reflection—all she could be sure of was that Emmeline was a girl lovely and sly enough to have won a coveted proposal from a wealthy and prominent young man. But she was a stranger to herself. The pretty features in the mirror did not seem to have much to do with whomever she was supposed to be, and her insides felt all washed out.

"My dearest?" This time Freddy's query was accompanied by a rap of knuckles.

"Yes?" She had been stalling in the dressing room, claiming she needed to remove her wedding finery before they talked, before he asked again where she had been. Of course he would—any husband would want to know. But she just couldn't bear for him to hate her too. Maybe, she thought, if she stayed in the dressing room long enough, he would forget about her little absence.

"Is everything all right?" Several moments passed before Freddy added: "I am worried about you. . . ."

"I'm fine!" she called brightly. She attempted a smile to match the sentiment, but the thing looked wobbly, then failed completely, and she began to cry. She put her forehead in her hands and let a big sob work its way up her throat and out her mouth.

Freddy must have heard, because he came into the dressing room. "Oh dear," he said. "Come, my darling, why are you hiding from me?"

"I don't knooooow!" she wailed.

He put his hands upon her shoulders, and urged her back into the bedroom, where he sat her down on a navy satin settee, and cupped his hands around hers. "Don't you trust me?" he asked.

She was trying her best not to cry anymore, and assiduously avoiding his gaze. Yet she sensed how he searched for her eyes. "Of course," she managed.

"It's all very sudden, isn't it?" he went on. "We hardly know each other."

Emmeline hiccupped and attempted a sideways glance at her husband.

"And you're very young to be married. I suppose I was your first beau, the first man ever to take a romantic interest in you."

Her head bobbed in vigorous agreement.

"That was your first kiss today, wasn't it?"

"Yes," she lied.

"I could tell." He sighed. "You're nervous. Aren't you? About what comes next."

When she could think of no answer to that, he patted her on the head like a child and crossed the room and fell into the velvet armchair.

With a ladylike lowering of her lashes, Emmeline replied, "I suppose."

"That is very charming of you, my dear. I confess it makes me adore you even more. It has been a very long, and very tiring, day. Why don't you rest now, and we can leave until tomorrow the business of being man and wife?"

This sign that he understood her delicate state, that he would be patient, filled her with gratitude. Maybe, even after everything, she still had some luck left. "Thank you," she murmured.

"All right," he said, unfurling himself. He stumbled a little on his way toward a heavy mahogany cabinet. The way he avoided looking at her told her that he was disappointed, and she thought how kind he was, to put her desires before his own. He poured himself a snifter of amber liquid, lit a small paper cylinder of tobacco, and returned to his previous position on the chair. "But there's one small matter I must discuss with you, before our wedding day is over."

She nodded in agreement. She wished all this regret and sadness and confusion would leave her already. Things would be better, she rationalized, if she could cheer herself up and accept Freddy's kindness. With Freddy, maybe, she could forget the awful mess of Fiona and Anders and what they'd done in the barn. "Ask me whatever you like."

"I have heard a rather wild story."

Emmeline straightened, making her expression alert.

The smell of the cigarette wafted toward her, but she didn't want to cough or appear otherwise put out by Freddy—not now, when he was being so attentive.

"It's about your maid. Did you know that she was hiding a boy in the greenhouse at your father's place?"

Emmeline's eyes widened and she moved her head slowly to the left. "You mean Georgie?" she asked.

"No." Freddy grimaced and focused his attention on the cigarette between his index and middle fingers. "I mean Fiona."

"Oh, yes, Fiona. . . ." Hearing the name out loud made her stomach tighten, and Emmeline felt a series of emotions wash over her: embarrassment, sadness, anger. "Well, no, I mean . . . yes. . . ."

"You were friendly with this servant, weren't you? Well, she seems to have absconded with many of your—and my—jewels."

"Oh." Emmeline swallowed hard. She had not thought about the jewels. It was she who had insisted Fiona sell them, but now she wanted them back, wanted never to have been daring and brave, never to have gone looking for something more than this. "I—"

"You don't believe it, because you have a kind heart. But I learned that she had help. A boy, who she was hiding in the greenhouse. A boyfriend, perhaps—"

"He wasn't *her* boyfriend," Emmeline shot back before she could think better of it.

Freddy blanched and then the strange light, the beginning of a realization, came into his eyes. "He . . . was . . . yours?"

"Oh, well . . ." Emmeline had accidentally told the truth, and she was too confused to figure out how best to twist it around, make it sound right and work for her. "Not exactly. I mean, it was all a long time ago. We were just children then."

"You knew." He gazed at her, aghast. "You *knew* they were stealing the jewels. Why, Emmeline? For what?"

Her heart was like a frightened bird in a too-small cage. For a few moments she was very busy trying to brush out the wrinkles in the lap of her dress. It was not yet midnight, on the first day of their married life, and she thought if she could only tell him the right story, they could begin again. That she could go back, and have the life that she had intended to have.

"They confused me," she began slowly. "Tricked me, really," she went on, half believing it herself. She did feel tricked, and badly used. "They came to me, and tried to convince me that Anders was my true love."

"Anders?"

"Anders Magnuson. He was my friend, back before—you

271

know, when I was—younger. He's a boxer, well-known in certain parts of town. You said yourself I have a kind heart, and I was a little simple, I suppose, and they convinced me I was making a mistake, and that I should run away with them. . . ."

"With *him*."

"But they must have used some magic! Because they convinced me of all manner of things that I can see were mistakes now. . . ." She had begun to babble, mixing truth and lies, half trying to convince Freddy of the nefariousness of Fiona and Anders, half wanting his pity and concern. She told him about the plan to go to New York, and the barn, and the desperate journey she'd taken just now, and what she saw, when she finally arrived on DeKoven. She tried to make Anders out as a wily seducer, and show how Fiona had always been more interested in money than in friendship. She tried to portray herself as a victim of their scheming, who had been coerced away from her true feelings for Freddy, who had been tricked into forgetting her best self. She was glad to think of Fiona and Anders this way. It made her feel that she had not lost so very much.

But if her story of woe moved him, it was difficult to tell from looking at his face. All the while Freddy sat impassively, and whether he was shocked or merely disappointed, she could not be certain.

"But I was wrong," she concluded. "I was confused, I

was sentimental, I was a little girl, I didn't know how lucky I was to be marrying you. But now we can start again. With no secrets and no lies."

When she was finished he stubbed the cigarette out in a black lacquered tray. "Your engagement ring?" he said as though it was this detail in particular that vexed him.

"Yes, but . . ." She stared at him helplessly. "I can get it back!"

"How?" he cried in anguish. "What a *fool* I was the day I bought that ring. I brought Ada's husband with me, and I could see how it amused him, how I asked to see every ring they had, and held them up, wondering which of these could possibly be good enough for my beautiful Emmeline? Oh, I knew what he was thinking: that I'd been taken in by a little social-climbing nobody. But I didn't care. I didn't care! My heart was full with Emmeline, and all I cared about was pleasing Emmeline."

"You did," she said meekly. "I loved that ring."

"And the crown! That crown had been in my family for four generations."

Emmeline shrunk into the settee. She had not considered the piece's provenance when she had handed it over to Fiona to turn into money.

"In what sordid place did you say you hawked it?"

"I—I don't know," she stammered. "Fiona and Anders took care of that."

"That barn, you said it was on DeKoven Street? On the West Side?"

She nodded slowly.

Freddy stood up and adjusted the high collar of his fine jacket. Earlier, the white tails had given him the appearance of a dashing hero out of a newspaper serial, but now it had a different effect. It was rumpled and sweat-dark, and she could see that he had been wounded by this day too. She had believed that depicting the events of the past few days as she had would win his sympathy, that he would see how tired and hurt she was, and they could begin anew. But now he seemed unlikely to say anything at all. The prospect of a silence without end made her desperate and doubtful of her own existence.

"You're not going to go looking for them, are you? Oh, please don't." She jumped up and came toward him. She couldn't stand the idea that her friends might learn that, along with everything else, Emmeline's marriage was already a disaster. Didn't want to give them the satisfaction of knowing how completely they had ruined her. "They didn't really have anything to do with . . ."

Freddy cleared his throat, as though he had just heard something but wished he hadn't, and moved away from her. As he paused in the doorway to the hallway she said his name, and when that didn't bring him back, she started saying anything she could think of to make him stay.

"They probably aren't even at the barn anymore," she said.

This seemed to get his attention. "No?" His voice chilled her with its abrupt force. "Where might those thieving ragpickers be?"

She had never seen Freddy so angry before. It changed the very shape of his face, and he appeared more wolf than man. Since he'd started courting her, she'd thought of him mostly as a man who was particular about what he wore, and who could be manipulated by always keeping herself just out of reach.

"They could be anywhere . . . out of the city, or . . . back in the old neighborhood, where Fiona's people are." The room's temperature had changed suddenly. Emmeline was having trouble making sense. But she felt certain that Fiona and Anders would never go to the old neighborhood. That was one place, on account of Gil Bryce, she was sure that Freddy would not find them. Plus, it was the last place Freddy, who dressed so fine, would ever go. "In the alleys near Jackson and Wells," she said triumphantly, as though the location alone would ward him off.

He assessed her. "Jackson and Wells?"

"Yes, but don't go there now. Stay with me. I'm sorry. I made a mistake, but I am still your wife."

He came at her so fast that she fell to the floor trying to get out of his way. He grabbed her by the roots of her hair and dragged her to her feet. His palm, when it hit her face, smacked like a frying pan just off the range.

"Yes." His breath was hot in her ear: "You are my wife."

She had no breath. The room, with its large, polished wood furniture and many gilt-encrusted objects, had a crushing gravity. Through the doorway, she could see the darkness of the fourth-floor landing, and wished to disappear into it. "To have and to hold, or did you forget that part? You will not humiliate me this way. You will not let them think they were right, that I was had by a con man and his pretty daughter. You are my *wife*, and I will get that ring back tonight, and you will be seen wearing it tomorrow, and the day after, and forever."

His shiny black shoes darted over the ornamented carpet. Emmeline touched her burning cheek, too frightened to make a whimper. She wanted to stop him, but she was terrified of what he would do to her if she drew him back. She wanted him to leave, but she wished she hadn't brought Fiona and Anders into it. Her temples throbbed, and her soul shrank from what she'd done.

The door closed behind him, and this time there was no mistaking the metallic whine of the bolt locking her within.

TWENTY-SIX

Born in the slums, died in the slums.
—Carved into the bar at Jem Gallagher's

They passed the Michigan Southern Depot and were in the old neighborhood again. A few city blocks, that was all it was, cut by crooked alleys, bordered on the west by the river, near where it hooked left and flowed on south to join the Mississippi. When she was small, these blocks had seemed the whole world. A glare was visible on the far side of the river, above the tar roofs and ship masts, its terrible reddish light reflected on an otherwise murky sky.

"They haven't been able to put it out yet." Fiona's bottom lip trembled as she sought Anders's eyes.

"Don't." Anders had seen her expression and read her

thoughts. He held her gaze as he gave a firm shake of his head. "It's not our fault."

But Fiona had seen the broken lantern, and couldn't help feeling that the conflagration had something to do with her.

As they turned onto the wide main street of the neighborhood, they were met by the strong westerly wind. A man, emerging from a laundry, was robbed of his hat—the current of warm air plucked it from his head, and sent it tumbling backward in the direction of LaSalle. But he was apparently in a rush, for he did not even attempt a retrieval. Fiona glanced over her shoulder to see where the hat would land, and noticed a boy about Jack's age, watching. He had been leaning in the doorframe of a three-story frame building, but he disappeared down an alley after she caught his eye. The inside of her mouth went dry.

Perhaps, she reasoned, the boy's haste was only to be on time for supper. But it was late for supper. As children they had been watchers, too. Ochs Carter would tell them who to look out for, and it would mean a half-penny if they could get the news of the whereabouts of certain persons of interest to Emmeline's father within minutes of spotting them.

"We can leave soon, I promise," she said. "Just as soon as I've warned my family."

"Don't worry." His eyes had a sheen by then, and the

ropey muscles of his arms tensed. "We'll be all right. Just stay close."

They went north, into the alleys, where three-story tenements of brick and pine leaned against each other, like trees that grow too close together and must fight each other's branches for the sun. In a few minutes, they would be at her family's place; and yet, in this part of the city, a hundred feet could be a treacherous distance. A whistle cut through the evening din behind them, and another sounded up ahead. Shutters banged, and a door opened.

"Don't look back," Anders said in a low voice. "Stay close to the wall."

He fell behind her, yet still she knew how to match his pace. Although he moved in silence, she sensed him, just as she'd sensed him the day she'd gone to Gorley's. This time he was even closer, and she felt the idea of his hand at the small of her back, urging her to move fast. Her hair crackled and her ears took in every tiny noise: the incessant blowing; the muffled voices within the shabby dwellings; the wailing of hinges; distant, high-pitched laughter; a rattling of coins; the heels of boots against a wooden walkway. The boots were getting louder; Fiona could feel them now, like a small hammer administering taps up and down her vertebrae.

It's probably nothing, she reasoned. *Soon we will come to the end of this street*, she thought. *Soon we will be home, soon my parents will know of the danger and take the necessary precautions, soon we will be back on the train.*

But these hopeful notions were no match for the uneasy beating of her heart. A few seconds passed, and she couldn't stand it anymore. She glanced over her shoulder and knew that the man with the heeled boots—he was tall and lean, with a bristly mustache—was on their trail. His chin was drawn into his throat, his gaze sought them like a marksman.

Anders's fierce posture and pace remained the same. His fingers brushed her hip, and she focused once again on the outlet of the alley, the place where they were going. But what she saw there made her stomach tighten into a fist. At the end of the way, standing in wait for them, was Gil Bryce. Although his greasy hat was crushed down around his ears, she knew him by the leather duster he wore and the broad menace of his shoulders. His eyes were just visible beneath his brim, flickering with blue-green rage, but his mouth curved with satisfaction upon seeing these two prodigal children of the neighborhood, returned to his territory.

"Hey there, Mag," he called, his voice a cruel imitation of friendliness.

Fiona felt like a deer hunted through a ravine. If Anders had not been right behind her, she would have stopped, frozen in her tracks. But they moved together, forward, as one. As though they, too, were hungry for a confrontation. She remembered Anders's sudden anger in the train station, and wondered if maybe he did want a fight. Another man appeared at Gil Bryce's side, and though she dared not look, Fiona had an inkling of others joining the one with the mustache to their rear.

"Hello there, you handsome boys!"

Fiona's gaze swung in the direction of the brassy voice. Above them, half leaning out of a second-story window, was a woman wearing sausage curls and a louche smile. Her elbows were folded on the sill, and she arched a painted eyebrow. The rest of the woman's face was painted too, and Fiona was momentarily distracted by the thought that she knew her, that if she could only picture this woman without makeup she would remember how. Then she had it: The woman's name was Maud, and she had been engaged at one time to Anders's older brother, Michael. But they said that, later, she had lost her way.

Anders! Fiona twirled in place, but he was gone. She was alone on the street, with Maud leering down, and Gil Bryce's men at either end of the alley.

"Don't look so beastly," Maud was admonishing Gil Bryce's gang. "I was hoping we could have a good old time."

Anders's fingers circled her wrist, pulling her off the street. The space between the two buildings was so slender, she hadn't noticed its narrow opening from the alley. But now they were running along between a wall of brick and a wall of pine plank. Gil Bryce was shouting after them, and she was relieved that he didn't seem to know precisely where they had gone. They had almost reached the outlet when he stopped, shoved his shoulder against a door that blended in with the rest of the pine edifice, and pulled her along behind him. Like that, they were in a different place.

"Hey, Mag, where you been?" called a man stumbling toward them. His face was dirty but he sounded friendly. Sawdust soaked with spilled beer rose to her nostrils. They were in Jem's place, she realized, and as before she was the only female in sight.

The second man to notice Anders sounded less kind. "Is that the kid?"

"Gil Bryce'll be wanting to know he's around," said another.

"Let the kid be."

"Don't you tell me who to let be."

To her relief, Anders pulled her in close, as though he might be able to shield her from view with his body, and hustled her along the same corridor she'd gone through that morning, a few days and a long time ago, when she'd come calling on behalf of Emmeline.

The crowd erupted in argument. A debate raged over whether Anders Magnuson's presence should be reported or kept a secret, accompanied by much shoving and cursing.

"They'll figure out where we went," she whispered. "They'll be right behind us."

"I know." Anders jerked his head at the scene behind them. A brawl had broken out in their wake. "But they'll have to get through that."

On they went, leaving behind the combustible atmosphere of the saloon and stumbling into the courtyard. At night the place was quiet as a secret. The walls of the surrounding structures rose up, framing a square of midnight sky that winked peacefully from a thousand different points of light. They gazed up. For a moment, they were the only two people left in the wide world.

He took hold of her hips, and his breath mixed with her breath.

"I'm sorry," she said, pressing into his chest. "This was a bad idea. I've put us in danger."

"Don't you understand, Fiona? I'd go anyplace with you."

Her shoulders relaxed and her body softened into his. They might have gone on like that—clutching each other, oblivious to danger—had a great whistling and cawing, like some mythical winged beast, not brought their attention once again skyward. The sweetness drained from Fiona's limbs.

The wind sent a blazing piece of roof—or what anyway had once been a section of roof—sailing overhead. It was

huge and bright as a comet, and it rained sparks on the surrounding buildings.

"Come on." Anders's fingers interlaced with hers.

At the back of the courtyard was a window. Anders
pushed it open and hauled himself up and through. Once he
was inside he reached for Fiona, lifting her by the torso. He
pulled her into a low-lit living room, where an old woman
dozed in an armchair, her knitting fallen into her lap. Fiona
turned, and closed and locked the window. Although she
could see no disturbance in the courtyard, she knew Gil
Bryce's people would find it soon.

"You're that boy who makes all the noise in the yard."
The woman's eyes were open, and she regarded the intrud-
ers with irritation.

Anders ignored this. "You have to get out of here."

"Are you aiming to rob me, young man?"

"There's going to be a fire," Anders said.

She batted his warning away with the back of her hand.
"There's a fire every night."

"We haven't had a fire in this section in a while," he
went on calmly. "We're due for one, and the wind is bad."

Fiona heard voices in the courtyard, and moved quickly
to dampen the wick in the kerosene lamp. She reached for
the old woman's hand. "Please, we wouldn't harm you,"
she said, and she must have sufficiently shown her worry
because the woman allowed Fiona to escort her to the front

of the house. As they reached the door, they heard the glass being shattered in the living room.

"We have to go," Fiona addressed the old woman. "We're in trouble if we stay. Promise me you'll leave this place. Go wherever you have friends, as long as it's south of here. If there's a fire, the wind will keep it moving north."

"Don't worry," she replied with a little cackle. "I've survived it all so far."

The houses and apartments and shanties of the neighborhood had emptied, and their residents filled the streets. Franklin was as crowded as at midday, and almost as light, for the stables on the corner of Jackson were now crowned by fire. All around them, they heard speculations as to when, or if, the firefighters would arrive on the scene. A man in a fine black suit and bowler begged for help in putting out the flames but he was mostly ignored. The building bore the name Parmalee, a stagecoach company that served the finer districts of the city. It had been erected that summer, on several lots where the homes of dockworkers and their families had recently been razed, earning the ill will of the local population. Nobody from around here would be sorry to see it fall.

Fiona heard a shriek, and turned to see the old woman whose living room they had just passed through pummeling the man with the bristly mustache. He was impervious to her attacks, however, and his eyes were steadily scanning the swarm of people. Suddenly he raised his arm and pointed right at them.

In the general chaos and confusion no one seemed to notice that the tall man in the leather duster was advancing through the crowd, his gun drawn and pointed at the sky. Her blood was thunderous in her ears and Anders's grip was strong. His eyes searched hers with their vivid light. "I'll find you at your family's place," he said, and let go of her hand. "Don't worry." He took a step away from her and his smile cut a dimple in his cheek. "Go!"

When she realized what he intended to do, her face went cold with dread.

His head was bent in determination and he was half running through the dense crowd of bodies, in the direction of the burning stables. After a second or two of helpless agony, she did the only thing she knew to do.

"You can't go in there!" called the man in the bowler— but meekly, as though he knew that keeping riffraff out was the least of his troubles. Anders paid him no mind, and neither did Fiona, following him through the small door off to the side of the locked, carriage-wide main doors.

She had let him go once before, and could not stand to lose him again.

TWENTY-SEVEN

Repent! For the bordellos and houses of chance that proliferate in the dark corners of every district of this city breed such hot lust, inspire such dancing with the devil, that the only cure shall be a great cataclysm, a fiery act of God that will level this city and cleanse its sin that all souls may burn with His righteous knowledge.
—Reverend Finney, All-Night Tabernacle of the Holy Evangels, *South River Street*

"I wish you hadn't done that," Anders said, but he didn't seem exactly surprised to find her still at his side. Fiona recovered her breath and smiled, happy to be with him again. "Those are reckless men, they won't hesitate to follow here. But we'll be gone when the roof caves in, all right? And they'll still be searching for us. Do you trust me?"

"Yes," Fiona whispered, although she wished she could be as sure as Anders that they would soon be leaving.

An aura of doom hung over the place. The interior of the stables was wide, the fixtures new and clean and redolent of varnish. It was empty of people, but not empty of creatures. The twenty or so stalls that lined either side of the space were still occupied by horses, regarding them from behind their gates with giant, shrouded eyes. Overhead, there was a hiss and rumble that made her breath quick.

Anders began to run back and forth, opening the gates so that the horses—which must have smelled danger already—went dashing through the main space of the room. The forces of nature swirled around Fiona, paralyzing her. But only for a moment, and soon she was helping Anders, pulling back the gates and freeing the animals. Their coats were slick and dark and their eyes rolled and their manes whipped back and forth. Fiona was close to the rear of the building—near the back wall hung with saddles, bridles, and other equipment—when they heard the first shot.

"You hear me, Mag?" Even over the stampede of horses that filled the middle space of the building, Gil Bryce's voice carried, sharp and cruel.

Move, Anders mouthed, and they began to crawl as one toward the corner. The mass of horses began to buck and neigh in terror.

"You thought I'd be too chicken to follow you in here? You thought I'd let you go, like that? There's no exit back there, you know. Only way out is through me."

The pack was wild in the main space of the room, and she feared that in a few minutes they'd be crushed under hoof. So she scrambled on hands and knees under the wall of one of the stalls, and Anders crawled behind her. The double-wide doors at the front of the place creaked, and another shot sounded from Gil Bryce's pistol, and the horses stampeded. The earth shook with the mad rush as Fiona and Anders crawled on their bellies from one stall to the next.

"Come on out, boy," he called. "It's just business, and you owe me money."

A few horses remained, which she and Anders must have missed in their haphazard attempt to free them. Fiona was afraid she and Anders would be kicked as soon as they reached an occupied stall, but they had no choice but to risk it. They came upon one just as the toes of Gil Bryce's boots appeared beneath the gate. A horse blanket was hanging at the rear of the stall, and on instinct she grabbed hold and used it to cover her and Anders.

"Hello, you," she heard Gil Bryce say.

Fiona dug her fingernails into Anders's arm before she realized he was speaking to the horse. His tone was gentler than the one he used for his actual prey—he must not have noticed the boy and girl, huddled behind the big, mahogany mare.

Don't breathe, she thought, and though she knew it wasn't really possible, she felt certain Anders had heard.

"Is it hot in here?" Gil called to Anders—farther on now, moving up the stables, toward the rear. "Who is that lovely creature you're dragging all around? Maybe you'd like to trade her to pay your debt to me?"

The others began to laugh again, as though they found the snap and crash of combustion overhead exciting. But Fiona remembered how quickly the barn on the West Side had been consumed—this place would be ash so much sooner than these men knew. They laughed again when the first flames penetrated the ceiling, and a blazing rafter fell to the ground—although their laughter became higher, wilder, and one of them yelped in pain.

"Hear that, Mag?" Gil Bryce called in his low, guttural rasp. "You'll be hurting soon too."

The horse trotted agitatedly in place. Through the blanket, Fiona felt the switch of its tail. She clung to Anders, trying not to shake.

"We're out of time." Anders barely put breath to his words, yet she heard him clear. "We have to get out of here. I'll go first, get their attention, then you go quietly. It's me they want, so they won't notice you. Just go quick and don't draw attention to yourself."

Fiona's heart darkened with understanding. Anders had never really thought he'd leave this place. It had always been a wild chance—he had drawn these men in for a final confrontation, knowing full well they were none of them likely to survive. "As soon as they see you, they'll . . ." she murmured.

"It doesn't matter," he said. "Soon none of this will matter."

The inside of her mouth was parched, and she was finding it difficult not to cough. The blanket was rough, smothering in the heat.

"You're making me angry." Gil Bryce was across the room. The way he growled, Fiona knew he meant what he said. "And I've been angry a time already."

"You weren't supposed to follow me." Anders spoke his words into her ear, so she felt their vibration more than she heard them. "You shouldn't have followed me at all. You already escaped the neighborhood, you know. You will again. The first day you saw Emmeline walking in the street with her father, you said 'That girl will see the world, let's be friends with her,' and she was like a promise that we, too, could leave. But it never mattered. You were always going to escape. I should have told you earlier. I've always known. I was just afraid you'd outgrow me, I suppose—have the dress shop you always dreamed of opening, or marry some important person. It wasn't Emmeline who was too big for us. You were always too big for us. For me. Me, I was never really going to get out. That's what I wanted to tell you, before—before everything. I wanted to tell you that you've already made it, and that I didn't think I should hold you back by kissing you again. But I am glad I did, Fiona. I love you."

She was so overwhelmed with emotion she couldn't manage a reply. But she felt strangely at ease, as though he had just explained everything to her, everything there was to know about Anders and Fiona and all the years they'd been friends, and was glad at least that her own heart was no longer a mystery.

She touched his face, the strong line of his nose, felt the tension in his jaw and the close crop of his hair. He put his mouth to hers, one last time. Then he threw off the blanket, and jumped to his feet. Fiona followed, crawling forward and taking the reins, whispering to the mare to stay calm. In the early days on Dearborn, when she and Emmeline had first learned how to ride like ladies, she had been afraid of the horses, and the horses had rebelled at her presence. But in time she learned to be confident with them, to lead with a sure hand. She murmured and waited to see what Anders would do. In a moment he bolted toward the center of the room, whooping in rage.

Her eyes darted as she crept forward, leading the horse. The stables were dark with smoke and drifting particles, yet she made out how Gil Bryce moved toward Anders, shrugging his leather duster from his shoulders and clutching his gun's grip. Fingers of flame pierced the ceiling in a hundred places, and the beam that had fallen close to the wide entrance created a nearly impassable wall of fire. Everywhere around them the hay and wood plank were ignited by the sparks that whirled like glowing orange snow.

"You want me?" Light shone on Anders's teeth when he grinned. "Here I am."

The gang closed in on him. They took no notice of Fiona, crouched behind the horse as she led it toward the entrance. Inside she seethed with despair, but outwardly she did the only thing she could do: she tried to go unnoticed.

The double-wide front doors were burning now, and they bent and swayed with the heat. She heard a popping sound, and the windows began to shatter, one and then another. The mare heard the breaking glass and reared, and if Fiona had not had a firm hand on the reins she would have lost her. But she was able to hold tight, and when the mare fell back to all fours, Fiona gave her a commanding pat and swung up onto her back.

She could not escape Gil Bryce's attention now.

"Hey there, little girl." He drew the tip of his tongue along his teeth. "I was wondering where you hid yourself."

The horse reared again, and Gil Bryce and his men stepped back. Any other day, Fiona knew, she would have been thrown. But her body was alive with panic and she felt possessed by a superhuman strength. Anders crouched, and took the leather coat that had been Gil Bryce's signature in hand. The horse charged and the men scattered, leaving only Anders, fearless in the mare's path, even as her front legs pawed the air and wheeled around.

The men stared, stunned by the crazed animal, watching how she trotted, snorted, tossed her mane, and readied to charge the door. Fiona gave a little nudge with her ankles. She did not have to look to know that Anders had broken into a run, that he was running alongside as though the horse were a freight train—running until he was hurtling, until he could launch himself onto the mare's back. Fiona felt him grab hold just as their mount broke into a gallop. Anders clutched Fiona's waist with one arm, and drew the leather coat around their bodies with the other, and Fiona held fast to the reins. They were hurtling into a ring of fire, but it was too late to turn back. Fiona flinched, and the mare leapt over the burning beam, through the ruins of the door, and into a mass of onlookers who had gathered to watch the conflagration.

The crowd screamed and scattered, clearing a path for the out-of-control horse and the two riders who clung to her back. There was no time to get one's bearings: a few seconds, and the people were shrieking about something else. Fiona glanced back and was flooded with relief, and at the same time choked with horror. The building in which she had just been trapped collapsed under the weight of its own fiery roof. A sound like rolling thunder shocked the onlookers into silence.

"He's gone," Fiona gasped. "All of them, they're—"

"Don't think about it," Anders said, and she knew how much he meant it. His features were hard and his eyes opaque. They'd meant Anders harm, she knew, but he had lured them in that place and to their deaths. He sat back, but did not relax his grip on her torso. The terrible light of the destroyed warehouse was mesmerizing, and for a moment he watched in the same dumb manner as the rest who stood with mouths hung open and eyes blank with shock. "Let's find your family, Fiona," he said eventually, and urged the horse on with a pat.

For a moment or two she couldn't remember how to say words. But it didn't matter. There was nothing that needed saying; anyone could see what would happen next. The fire was too voracious—it would spread to the nearby buildings, maybe to the entire neighborhood, and those who lingered would lose their lives along with everything else.

TWENTY-EIGHT

You can't put out a high wind with water.
—Overheard on the corner of Jackson and Wells

Fiona had not known there were so many people in the whole world. Even at high noon on a busy Friday she had not seen the streets as densely populated as now. From atop the horse's back, she surveyed the impassable sea of bodies that filled the avenue, along with wagons piled high with shop goods and trunks, animals, and wailing children. Piano benches and spinning wheels were passed overhead across the tide. She checked her watch, and so knew it was nearing midnight. It had taken her and Anders half an hour to make their way from Franklin onto the alley where her parents kept their home.

Panic was general through the old neighborhood. Talk

of the fire and its path was everywhere. Her eyes darted through the mass, hoping to see one of her siblings. As the minutes peeled away with no sign of them, fear over her family's whereabouts tightened in her throat. If not for Anders's hands resting at her waist and shoulder, she would certainly have panicked, too.

But on the street where she used to live, no one spoke. Eddies of cinder and ash whirled in the air, and men and women hurried by without meeting each other's eyes. Despite the heat, they wore layers of clothes—whether to protect themselves from sparks, or to preserve the coats and jackets and dresses they could ill-afford to lose, she was not sure.

"Here," Anders said, and swung himself to the ground.

Fiona's face went pale. The facade of the three-story frame structure was plain and solid as ever, but she was afraid of what she would, or would not, find within.

"Remember?" Anders pointed to the place where, some months ago, he had taken her against the wall and his lips had touched hers. His eyes were bright and reassuring, and the memory of a cool quiet night, when they had stood together on this spot, gave her some courage.

"Yes," she said, and jumped to the ground.

Anders tied the horse to the railing and they went up the porch steps.

"Hello?" she called, although she knew as soon as she

stepped through the door that it had been abandoned. Nothing had been touched. The furniture was as it had been the night before, the book of verses lay on her father's chair, her mother's crochet basket was placed neatly on the shelf. But the life had gone out of the place. It was like some house on the prairie, abandoned after the crops went bad, never to be a home again.

"They've left," Anders said. "That's good. That means they sought safety."

"I just want to see them." Fiona couldn't seem to raise her voice above a whisper. "I need to know they're all right."

An eerie quiet hung over her family's possessions. The bluster outside was forgotten here, but not the heat. The skin of her face flushed as though she had just leaned in to check a loaf of bread baking in the oven. Her eyes were dry, her throat parched. She walked through the apartment and into the room where her parents slept. The bed was made, the blanket neatly tucked around the mattress, and the white enamel washbasin and pitcher, which she had given them for Christmas—the Carters hadn't wanted it anymore—remained on the bedside table, as though waiting for someone to retire for the day.

Anders came in behind her. She turned, and met his gaze. How she wished it were a few days ago and that she had told him how she felt instead of summoning him on behalf of Emmeline. She wished they had come here, tonight, for a simple dinner with her mother and father. But that seemed too much to explain, and anyway, from the way he watched her, she knew he already understood. She went to the pitcher, poured its contents into the basin, and lifted the basin over her head.

As the water trickled from her hairline over her forehead—washing the soot from her face, the tension from the muscles of her shoulders, the flurry of agitation within her rib cage, and her many, many mistakes—Anders stepped in close so he, too, could be cleansed. The tips of their noses touched, and she felt his chest rise and fall under the cold bath. She realized her thirst, and opened her mouth to the water, and he opened his mouth, too. When the basin was empty, she tossed it to the bed, and he pulled her against him.

For a few moments, with her body pressed to his body, they were in some before-time where there was no danger and only sweet possibilities.

"We shouldn't stay," she said, withdrawing from the kiss.

"I know." He exhaled, and put his lips chastely against her ear. "Don't worry, we'll find them."

As they came onto the street, she saw Magda Dorrans, pushing a wheelbarrow piled high with all manner of bedding and kitchen things.

"Mrs. Dorrans!" she called out, but the old lady kept on

in her slow, stooped way. "Mrs. Dorrans, wait!"

As she approached, old Magda paused and looked up at her. A dusting of ash darkened her nose and cheeks, and she was already out of breath. "Fiona, there you are, you lovely girl. We've missed you," she said cheerily, as if they were meeting at a baptism on a sunny spring afternoon.

"Have you seen my family?" Fiona blurted. "Are they all right?"

"Oh yes. When they heard how bad the fire was, they went on to the lake straightaway. Lots of folks are there, waiting by the shore till it blows over."

"All of them?"

"Yes, all of them."

"Jack, too?"

"All of you Byrnes."

Fiona closed her eyes and for the first time in hours she felt the tightness in her chest soften. She nodded, as though to reassure herself it was true, that she could relax a little now. "Why didn't you go with them?"

Old Magda tilted her head toward the cart.

"You should leave that, Mrs. Dorrans," Anders said, but she shook him away.

An explosion rang out to the north and west of where they stood, and their attention snapped in that direction. Lights flickered, and they heard a scream carried on the wind from far away. Meanwhile, Mrs. Dorrans had moved on.

"It's all I have," she was muttering. "All I have."

They watched her as she proceeded down the alley, toward the wide street, pushing her wheelbarrow. From where they stood, the chaos on the thoroughfare was clearly visible. Four-poster beds were being handed down from second-story windows and the shouting was general. She had not thought ahead of reaching her family home—but now, seeing how widespread the unrest was, she thought perhaps the train might be delayed, perhaps they might make it just in time and be able to leave tonight after all.

"Who's that?" Anders asked.

Fiona followed his gaze. A white landau pulled by a pair of blindered horses had broken through the crowd on Wells and was coming toward them. This was not a class of carriage one often saw in their part of town. It was only then that Fiona noticed that the horse she and Anders had ridden out of the stables was gone—whether it had been spooked or stolen, she'd never know. The man sitting on the coachman's perch was also wearing white, although the brimmed hat tipped over his eyes was black.

"That's Frederick Tree," Fiona said. "Emmeline's . . ."

"Oh." Anders's jawbone tensed.

Freddy made a sharp, loud noise from the back of his throat, halting the pair of horses. He rose to his feet and lifted a shotgun from the seat, pointing the barrel at Fiona. She stepped back, bracing herself. "You're the maid," he said.

She nodded stupidly.

"And you're young Anders?" Freddy's mouth curled up at the corner. "The boxer."

Anders stepped forward and lengthened his neck. "Who are you?" His voice was steady, but his hands had formed into tight balls.

Freddy didn't answer, he just took a rope from his pocket and tossed it to Fiona. She didn't want to catch it, but it hit her in the chest and she grabbed for it instinctively.

"Tie his hands," Freddy said. When she hesitated, he fixed the gun's aim more precisely on her. Inside she felt like a pot of water that had reached a high boil, the bubbles snapping violently at the surface. Anders offered her his wrists and she did as Freddy wanted. Once Anders's hands were bound, Freddy jumped to the ground. With a wave of the gun's shaft, he indicated where he wanted them to go. "Get in."

"Why?" Anders demanded.

Freddy marched toward him and jabbed Anders's chest with the mouth of the gun. "Would you like to ask me why again?" Fiona had seen men handle guns before, and she could see that Freddy was not particularly adept, but this was no reassurance. He was angry enough not to care what he did, and whatever it was would be messy and imprecise. Freddy kept the gun nudged between Anders's shoulder blades as he walked him to the landau. "Not you," Freddy said, when Fiona moved to follow Anders into the backseat. "You drive," he commanded, and she smelled the whiskey on his breath. "Take me to the shop."

She stared in confusion. "The shop?"

"The shop!" Freddy screamed, and his face got all twisted up like he might cry. "The place where you sold my wife's stolen jewels."

"But they weren't—"

"Take me there or god help me, you will find out what this gun can do to your friend's face." Freddy had control of himself again, but she could see the anguish in his dark and shining eyes. "I already have plenty of reason to wish him harm."

Fiona could no longer see Anders's expression, but she felt Freddy's eyes trained on her, waiting to be sure she climbed onto the coachman's seat. She didn't know how she'd be able to maneuver the large carriage through the alley's outlet, but fear was strangling her voice.

When they reached the crossing, Freddy leaned out and barked, "Out of the way," in a loud, curt manner that expected to be obeyed. And they did obey. The neighborhood denizens who had streamed from their homes and onto the streets kept up their shouting and shoving, but they moved aside so the grand vehicle could make its way north on Wells.

At the next intersection, she saw that a corner had been occupied by a group of men openly drinking whiskey from bottles they must have pilfered from an abandoned saloon. Two policemen stood watching in their navy uniforms with the hats like upside-down bells, yet still this gang heckled the passing families and bellowed at the smoke billowing overhead, daring the sky to rain fire upon them. A girl of about twelve went rushing by carrying a drawer full of frilly things, and one of these men stepped forward and kicked it from below, so that pastel silks went flying through the air. The poor thing knelt on the ground trying to pick them up, but a live ember was blown down from a nearby roof, landed on her skirt, and the fabric caught. When she realized she was on fire, she screamed, abandoned the drawer and its contents, and disappeared among the hordes. Not only the rogues on the corner, but the two policeman, roared at her misery.

At the crossing, the pair of horses hesitated. Amid the sea of rough carts, their fine carriage rose like the moon. It soon caught the attention of the corner boys, and when Fiona saw the policeman looking at her she gestured wildly. He spoke a word to his partner and ambled in her direction, smirking and thrusting his thumbs through his belt buckles. Her hands gripped the reins so hard that the leather marked her palms, and she was afraid he would address her, and that she wouldn't be able to speak. But she hoped that as soon as he glanced in the cab, he'd see that they had been kidnapped by Freddy and were being held at gunpoint.

"Evening, Officer," she heard Freddy say. "It's quite a fire tonight."

The officer whistled in agreement. Fiona closed her eyes and prayed for him to notice the gun, to notice the rope around Anders's wrists. "Out of control on the West Side. Damn fire jumped the river, blew up the gasworks. The firemen can't do nothing around here—too many shoddy buildings, too much wood. Don't worry, though. When it reaches the big stone buildings downtown it will be stopped for sure."

"That's very interesting," Freddy said curtly.

The policeman comprehended his tone. "How can I help you, sir?"

"I am Frederick Tree, of the North Side Trees. My father is Judge Orwell Tree. I introduce myself so that you know I am a gentleman and would not deceive you."

"Course not."

"These scoundrels have absconded with my property, and I must make haste to retrieve it before the fire destroys everything."

The officer pushed up the little brim of his hat, and glanced at Fiona. She tried to think of a way to signal to him that they were in trouble, that they weren't thieves. But all the parts of her face were immobile with fear, and she could only manage to stare back blankly.

"Yes, yes, go on, Mr. Tree," the policeman said, and turned his broad back to them.

The little window onto the cab opened, and Fiona's head was wrenched backward. With a firm grip on her braid, Freddy said: "Go. Go on, straight north, and do not try me again."

Tears sprang to her eyes with the pain. She longed for one glance from Anders, but was afraid of what Freddy would do if she looked back.

So she urged the horses on into the chaos.

TWENTY-NINE

Do not pry into your husband's private life,
lest your modesty be scorched.
—*Cressida Marr,* Advice for the Young Bride,
Ostrich Press Publishers, 1870

The courthouse bells had been ringing so frequently that she became deaf to their clang. The gas had gone out, and Emmeline, alone in the darkness, was forced to rummage for candles to see anything at all.

Freddy was out somewhere in the sprawling city, one of back alleys and towering buildings, of speculators and strivers, looking for Fiona and Anders. She had babbled on to him about Fiona and Anders, the long history of their friendship, as well as the convoluted series of events of the past few days. Because of her, he knew a lot about them.

Who was chasing them, and where they might hide.

Emmeline's heart was still bruised by what she had seen in the barn. During the hours since, she had several times told herself that they deserved whatever they got. But, after a little time, she knew she could not bear it if any harm befell them.

At last there was no more wondering whether they deserved her help, and only the need to do something. So she hurled herself at the locked door full force. But it did not even register her weight. She ran into the lady's dressing room, and pushed open the window, but the ground was four stories down, and there was not even a vine to grab hold of. The very idea of a fall stole her breath. She rushed back into the main room of the master suite, to the windows that faced Michigan Avenue, but these, too, opened onto a sheer drop. Half tripping over her cumbersome skirt, she hustled back to the far side of the suite, into Freddy's dressing room, where shoes of polished leather were lined up by the dozen. Shiny, black jackets hung along the wall, beside every variety of collar. Desperate for an outlet, she pounded the walls with her hands, throwing folded trousers through the air. But this too was a dead end.

A full-length mirror occupied the far wall, and she caught a glimpse of her wretchedness. Her hair had gone lopsided, falling loose on one side but still pinned up on the other. Several of the bows that decorated the lower sweep of her skirt now hung by threads. Her cheeks were flush from rushing back and forth. The girl she saw in the reflection was nothing like the elegant society lady she had tried so hard to be. How she hated what she had become! She grabbed the mirror's gilt frame, and rested her forehead on the cool glass.

To her surprise, the mirror sprang back.

Her blood was alive with fresh hope. Behind the mirror was a narrow stairway that led into a secret library. The walls were lined with books, a skylight and chairs upholstered in cowhide. Over the small fireplace hung a painting that was almost as tall as Emmeline herself, depicting a girl about her age wearing a fur coat and nothing else, her eyelashes dark and drooping. An angry blush crept over Emmeline's face, but she resolved not to be deterred. Her friends were in trouble, and if she could find a way out, then she might be able, somehow, to help them.

She pushed the bookshelf ladder into the center of the room and climbed up to the skylight. Balancing nimbly on the top step, she thrust the window open, and found herself teetering in the night. The strong wind picked up her voluminous skirt and it filled like a sail, so that Emmeline was almost knocked over, and had to crouch down to keep from being blown away. What she saw made her stomach weak. To the west the sky was a sickly orange glare billowing with black smoke. Countless buildings were engulfed in flame, and the glowing embers swirled in the gale. It was as though the city that she had known her entire life were just a little toy diorama at the bottom of a vast and blazing hearth.

With care, she brought herself and the enormous dress onto the sloped tar roof. She crawled toward the edge, but found that there was no way down from there. Her hope was mostly gone, but she crawled to the other side anyway, and saw that there was no exterior stair on that side, either.

As she was lowering herself back down, she saw something that chilled her heart. The courthouse, which Father's associates had always braggingly called "fireproof," had succumbed to the northward sweep of the conflagration. Its high windows belched smoke, and the cupola, which stood above all the surrounding buildings, was alight with flames. While she stared, trying to comprehend the destruction of a building that, to her, had seemed as permanent as the sun, the cupola disintegrated entirely, erupting into a torrent of sparks and flying debris, and the great iron bell which had rung consistently through the night fell. The sound was terrible, a thud so heavy that it shook the surrounding buildings. Even at her safe distance, Emmeline felt the crash rattle her teeth. She closed her eyes, went down the ladder, down the secret staircase, into the prison of her marriage bedroom.

★ ★ ★

Five hours after the fire began, the great courthouse bell crashed to the ground, and its awful thud was heard for miles. Water Street was crowded with people moving determinedly east and north, but they stopped and gazed downtown when they heard it. By then, Georgie had made it to the North Side—the river was busy with boat traffic and there was much commotion over whether the Rush Street Bridge should remain open to allow their passage, or stay closed so that the fleeing hordes could cross on foot. There was great confusion about where to shelter, with some heading to the lakeside strip they called the Sands and some to the cemetery at Lincoln Park, but Georgie kept on up Rush Street, clutching the envelope with the twenty-dollar note Emmeline had given her that morning.

The city was in chaos. She had seen men put torches to carts packed high with lumber; she had seen women, bulky with the three evening gowns they wore, one on top of the other, step over the bodies of dogs in the street as though they didn't care at all; lost children screaming for their mothers; and men with legs broken by falls from roofs or high windows, crawling on their elbows to get away. She had seen a ghostly tower of blue flame rising from a spilled barrel of whiskey, while the whiskey drunks toasted in celebration of the fire and all the bounty it had given them. She passed so many oil paintings, harps, settees, and other discarded finery that she lost interest in such objects.

The lawns of the fine mansions that had lately been the sites of picnics and evening soirees were now the destinations of refugees from the better neighborhoods of the West and South Side. Their pianos and hutches and dining tables were strapped atop wagons, and the residents came onto their porches and ushered those who had traveled through the flaming city inside, to wash up and rest, saying they were all safe now.

With a set and determined jaw, Georgie returned to the Carter residence, where the wedding trappings were still evident, relics of a now lost time. She found Ochs Carter at the back of the house with his man Malcolm, and told him in a rush what she had seen on Terrace Row: the slap, the taking of the key, Emmeline locked within, and Frederick Tree, who had so abused her, raging in the town, trying to find her engagement ring. It was not Georgie's way to do for others—she had learned early on what that got you. But after her affair with the future duke had been discovered, his mother struck her face and ordered her locked in the basement, then transported in a trunk to the wharf. The last she saw of England was the inside of that box, and it had held her like a coffin. The terror of that experience still woke her in the night. She had never seen home again, and only been released into steerage, where for weeks she sat among colicky babies and moldy clothes. If she survived, she promised herself, she would one way or another acquire enough that no one would ever cage her again. And she could not stand the idea that a Frederick Tree had locked a young woman in a tower, that he had humiliated her, and might get away with it.

Georgie wanted to know that he would be punished, and embellished some, telling Mr. Carter of the beating Frederick Tree had given his daughter. She knew that she had done a good job describing the horror of the episode when she saw how enraged Mr. Carter was. When he asked where she thought Mr. Tree was headed, she showed him the envelope, the one Emmeline had absentmindedly given her with a little money to keep her quiet about all her odd behavior.

"Gorley's," he said, and cursed. Then he assured her that Emmeline was in the safest part of town, for the wind was blowing from the south and west and the fire would not go her way. With a pat on the head, he returned the twenty-dollar note to the envelope, and told her she was a valued member of the Carter household. And Georgie, satisfied that she had done Emmeline a good turn, went out into the North Side blocks. The mansions stood solid and proud, and the oak trees kept their sentry along the properties' borders. One would not think, from the look of things, that any harm could come to these elegant houses. But when she glanced up at the sky—she had been awake a long time now, and thought the stars might give her some sense of the hour—there was nothing to see. The fire's smoke covered everything, even here, and Georgie hoped Mr. Carter was right, that Emmeline would be safe in her tower.

Emmeline, for her part, felt so alone that it would not have occurred to her for even a flickering second that anyone in the world was thinking of her. Anyway, if there *had* been someone to tell what she had seen, up on the roof, she would have burst into tears trying to describe it. Perhaps it was right that she be here, she thought, and belong to no one. So she lay on the bed, and let the tide of rotten help-lessness wash over her.

THIRTY

The fire department of this city is woefully underfunded. They have requested for some time a few boats equipped with hoses to patrol the lumberyards on the river shore. Those who would save a few pennies in City Hall argue that the downtown is populated more and more by fireproof buildings, but these are really only fireproof facades cloaking wooden interiors, and we must pray that the claims of their builders are never truly tested.
—Chicago Evening Journal *editorial, October 8, 1871*

They were heading north, after several detours to avoid new outcroppings of fire, and approaching Courthouse Square, when they heard a sound like a giant anvil dropped from heaven. The nearby buildings shook, and bricks fell from high stories, and the popping of glass windows shattering from their frames was heard on every side. The blaze was so intense that in all the surrounding streets it was bright as noon. Fiona could no longer control the pair of horses. They reared and raced, so that the landau jerked and swayed, and she was thrown from the driver's perch.

The ground smacked her face, and her hands smarted, but she was otherwise unharmed. The carriage, however—with Anders and Freddy still inside—was overturned and dragged by the frightened horses.

On any other day, an accident like this in the middle of the broad intersection would have brought people running to help or to watch, and police would have descended to clear the obstruction. But tonight theirs was only one of many overturned vehicles. Collisions seemed to occur by the minute, as wagons packed with the inventory of entire stores rattled past hackneys and wheelbarrows pushed by boys no older than Jack. A broken-down steamer lay in the middle of the intersection, and those people who were not consumed with their own escape stood gawking at the flaming ruins of the courthouse. Someone had thought to let the prisoners out of the basement jail—they were easily identified by their striped smocks—and they ran wild through the square, grabbing for the valuables that had been abandoned here and there. As Fiona rushed to see if Anders was all right, Freddy climbed through the landau's window onto the street, holding the shotgun by the barrel.

"Idiot!" he shouted as he approached Fiona. He had lost

his hat in the fall, and his hair fell, stringy and unkempt, around his face. "Why didn't you stop them?"

It took a few seconds for her to realize that he meant the horses, which had by then fled into the night. The world was on its head, and there was no fighting nature, now— but such reason would have been lost on Freddy, so Fiona stared at him in hostile silence.

"Don't look at me like that!" he screamed.

Frightened as she was, Fiona could not allow herself to be cowed. "Like *what*?"

"I will not be made a fool!" he ranted on. "I know what they say—Frederick, the fop, Frederick who can't do anything right, Frederick who has no mind for business, Frederick who is useless on a hunt. They shall not say that Frederick flopped as a groom, too. That his marriage was a sham. That he chose badly and was tricked. You will not humiliate me. You will do what I want!"

If he were not holding a gun, Freddy's wild and blabbering speech might have been laughable, as though the wounded and hapless child he carried in his man's frame were suddenly free to throw a tantrum for all to see. Later, she heard of such stories—how, when the whole world went up in flames, many showed their true and ugly natures. Freddy's frustration was making a comical mask of his face, and he came at them with his weapon, striking Anders in the face with the butt of the gun. Anders's head was knocked back with the blow, but in a moment he had recovered sufficiently to give Freddy a placid smile, as though it had just been a little accidental push.

Fiona's body was weightless with rage. "Don't you ever," she warned, advancing toward Freddy. "Don't you ever do that again."

She felt the butt of the shotgun in her belly almost before she saw what he intended to do with it, and doubled over in pain. Anders lost his taunting manner, and rushed Freddy, knocking him backward. If his hands had not been bound, she knew, he would have beat Freddy like he beat the man on Market Street, after she'd sold the jewels. But, things being as they were, Freddy regained his footing and put the muzzle of the shotgun into Anders's chest.

"Would you like to try again?" Freddy had somewhat regained his composure, and affected the dry manner popular in drawing rooms. "I think I'd enjoy hurting something right now."

Although Anders's teeth were bared, he heard the ferocity in Freddy's tone and heeded it.

"Good," said Freddy. He reached for a cigarette from the interior pocket of his jacket, and crouched to light it with a live coal that had fallen nearby. "We continue *à pied*."

They began to walk west on Washington. A tornado of wind and fire howled above the smoking skyline. "We'll get ourselves killed going to Gorley's," she murmured.

"The fire is everywhere now."

"Are you afraid?" Freddy called from behind. Fiona glanced over her shoulder and saw that Freddy, some paces behind them, had the gun aimed at Anders's head. "I don't suppose courage is something your kind understand very well. That crown was in my family four generations." Until then he had sounded rather reserved, almost mocking, but at the mention of the crown, his voice spiked. "I suppose you don't understand that, either. What it is to come from a proud family, a storied family with great responsibilities, a family that stands for something. Do you know how many people like you live off the Tree family?" He cursed under his breath. "Not that any of them appreciate it, and I see you don't, either. Common people who work with their hands, knowing nothing of their origins, leaving nothing for the next generation, ignorant of manners, refinements . . ."

Actually, in the days when they were new to the North Side and Emmeline had no friends, Fiona had studied manners and refinements as an explorer studies maps. She knew a few things. But Freddy was fuming to himself, and would have taken it badly if she corrected him.

"The ring I gave Emmeline for our engagement is from France. It was made by the finest jeweler in Paris, but you couldn't comprehend a treasure like that, could you? A symbol of love and devotion. You just saw something that was easy to pocket, and turn into tawdry cash."

After that, Fiona tried not to hear him. She marched stoically through the streets and listened to the sound of Anders's feet as they struck the pavement. She listened to his breathing, sharp through his nostrils, and knew that Freddy's speech infuriated him, too.

The heat was terrible. Although they had passed away from the inferno of the courthouse, and though the fire seemed to have blown north and east of them, the stones of the buildings they passed and the pavement of the roads they walked gave off warmth like metal tools left too long in the sun. It was not her city anymore. This was a new and monstrous territory. Instead of rain, gold sparks fell from the sky, and unless they were larger than a silver dollar, she was not even afraid of them. One such cinder drifted into the loose weave of her braid, and she did not heed it until Anders clapped it out with his hands.

"I suppose I'm lucky to have no family left to worry about on a night like this," he said, and she suddenly felt very selfish for having made him run all over town to make sure her people were all right. He kept his thoughts to himself; he was sad, that she knew for certain. He couldn't look at her, so she let her fingers slip down his forearm, and over his bound hands.

Freddy had noticed. "You like him, don't you? He must be quite a charmer, to have deceived Emmeline—however briefly—and when she came to her senses and realized she would much rather be Mrs. Frederick Tree, convinced you to whore yourself in consolation." Freddy laughed his grating laugh. "And you might have been a great boxer! Now see how low you've stooped. Ruining *servant* girls."

Anders wheeled around and charged Freddy. Freddy flinched, and his hands grappled awkwardly with his weapon, but before Anders reached him, he stopped short.

"Here it is," he said. "Gorley's block."

The hordes had been through this place. A gang of looters rushed past, but the stretch was otherwise abandoned. Merchandise from furniture stores and dry goods stores, dress shops and furriers was strewn across the street, already trampled by horse hooves and wagon wheels. But the quiet was eerie, temporary. Soon the roar of flame would rush through here, too, like an angry storm.

Ash and cinder fell like rain over what was once a city, as though Chicago were the center of a meteor shower. Her people had become deft at knocking burning bits from their bodies, and glanced habitually upward, fearful of what might fall from on high. They hurried in all directions for information changed almost as quickly as the skyline, and there was no clear directive of where they could be safe. Maybe there no longer were safe places.

Like a litany, people said the names of great structures that were no more:

"The Opera House."

"The post office."

"The First National Bank."

Rumors were contagious, but there was no longer anything that sounded too bad to be believed. A whole section of downtown had been destroyed in a matter of minutes. The State Street Bridge was thronged with frightened refugees one moment, and the next it was an arch of flame. Soon thereafter a brand carried on the gale found its way to a train car loaded with kerosene, and then the North Side belonged to the fire, too. The fire by then seemed to have grown its own mind. It seemed, almost, to know where to go. Later, it was known that only a short while separated the felling of the courthouse and the destruction of the waterworks. After the water failed, people were not sure what to pray for.

On the South Side, a soldier who was trying to quell the hysteria by the riverbank noticed the business leader Ochs Carter loudly demanding to know what had happened to the wind. He had emerged from a skiff, a ride for which he had paid exorbitantly so that he might avoid the hordes on what remained of the bridge crossings, and was furious to see that the wind had no clear direction. So consumed had he been with getting across the river, he had not at first noticed that the wind no longer moved exclusively north and east. Meanwhile, the whirl of fire howled, and stone turned to powder, and trees exploded from the heat of their own resin.

"Where's it going?" Ochs Carter demanded of the soldier.

"Everywhere," the soldier replied, shocked to have a person of such importance address him at all, much less in such obvious panic.

"To the south?"

"Everywhere. But General Sheridan's coming, don't worry—he will bring explosives from the army's stores, and plans to blow up a section of South Side buildings to make a line the fire cannot cross, because without those buildings, it will have no more fuel."

Ochs Carter seemed to shrink with this news. "Where?"

"He's coming up from the south . . . starting somewhere along Michigan Avenue, I'd think."

"What's the fastest way to Michigan Avenue from here?"

"Oh, there's no way, sir, it's all burning between here and there."

The soldier had never seen an expression as wretched as the one Ochs Carter wore just then. He would recall it later, when stories of the fire were being told, all the strange happenings, the way fine folk had been brought low. But at the time, the great man was just gone quickly, and there were other hard cases to worry about.

★ ★ ★

The rain of ash and cinder fell on Fiona and Anders too as they made their way slowly up Gorley's block. When she was last here, it had been a heavily guarded place. Eyes had peered from every window, and Gorley's people had threatened from every stoop. She wondered where they were now. As they passed the stonecutter, she gasped to see a boy of about Jack's age, with the sweet and delicate face of a fox, lying on the ground, mouth open, a trickle of blood down his chin. A great marble slab, which may have come from the second story, had crushed him. He wore white kid gloves, and his hands still clutched the gilt candelabra that he must have stolen—perhaps from a fleeing family, or maybe from Gorley himself.

"Don't look," Anders whispered to her.

She nodded, but the image kept flashing in her mind, and she shuddered to think that that could happen to a child. "There it is," she told Freddy, and pointed to the storefront with the plate glass busted out.

Freddy groaned in anguish and rushed inside.

Fiona and Anders, stunned to see the place so transformed, followed him. The walls, which had been covered in paintings, trophies, fine rugs, antique rifles, were now just a pockmarked field of hooks, nails, and holes. The case, which had displayed watches and cuff links and brooches, writing implements of rare origin, ruby buttons and sapphire pendants, was entirely emptied out.

"Where is it?" Freddy screamed.

Anders turned away from him, and tried to usher Fiona out of the shop. But the shot split their ears, and the transom shattered, raining glass over the already destroyed doorframe.

"Where is my ring? Where is my crown?" Strands of spit flew from Freddy's lips, and his face went crimson. "What have you done with them?"

"They're gone," Anders said. Fiona was amazed at the evenness in his voice. She was shaking all over. "They're gone now."

"Get down. Get on your knees. On your knees!"

As they sank down, Fiona heard the terrible metallic shift, the click, as Freddy reloaded the gun. The smell of buckshot mingled with all the other smells: burning hair, burning pipe, burning sawdust, burning silk.

"Now tell me, which one of you would be most pained to see the other die? It's you, isn't it, Fiona? She was just a romp in the hay for you, wasn't she, young Anders? She might as well have been anybody."

Through this long night, this parade of horrors, this reversing of all goodness, Fiona had felt Anders at her side, his fierce gaze and light touch. But when Freddy put it that way, she couldn't help but wonder if it weren't a little true. Even if it were mostly a lie, that little shard of truth would crush her heart.

"In a *barn*," Freddy muttered in disgust.

"How did you—?" Anders began. But Fiona did not have to ask. That broken lantern, which should never have been lit—Emmeline really had been there. She had, somehow, been in the barn. She had seen them together. The barn itself was gone now—it had been reduced to a thousand flying, burning specks—but the image of what happened there would still be solid in Emmeline's mind's eye.

"He knows," she whispered. "Because Emmeline told him. Emmeline knows."

"He doesn't know anything," Anders said, and the way he held her gaze banished the fear that he had used her.

"Very noble of you to reassure the lady. But you'll die as you lived—a slum rat."

The floorboard creaked, and Freddy sucked air through his teeth.

Every tiny thing screamed in her ear. The soreness of her feet, the ache in her throat, the sting of her eyes, the way the heat had made her underclothes stick to her skin, Anders beside her, his smell, the places on her body where his lips had been. In a moment it would all be gone—her city, her Anders, her Emmeline, all the yearning and secrecy, all the striving and seeking. She only hoped she would not have to see him hurt.

The shot exploded in her ears. A sob choked its way up her throat, and the color left her face.

But when she glanced at Anders, he was in one piece. Shocked, but unharmed. His chest rose and fell, and his gaze swung to meet hers.

"Put that down," a man said. His voice, which carried from the street, became more urgent the next time he spoke: "Put your gun down!"

Freddy must not have obeyed, because the next shot came from in front of them. Fiona raised her eyes to see, through the shattered doorframe and scrim of gun smoke, the familiar figure of Mr. Carter, wearing the coal-colored velvet jacket that he always donned for special occasions. His face was ruddy and pained, and he stepped into the shop almost without acknowledging Fiona and Anders. His eyes blazed, and seemed to see only Freddy, who had fallen to the ground. The bright red stain was spreading across his dress shirt, and his breath had become short.

"You," Mr. Carter growled.

"What?" Freddy whimpered through labored breaths as he tried to get hold of the shotgun.

Mr. Carter kicked his gun away. "Emmeline Carter is not some piece of trash, some girl you bought to make you seem like a man. She's my *daughter*."

"No, I—but . . ." The garbled words were Freddy's last.

Emmeline's father faced Fiona, grimacing. In his hand he clutched the envelope, the one she had demanded from Gorley, with its itemized receipt and the fancily scrawled address of the proprietor.

"Mr. Carter," Anders said, scrambling to his feet. "He's dead."

Mr. Carter shook his head. Blood had soaked the side of his trousers, where Freddy's shot had nicked him. "He locked up my Emmeline. That girl who works in the kitchen—Georgie—she told me. I thought she'd be safe there on Terrace Row, while I got the key, while I showed Frederick Tree that we Carters are not to be pushed around . . . but I made a mistake. Oh, what a mistake. I *could* have gotten to her, if I'd gone that way immediately, but now there's no way, no way . . . they're going to blow up the South Side, did you know that? They're going to blow up my Emmeline, to stop the fire. Anyway, what does it matter, we'll all soon be dead. . . ." Anguish had made his face unrecognizable. "He destroyed her, my perfect Emmeline."

Anders offered Fiona his hand, and helped her to her feet. But he didn't meet her eye. His mind was occupied with someone else. Though she knew what he said next was right—"The fire's too big to know where it will go, the wind's too strong for it to die, and it's moving faster than can be kept up with"—the old sorrow welled within her, and she was afraid that if he saw Emmeline, she'd be robbed of all that happened between her and Anders over the past hours.

"But," Anders concluded, "we have to try."

For a moment, Mr. Carter seemed not to hear Anders. Then he howled into his hands, a sound Fiona had never heard from him or any human being. Eventually he nodded, said, "All right," and with a wince began moving to the door. "You're right, you're right. Check his pockets for a key—Georgie said he must have the key to the room where he locked up Emmeline."

The alacrity with which Anders bent and rummaged through the pockets of Freddy's formerly white jacket pained Fiona, though she tried not to show it when he stood, held the key aloft, and said: "Here, I found it." And she had to be stern with herself not to feel forgotten when he added, "We must find her. We had better find her right away."

Anders turned to Fiona then, and though his face was torn with worry his eyes were searching hers for what to do. He wanted to know what she thought they should do, just as he said he always had. She gave him a little nod of agreement—he was right, they must try to reach Emmeline—and he drew his hand along her jaw, and pressed his lips ardently into her cheek. Then he clasped her hand, to lead her out of the abandoned pawnshop. Everything he did suggested he loved her, but Fiona couldn't help but remember what he'd said before. Once upon a time, so he said, she had insisted he be sweet on Emmeline until he was—and she couldn't help but wonder if that sort of feeling can easily go away.

THIRTY-ONE

Chicago shall stand forever, for she is the unbeatable city.
But if she should fall, she will fall completely, for Chicago
never does things by half-measures.
—Aphorism of Ochs Carter

Six hours after the fire began, what was once downtown had been ravaged, and the path of the flames had herded refugees into curious sanctuaries. The fire had sometimes leapt over buildings, over whole blocks, leaving safe patches in its wake. But they were not really safe—the fire was often blown back, thus consuming what it had missed the first time. The lobby of the Nevada Hotel was such a place, where the fine and the lowborn clustered together with frightened families in bedclothes and defeated firemen, telling stories of what they had seen. The room was lit with candelabras, for the gasworks had long ago ceased functioning, and those who remained there occupied its pretty corners with a reckless fatalism, as though it were the last place left in the whole world. Even this place, with its fancy furniture and rose-patterned wallpaper, might soon be gone.

The waterworks was out, and the firemen could no longer do what they had been trained to do on nights like tonight. Except—there had never been a night like tonight, a fact that everyone in the room knew, and felt no need to say. The Illinois Hook and Ladder Company's last stand had been another hotel, the St. James on the corner of Washington and State—they had dragged the occupants from their rooms, while others scaled the mansard roof to try to put down the flames there. But there was no water, and they'd been reduced to stamping out embers with their feet. In a little while, they were forced to watch from the curb, among the shocked patrons and staff, as the place went up like a piece of paper put to a candle's flame.

The Nevada took them in, serving coffee out of large silver urns. But the firemen wanted only whiskey, and darkly warned those who rested upon their trunks and salvaged possessions that they might soon have to move again. Among these was Gabriel, who had tried hard to exhaust himself by joining every battlefront against the fire that he could. Since that terrible moment when he misjudged the location of the West Side blaze, Gabriel had tried never to rest for a second, never to pause long enough to think, lest the terrible, inky guilt stain him.

Later, when the city was a charred ruin, as stark and barren of purpose as Pompeii, when causes were being determined and assessments made, it would become generally known that as many as seven companies had seen the burning barn from their own stations and arrived on the scene within twenty minutes. Those who had witnessed it on the street said that it had moved too fast to be contained, for that part of town was all sheds and dry wood. That there was no one person, really, to blame. Yet, for many years, whenever Gabriel paused to think long enough, he felt a stab of responsibility for having slept at the wrong time.

Though he was not the first of the firemen in the Nevada lobby to notice the odd trio demanding the use of a vehicle at the front desk, he was the first to recognize them. It was his cousin Anders, and Fiona Byrne (with whom Anders had been inseparable as a child), and Ochs Carter, who had once been a person of importance in the neighborhood, and was, like all people of importance there, an intimidating figure. His fortune, they said, originated in the backroom card games of the old neighborhood, but now included stockyard and railroad holdings.

"Anders!" Gabriel exclaimed. Even now—weary from

whatever he had been through, his clothes burned and blackened—you could see the best of Anders's parents in him. The determination of his father, the big, blue-eyed Swede, with those made-of-stone features; and the quickness of his mother, Gabriel's mother's sister, who had been delicate yet sharp of tongue. Gabriel's aunt had died—it must have been more than five years ago. And afterward, old Magnuson just walked off.

Gabriel would never know the comfort he gave Anders when he called his name, and reminded him that he did have a relation in the city, and that that relation had so far come through the night alive. He only knew how grateful he himself was that the great Anders Mag responded by calling his name in happy surprise, and striding across the room to embrace him.

"Gabriel!" he said again. "Thank god."

And Gabriel, thankful to be recognized and so warmly greeted, and perhaps to be of some good purpose, said, "I will help you get where you want to go. A few bridges are still open. It won't be easy, but we'll try."

Outside the fire had become its own weather. A tornado of sparks and debris whirled overhead, hurtled through the canyons between the buildings, pulled Fiona's braid apart and whipped her clothes against her skin. Despite the fury with which the elements beat her body, she could not escape the idea of Emmeline, holding that lantern in the barn that was no more, finally learning the secret Fiona had kept from her, and in the worst possible way.

I am the one who has been untrue, Fiona thought, and tried not to let herself imagine the danger her friend was in, nor the sense of betrayal she must have lived through on what might be her last night on earth.

THIRTY-TWO

She left the web, she left the loom
She made three paces thro' the room
She saw the water-lily bloom,
She saw the helmet and the plume,
She look'd down to Camelot.
Out flew the web and floated wide;
The mirror crack'd from side to side;
'The curse is come upon me,' cried
The Lady of Shalott.
—Alfred Lord Tennyson, "The Lady of Shalott" (1842)

A listlessness came over Emmeline that she could not shake.

She had shouted herself hoarse trying to get the attention of the people on the street, but the wind had changed directions, and was now howling in her face, shouting her down. The world was in a kind of daze, every soul lost in its own horror and panic. Perhaps Emmeline was already a kind of shade, invisible to the living.

Below, on Michigan Avenue, the residents seemed to have comprehended that the conflagration would reach them, too. It was not—as was so often the case—a fire of the lower classes. Here, on Terrace Row, they were dragging their rosewood furniture down the stoop, their rolled oriental rugs, their vases and mirrors, their portraits and statuary, and piling it all across the street, draping blankets over the treasure, as though that could save them. They sat upon their couches in the open air to watch the end. It was, Emmeline had to admit, something to behold. The awful spectacle she had witnessed from the roof was unlike anything she had ever seen—terrible and beautiful at once, like a glorious blaze set by some pagan goddess bent on destroying her worshippers for their insufficient ardor.

At times, she told herself that she was safe here, in this fortress of a house. It had solid stone walls, didn't it? But she had indulged in a great deal of self-deception in the last days and months, and had lost her capacity for it. After she saw the courthouse succumb she knew that the destruction would, at last, come this way. That it was her fate. This room, this day, this fire. She had tried, in her way, to have a glamorous life, but she had lacked conviction when it mattered most. Perhaps it was a suitable end, to be locked in a tower, like the Lady of Shalott in the poem her tutor had insisted she memorize.

"You cannot sing, you cannot play piano," Miss Anjou had admonished her. "The least you can do is have a poem or two to recite."

Now Emmeline whispered the words to herself as she saw to her appearance.

"I am half sick of shadows," she intoned as she took down her hair, and brushed it, plaited it, and arranged it around her head. She removed the dangling bows from her dress, and redid the buttons at her wrists. She painted her eyes and mouth, and put a little dab of perfume behind her ears. When she had first read the Tennyson poem, she had not understood why the Lady should be so lonesome, dwelling by herself as she did, occupied with her loom and her dreams. There was so much to do, and so much to see! And anyway, wasn't the point of being a pretty girl to go into the world and be admired while you could? But now she saw that a girl doesn't decide what kind of life she will have. That was a decision life made for you. And if you tried, as the Lady did, to be free, a tragic death would swallow you soon enough.

When she was suitably made up, Emmeline went to the polished oak escritoire and took out pen and paper. In her practiced hand, she wrote: *I, Emmeline Carter Tree, do leave all my worldly possessions—dresses, shoes, furnishings, books, etc.—to my best friend, Fiona Byrne, as well as any currencies, investments, or properties held in my name.* Then she signed it, and lay herself down on the bed. She knew of course that such a will would most likely be destroyed along with everything else, but it made her feel better to have provided for Fiona, or intended to, anyway.

Even now, when she thought of Fiona, her eyelids squeezed tight with the painful memory of what she witnessed in the barn. But she found that the pain was somewhat lessened when she wished Fiona good instead of harm.

So she clutched the hastily written will, closed her eyes, and waited for the worst. The crackle of flame and the sweat that pooled between her upper lip and the tip of her nose were frightening. But the piece of paper in her hand gave her courage, and as the minutes passed, a memory came to her of a clear, sunshiny day when they had climbed to the roof of Mr. Carter's office, and looked out across the whole city, with its marble stores and limestone monuments and spires and clock towers. The city had looked clean and permanent at that time of day. Fiona and Anders and she had pointed out the big houses they particularly liked, and said that when they were grown they would live there, and they had been very happy in the belief that they really might.

"You shall always be welcome in my home, Miss Byrne," Emmeline had said, in the fluty voice of fancy folks.

"And you shall always be welcome in mine," Fiona had replied, and they laughed, because they'd known it would be true no matter whether they lived in one of those grand places, or in a garret somewhere. The memory made Emmeline's heart placid, and she thought that if she could only stay in the sweetness of that memory, death would not be so terrible after all. Perhaps, if she concentrated very hard, her soul, released from her body, would travel through the air and rest eternally in that happy day with Fiona.

THIRTY-THREE

My dear one,

When you are gone, my heart is poisoned thinking you will leave me for another. Promise me you will return and not forget me.

Yours,

Bunny

—Family letters found scattered on Twelfth Street, October 9, 1871

At last the sun came up, and she knew their buggy was moving east once again. In the course of a long night their little band had stopped remarking on the sights, but it was alive in her memory, more real than her own slack limbs and weary eyes. She kept trying to catch a glance from Anders, but he had remained stoic all the while, fixated on the road ahead.

Upon first leaving the Nevada Hotel, they had lost a quarter hour in securing the buggy. The price had been a hundred dollars, and the previous owner was a man who seemed likely to have acquired it by force. At first they'd traveled east, hoping to take the most direct route to Terrace Row, but they had been dissuaded from continuing on by a policeman who occupied a corner of Wells. Mr. Carter was determined, and argued with the officer, and might even have ignored his command, had they not glimpsed the sea of flame that filled the street beyond. They were warned that all the bridges of the main branch had been destroyed, so they could not go around by a northerly route, either. Fiona had always known Mr. Carter to be fastidious in the maintenance of his property, but when they began to hear rumors that the fire was raging on the North Side, that it was spreading voraciously through the genteel blocks and had already destroyed Lill's Brewery—which was situated near the shore, beyond the Carter residence—he did not seem to consider that this might have anything to do with him.

He spoke only of Emmeline, and how to reach her.

The streets were no less thronged than before, although the faces they saw now were dark with ash, and everyone had singed clothes or hair. The rumors were wild, but consistent enough to be believed: the courthouse, the post office, the Palmer, Field & Leiter, the First National Bank, and the Opera House had all been swallowed in flame. As they reached the south branch of the river, they learned that the Madison Street Bridge was impassable, and they had to travel north again to Randolph Street, the span of which was filled with hundreds, pushing and shouting as they made their way across.

The river below them was full of tugs and skiffs, as busy as high noon. When they reached the far side, they glanced back and saw the Nevada, where they had rested, go up like a book of matches that has been ignited all at once. In a matter of minutes, the facade caved in. A tower of flame shot up in its place, hundreds of feet into the air, and the wind caught it, and carried its furious heat to another high roof.

In the end, they'd had to go south all the way to Twelfth Street to cross the river again.

Now, with the new day rising, they had finally turned north. They were approaching Harrison Street when they heard the first explosion. Fiona instinctively put her hand over her ears, although loud sounds no longer surprised her.

"General Sheridan," Gabriel said, his face fearful and impressed.

"That must have been damn close," Mr. Carter said, and urged the horses on. "Wabash, probably. Maybe the Methodist church. What else would make such a bang?"

By then they could see Terrace Row, the impressive

stone facade of those eleven contiguous town houses, as well as the smoke that rose from the back buildings, the flames that licked the rear walls. Across Michigan Avenue, the lagoon was full of debris, scattered there by the wind and waves. The residents of that part of town had not been careless with their things—they had carried down dining tables and sofas, pianos and china sets, and now sat among them, as though they were waiting to board an ocean liner.

"That's the one!" Mr. Carter said, and jumped down from the buggy.

But as soon as his feet met the ground, his legs failed him. He cried out in anguish and pain. Gabriel followed, lifting him from the street, and Anders bent to assist from the other side.

"Which one?" Anders asked.

Mr. Carter pointed an accusing finger at the house that had once belonged to Freddy Tree. Another explosion shook the earth, south of where they stood.

"Please, Fiona," Mr. Carter said. "Please help my Emmeline."

Fiona had not imagined she would be the one who would be called upon to free Emmeline. A long while ago, on a warm October night, in a barn in a dusty and unimportant part of town, Emmeline had seen something that made her drop her lantern and run away. That thing, Fiona had believed, would break their friendship apart forever.

But it hadn't, somehow.

"Yes, of course." Fiona's body felt cold and clear, as though her fate were already sealed, and there was no sense in fighting it anymore. She climbed down from the carriage, and tied her hair back from her face. When she had set out that morning, her skirt had been black and her shirt had been white, but now they were more or less the same color. She was all smudged with the dirty snow that continued to drift from above.

"Wait!" Anders called after her, but Fiona knew she would lose her resolve if she looked at him. If she let herself remember his easy smile or the sweetness of his touch. She was halfway up the limestone steps, and had resolved not to stop until she found Emmeline. "You can't go in there."

"I have to," she said at the door. "It has to be me. I can't abandon her now."

His fingers wrapped around her elbow, and for the first time in some hours Fiona felt her shock and terror thaw. Felt a little glow of hope that, at the end of this, Anders might still be there, that they might resume what they started in the barn. "Please let me be the one," he said.

Although his hair had gone prematurely gray with dust—though his shirt was creased, stained with sweat, and hanging loosely from his lean, strong arms—his face still had the capacity to change her heart's rhythm. His eyes flashed, and the dimples appeared in his smudged cheeks.

"You have to," he said, producing the brass relic they'd taken from Freddy's white jacket and giving a little flourish. "I'm the one who has the key."

It was some kind of miracle, Fiona knew, that he could still, after everything they'd seen, make her laugh with a silly gesture. "I'm coming with you," she said.

He inclined his head—as though he knew better than to argue with her—and they pushed back the imposing front door.

Inside, the air was dense and dry and the walls gave off an awful heat.

"Emmeline!" they howled as they hurried up the stairs. "Emmeline!"

As they ascended, the smoke that hung in the halls became thicker. On the second floor, a bedroom door opened easily, but they could hardly see for the haze. Anders ripped the coverlet back from the bed, and draped it over Fiona. As they came back onto the landing, a seam opened in the wallpaper. In seconds, the hole widened, sending flames upward toward the ceiling, leaving black streaks against the white-and-gold-flocked pattern.

"You have to go back now," Anders said.

"No." Fiona shook her head. She wasn't certain if her reluctance was leaving Anders in danger, the possibility of Anders caring more for Emmeline's safety than her own, or the sense of responsibility to her old friend that, even now, had a strong pull. These had all become hopelessly melded together.

"Yes," he said. "You must."

Ribbons of flame had reached the ceiling, so that the plaster blistered and cracked. Every breath seemed to scorch her from the inside, to lodge sparks within her chest and the pit of her belly. Even so, Fiona shook her head. The tears came fast and hot now—they sprang up with the smoke, but also at the suggestion of their parting.

"It will be easier for two to come down than three," he said. "And anyway, I couldn't stand myself if you got hurt."

"But—"

"Yesterday, I didn't think my life was worth very much. I would have given it away for any price. Not anymore. It all seems bigger now, and sweeter. When I look in your eyes, I see my own goodness. Do you understand? I know what it's all for."

The skin of her cheeks was damp, and she couldn't bear to leave him. The roof would cave in soon, she thought, the walls would catch and come crashing down around them. When that happened, she would rather be with him. He lifted the corner of the bedspread, and used it to wipe the mixture of ash and tears from her cheeks. His hands traveled along her neck, his fingers pushed through her hair, taking hold of the base of her skull and bringing her mouth to his. His lips were moist and tender, and their sensation stoked the old longing. He kissed her, and kissed her again, as though she could take away his thirst.

"I don't think you know how beautiful you are."

"That can't matter very much now—"

"But it does. It matters now more than ever."

"I can't," she murmured. "Can't leave."

"You have to go," he said. "Because I love you—go now."

"I love you," she whispered.

He kissed her once more, with exquisite force. "Now go, get safe. If you're safe and waiting for me, I'll have a reason to make it out of here alive."

He stepped up, his hand slipping from her shoulder, to her forearm, to her fingertips. In a moment, he was two steps higher. His grip opened and released hers. At the third-story landing, he paused to look back. The corridor was so dim with combustion that she could only make out his general outline. But his eyes still shone blue and bright. When she saw them, she thought that she could not stand it; she would have to follow.

But the staircase to the third floor was burning by then, and she had no choice but to retreat, down the stairs and into the bleak morning.

THIRTY-FOUR

Let me be redeemed.
—Diary of Emmeline Carter Tree, October 9, 1871

The world had gone violet and bronze. It was breaking apart in a million tiny pieces that swirled, like fairy dust. Or stardust. Yes, stardust—she liked that better. Soon the city and everything else would disappear in a burst of sublime light, and Emmeline would be no more. Her thinking, and her vision, were not entirely reliable—she knew that much—and so when she saw Anders opening the door, very smoothly, as though he himself had designed the key, she thought it must be her eyes playing tricks. Either that, or she was already dead.

"What are you doing in there?" he said as his mouth cracked open. She had forgotten that smile.

She sat up very quickly and was seized by a coughing fit. Then she knew she was still alive. She had to be—the pain was too sharp for her to be otherwise. It was as though burning bristles had lodged themselves in her lungs. As though she were on fire on the inside.

"Are you here to tell me that you hate me?"

He shook his head. "Come on, the roof is on fire."

"I'm sorry, Anders, I should have come this morning."

He made a funny gesture at her wedding dress. "You had someplace else to be."

"Oh!" She smoothed her hands over the bodice. "But that was a terrible mistake."

He nodded, averted his eyes. "Come with me," he said, extending his hand for her to take. "It's dangerous here."

She allowed him to draw her out onto the landing. A little side table stood beside the door, topped with blue linen and a lacquer vase full of white roses—he threw the flowers away, and doused the cloth with their water.

"Here," he said. "Put that on your face."

She did as told. But even with her mouth covered, she could not help asking the thing she had wondered all these hours. "But if I had come, would it have been me?"

He thought a moment and said, "I did love you, Emmeline." His eyes darted over her face, as though he wanted to make sure she was all right. "You were my first love. But—"

"I understand," she whispered through the cloth. She did not want to hear what came after *but*. During the long night she had had many hours to contemplate what she had done and the consequences, but it still crushed her, now, to find herself at the final end of that beautiful idea. Her head jerked, as though she were swallowing a bitter pill. "It was a lovely time, wasn't it?"

"Yes." He lifted her hand and, holding her gaze, brushed his lips over the top of her hand. "But please, we can't talk about that now."

Anders had her hand in a firm grip, and pulled her down the stairs. The long white train trailed behind, catching against the hot walls, and by the time they reached the third-floor landing, it had been infected with flames that had to be stomped out. They tried to continue, but the flight between the third and second floor was a riot of yellow licking light.

"The servants' stairs," she said, and they hurried toward the back of the house.

But they had only gone a little way before their inability to see or breathe told them definitively that there would be no escape that way. They came back, through the linked parlors that would have been hers to have little private afternoons with Ada and Daisy and their kind, toward the front. The middle stairwell was now a tower of flame, the wallpaper peeling off and whirling, making little boats of fire that coasted up and down on the current.

"Close the door," Anders said. "All the doors."

Once they had sealed the exits to the room, she gestured toward the window. "It's the only way. Maybe we'll be lucky."

But Anders hung back, assailed by an attack of coughing. "We're too far from the ground."

"Don't be afraid," she said. She hurried toward the big front windows, where shouting could be heard down below. The voice sounded familiar, and before she knew to think otherwise, she was heartened by the realization that it was Fiona. "I'm always lucky."

Down below, Fiona had commandeered a crew of Terrace Row men, and they had picked up a large wooden cart—the kind used to transport produce from one side of town to the other, with a large square frame covered in canvas—and placed it in the rose garden beside the front stoop.

"Closer!" Fiona was shouting to them. "As close to the building as you can."

"Anders!" Emmeline exclaimed. "We're going to be all right—"

But when she turned, she saw that the ceiling was no longer a ceiling. It trembled and swelled and finally a beam cloaked entirely in fire fell through the white plaster. Anders looked up in time to see it, but not in time to move. The beam struck his back and knocked him to the floor. Emmeline screamed and rushed to kick the wooden torch away so she could roll the rug over him, crushing the flames that grew from the back of his shirt.

"Anders?" she wailed. Her heart was pounding so loudly that she could no longer hear the encroaching fire.

"Go," he said, scrambling to his feet. His irises were like the lake when it froze in winter, glinting with cool, spectral light. He pushed her, so that she reeled toward the window. "We have to go now."

"But—"

His hands were guiding her. Her feet had gained a foothold on the sill.

"Go," Anders urged her.

When she opened the window, the cool air rushed in and the unbearable heat surged, expanded, pushed outward. She did not have time to wonder if she was afraid to jump because the force of that hot gust sent her flying. Her skirt ballooned, and her heart surged up, and a moment later she bounced on the wagon's stretched canvas, slid down the side, and found herself in her father's arms.

"I'm sorry, Emmeline," he said, kissing her forehead. "So, so sorry for all I've put you through."

She knew it was bad, then, what had happened in the

world while she was locked up. Her father was never discomposed, but his face was stony with shock now. Across the avenue, the people who would have been her neighbors stood among their fine furniture, their heads tilted back, their mouths hung open. They, too, were stunned by what they were witnessing, and when Emmeline revolved slowly she saw that all their grand houses were crowned with flames. Then she heard the scream.

The window that Emmeline had fallen from was like the mouth of a mythical beast, breathing fire in a long, furious red-and-orange tongue.

"Stop her!" someone yelled.

Emmeline heard that anguished scream again, and turned to see Fiona and one of the men who had carried the cart, trying to hold her back from running into the burning building. Emmeline threw her arms around Fiona's waist, and held tight as she marched her down the stairs, through the iron gate, into the middle of Michigan Avenue. All the while Fiona struggled and screamed, her eyes huge but unseeing. At last her body went slack, and the two girls collapsed into a pile against the pavement.

The sobs had begun. Emmeline felt them shuddering through Fiona's shoulders, and knew what they meant. Anders was gone. He had been there, with his mischievous smile and strong hands, urging her to seek safety, but now he was no more. It didn't seem possible, and Emmeline tried very hard to keep the realization at bay.

Later, there would be time for her own tears. Now she held steady and let Fiona shake and weep in her arms. Let Fiona's grief be hers, too. Let it be a storm that could wash over them, wash away the sooty stain of all they had done, wash them clean.

AFTERWORD

The rain was falling again. Fiona touched the window glass in the salon of the hotel Mr. Carter owned by the stockyards and gazed out at the big drops. She knew that these showers from above were necessary and good—the rain had begun Tuesday morning, and put out what was left of the fire, although its power was already much diminished by then. On the North Side, the blaze had reached the edge of town by Monday night, and there was nothing left to burn, and on the South Side it met with the line of buildings General Sheridan had exploded so that the mountain of flame, starved of fuel, was reduced to piles of cinder. And the rain had dampened the ground, which held its terrible heat for days and days after. Yet the rain made her angry. This rain had come too late for her, too late for Anders.

The rain was also the reason that she had been persuaded to leave her vigil at Terrace Row, and even now, she regretted it and wished she had stayed there until what remained of that terrible house was cleared and she could see for herself that he had not survived its fiery collapse. Wished she had found some tiny relic of Anders, wished she had done him the honor of staying until she was soaked with the rain that came too late, and caught her death of cold, just like everyone said she would, and could thus disintegrate into the atmosphere as he had.

Emmeline had been at her side the whole time, and when the men who worked—at first to make sure the hot embers did not catch and spread fire again, and then to clear the rubble—started urging them to leave, she had spoken for both girls and said they would stay until the house at No. 5 Terrace Row was cleared. On Wednesday morning, General Sheridan marched his troops up Michigan Avenue to take control of the city, and Gabriel, Anders's cousin, finally prevailed upon them to get some rest.

"He would not want you to destroy yourselves," Gabriel had said. His face was as young-looking as before, his body as frail, but he seemed ten years older now. Overnight, he had become capable of giving wise advice and issuing commands. Like so many others, he worked tirelessly to clear the debris and make ready for a new city to rise over the old one.

Emmeline squeezed Fiona's hand. "He's right," she had said. "We can come back tomorrow."

Fiona's heart screamed *no*, but her body followed obediently as Emmeline led her to the carriage that Mr. Carter had sent with orders to wait until the girls were ready to leave. They had washed and slept and changed clothes and returned to the last place they had seen Anders. But by then what remained of Terrace Row had been razed, and Fiona began weeping uncontrollably once again, and was forced to finally admit what she'd known since they dragged her back from the burning house. Anders was not coming out again.

In the days that followed, neither said his name. Fiona could feel Emmeline's worried gaze on her, but she did not want to look back. Fiona was having difficulty speaking at all, and she did not want to have to talk about Anders. If they spoke about him, it would be in the past tense, and she wanted to hold the feeling of him alive in her heart as long as she could. She did not want to risk breaking the spell of his living presence. But when Emmeline said there was work to do, Fiona nodded and asked where they ought to start. Children had been separated from their parents when they fled to the Sands, the prairie, and Lincoln Park, and they required looking after until they could be reunited. Thousands were in need of food, clothing, and shelter, and they were both glad to be busy for many days with the relief effort.

It was a cold comfort that they were well taken care of, while so many others suffered—once the fire had begun to spread, Mr. Carter had ordered Malcolm to bury his many deeds and claims, as well as much of his fortune, deep in the sand and clay beneath the Dearborn property. He led the city in funding new construction, hiring the men who had been left homeless by the disaster, hosting charity balls in barns and construction sites and anywhere he could convince those with money to gather for a good cause. But Emmeline did not seem interested in such events, and Fiona was glad that they did not have to attend to her social status as they had before. She was glad of her friend's company in the quiet evenings, even if neither was ready to discuss the breach that had seemed sure to destroy their friendship, or the secret that was now their shared burden.

In those days, many people said that despite the terror

they felt while the fire consumed the city from one end to the other, it was the most spectacular sight they ever hoped to see. That the fire's ghastly light, its otherworldly colors, its singular weather, its whoosh and boom, might almost be described as beautiful. Almost—for how could something that left 100,000 without homes, and robbed three hundred of their lives, be beautiful? Three hundred was the official number given by the commissioner's report some months after the ground ceased smoking, although it must have been many more. For how many men and women were consumed in their sleep, buried in rubble, became ash and floated over the lake, dispersed finally into the upper air? Who could count them all?

And then there were those who, on Tuesday, when they saw what had once been the whole world leveled, their houses swept away, their businesses gone, their families broken, took the opportunity to begin again. It is impossible to know how many looked at that grim morning and decided to simply walk away, but there must have been many.

Other lives became legendary, for their fortunes were made or destroyed overnight. Millionaires who became paupers, and the other way around. One such was a girl named Georgie Kelly, who came walking down Michigan Avenue on that strange unending day, saw where the fire was headed, and offered a twenty-dollar bill for the deed to the Michigan Avenue Hotel. The proprietor laughed, for he could see that the fire was already ravaging the building two doors north, and he was only trying to salvage some of the fine pieces from the front parlor, and agreed to the deal. After the transaction, she told him he would have to leave what was in the hotel, for it belonged to her now. The next day, everyone knew that the fire line was marked at the Michigan Avenue Hotel—later known as the George—and Miss Kelly was afterward known as a woman of property in Chicago, not to be crossed.

Fiona listened to these stories in vain, hoping to hear Anders's name.

And then, on a rainy afternoon—after many days serving the destitute in the ruined city—when the girls sat in the salon, staring out at the rain and trying to rest, a stranger came to call.

Miss Lupin announced him from the front room of the hotel, and the girls revolved in their armchairs to see a gentleman removing his hat as he approached.

"Emmeline Tree?" he ventured uncertainly.

The girls were dressed in similar plain, dark dresses, and they wore their hair in the same simple braid, so Fiona supposed he could be forgiven for the confusion. Emmeline stood and said, "Pleased to meet you."

"I am Ephraim Brown, of the Metropolitan Life Insurance Company, and I represent your late husband's account."

Emmeline lowered her eyes, and murmured, "Yes, well, I never knew much about that."

"No, he didn't want to trouble you. But his sister has recently filed a claim—did you not know?"

Emmeline shook her head. "I did not know."

As if remembering the sad state of everything, Mr. Brown said, "I am sorry for your loss, Mrs. Tree."

"Thank you."

Mr. Brown cleared his throat. "Ordinarily, we would require more proper documentation of a death in order to proceed—a certificate, a body—but in the case of the Tree family, they have held many policies with us over the years, and we of course wish to proceed on good faith. But, after looking into the matter, I had to inform Mrs. Garrison that Frederick had recently made *you* the beneficiary of the policy on his Terrace Row house, and also of his life policy, effective as soon as you became man and wife."

"Oh."

"I should tell you that Mrs. Garrison was rather displeased with this news, but my firm does a great deal of business with your father, as well as with the Trees and the Garrisons, and I of course want to assure your family like all our customers that as a company we pay out our settlements to the letter of our policies."

Emmeline glanced at Fiona, as though for some indication of what she should do, but Fiona was confused as well, and simply nodded that she might as well accept the check he was placing in her hands.

"Thank you," she said a little doubtfully.

"Thank you," Mr. Brown replied, and produced a card from an interior pocket. "If you have need of my services in the future, do please call."

Emmeline watched him leave the room before she glanced at the check. When she saw the amount, she reached for the chair's back, and then sank heavily into its well-worn seat. Fiona watched her friend, waiting for her to say something. She had told her, that first day, while the fire was still burning, that she had seen Freddy on Gorley's block, and that her father, in his fury and fear for Emmeline's safety, had shot Freddy. Emmeline had nodded stoically, but had not seemed to want to hear more. Perhaps she could not bear to think of her father that way.

Emmeline frowned and stared at the check as though she wasn't sure she wanted it. "He was not a particularly good husband. . . ." she remarked.

For some reason this struck Fiona as absurd, and a peal of laughter escaped her mouth and a tear rolled from the corner of her eye. Emmeline glanced at her, and she began to laugh and cry, too. "Oh," she wailed, "it's all too much, isn't it?"

"Yes," said Fiona. "It's too much for any one heart to take."

"He didn't deserve to die, though," Emmeline murmured.

Fiona thought a moment. "No, he didn't. He wasn't himself, though, in the fire. So many people weren't themselves. Your father . . . he wasn't himself, either. He lost reason. But he was thinking of you—he was crazed thinking how he could save you."

Emmeline nodded sadly, and turned the check over in her hands, as though it could make sense of all the awful things that had happened. "I don't know if I want this. It doesn't really seem like mine."

"You could return it to Ada—she'd be pleased, but she also might take it the wrong way."

Emmeline gazed at the window, where droplets went on beating a pattern against the pane. "During the fire . . ." she began, without shifting her eyes to meet Fiona's.

The phrase made Fiona stiffen, and she wasn't sure she wanted to hear what Emmeline had to say. But she was speaking in a deliberate fashion, and Fiona thought she had better just listen.

". . . when I was locked in that room, I felt sure I'd die. I thought about all kinds of things there. Thought about . . ." She trailed off, and her brow flexed in pain. "Anyway, when I thought about it, I realized that I was always happiest when I was with you, you and . . . With Father, we were always thinking about the future, and what we would someday become. But with you two, we were just our-selves. So I made out a will, and I left everything I had to you. I was angry, but when I thought about you having my things, it made me happy. It doesn't make much sense, does it? Because if I died in the fire, my will would have burned up, too. And now I'm alive, so the will wouldn't mean any-thing, anyway. But when everything seemed rotten and at the end, it made me feel better to think of giving what I had to you. Well, everything still feels rotten, and I still think it will make me feel better to give it to you."

"You can't—" Fiona started.

"Of course I can!" Emmeline's face was sad and wet with tears, but she was smiling, too, and she seemed quite sure of herself, and Fiona had known her long enough—if Emme-line was sure, then there would be no stopping her. "But you have to do something beautiful with it, all right? I will absolutely die if I don't see something beautiful in this god-forsaken city soon."

Then she marched into the lobby to find a pen. When she returned, she had signed the check over to Fiona, and put it into her hands before she had a chance to refuse. The check was for such a staggering figure, Fiona didn't really believe in it, that any of it would ever be hers. She was just relieved that they had started talking again, really talking, and didn't want to refuse Emmeline when she had thought of something that made her smile.

"Remember Mr. Polk?" Emmeline asked.

Fiona glanced up from the check in her lap. "Yes," she replied, although he seemed like a habitué of a long-lost world.

"You make much better clothes than he does. Why don't you have your own shop? You could call it Madame Mag's."

Fiona nodded at this suggestion, but it hurt her heart. She knew that it was ridiculous to feel this way now, when he was lost to both of them. But she couldn't do away with that old fear, that Anders was Emmeline's, and that, no matter how he had spent his final day on earth, he had never really belonged to Fiona.

"I loved Anders too, you know," Emmeline said very gently as she searched for her friend's eyes.

Fiona gazed back at her, and something inside broke open and made way. They had both loved him, and they had both lost him, and she was suddenly very glad that she did not have to be the only one. She was glad just to hear his name. "I'm sorry," she whispered.

"I'm sorry, too."

"I wish Anders was here."

"Me too." Emmeline leaned forward and laced her fingers with Fiona's.

Fiona could not have guessed, on that gloomy Monday, that by the end of the following summer, when the ladies of Chicago were ordering their new clothes for a season of galas and balls, she'd have established her own dressmaker's shop in one of the new marble-encased State Street buildings. That her siblings would all be employed there, and well able to pay the rent on a new house on the West Side, or that Emmeline would have found such a calling in running the showroom. In time, they found that they could not be as they had been before—one serving the other, one living and the other half dead. They built the place up, side by side, until it was regarded as one of the fashionable symbols of the new Chicago. The blaze had cut a path through the city, clearing away who they had been, and all they had ever known. But it had cost them the same love, and forced upon them the same secrets. In this way, the fire bound them more closely together, so that in the end they became true friends.

The girls were still holding hands when a figure appeared in the doorway, backlit so that all she saw was his silhouette. Her skin flushed and her heart lifted. One heard so many stories in those days, of people who had disappeared when a structure went down, but were discovered days later, a little thirsty and frightened but otherwise quite all right. For a few moments she believed it was Anders, come back to her, and a shiver shook her shoulders. But then the figure came forward, and she saw it was only Jeremy, who had worked in the stables on Dearborn but since the fire had been involved in all manner of business for Ochs Carter.

"This came, addressed to the house," he said, coming forward to put a card in Fiona's hand. Although he had been elevated by the disaster, he was still afraid to look directly at Emmeline. "Mr. Carter said he didn't know what it was and that you girls might as well have it."

Another shiver passed through Fiona when she held the postcard. She studied it, and her eyes rose to meet Emmeline's, which were shiny mirrors of her own wonder, and her heart became buoyant. On one side of the card was a color illustration of the view of New York Harbor, with the ocean flowing, rich blue and turquoise around the tip of the island, and dotted with little boats and white caps. The other side was postmarked some days ago from Manhattan, and written in simple, strong letters was the message:

> *All New York talks about is Chicago,*
> *and its heart is full of her*

HISTORICAL BACKGROUND OF
WHEN WE CAUGHT FIRE

There are two big reasons I love historical fiction. One is that as a reader and as a writer, I want to be transported to places I can't go in real life, and novels set in the past give me access to strange and fantastical worlds that no longer exist. The other is that when we reach into the past, we find dramatic settings that push characters to the extreme, that challenge their moral and physical selves so that their true identities emerge.

Chicago in the fall of 1871 delivers on both accounts. The fire that began on a Sunday evening in early October destroyed all of downtown Chicago. While much of the city was spared, its core institutions burned to the ground. The Great Fire is legendary in part because it cleared the area now called the Loop to be rebuilt in grand fashion, and for Chicago to become the leading city of architecture in the United States. The city that was there before is quite literally a lost world, and thus a very exciting place to imagine. The people who witnessed its destruction—especially the young people who were born there—were survivors of incredible terror, and when the fire itself died down, they had to face the destruction of their homes, their way of life, and the landscape that until then had been their whole reality.

In 1871, Chicago's population had undergone fifty years of exponential growth, from fewer than three hundred at the city's founding to more than three hundred thousand. It still possessed something of a frontier town spirit, and it was most certainly a boom town—the crucial stop-off between the wheat, hog, and lumber producing regions of the Midwest and the big urban centers of the Northeast. Real estate speculation was notoriously wild. Buildings went up quickly and cheaply, with little regulation, and property owners relied on insurance rather than sound construction to protect their investment. Like all cities, the criminals and the city boosters, the civic heroes and the new immigrants (in 1870, over half the population was foreign born), collaborated in creating the special spirit of the place.

The one detail everyone knows about the Great Fire of 1871—the part that makes it into songs and poems and cartoons—was that it was started when Mrs. O'Leary's cow kicked over a lit lantern. Some elements of this story are true—the fire did begin in a barn adjacent to the O'Leary family home, a lantern was possibly involved, and Mrs.

O'Leary did have a dairy business. But the official inquiry cleared the family of wrongdoing—they were not in the barn but asleep in the house when the fire began—and the story was probably seized upon because of the strong anti-Irish sentiment in the city at the time. Then, as now, everybody was looking for somebody else to blame.

In real life, as in my fictionalized version, the night watchman in the courthouse tower mistook the location of the fire and called the fire trucks to the wrong location. Although Mathias Schaffer (Gabriel's real-life counterpart) soon realized his mistake, the telegraph operator refused to correct it, saying that it would only confuse matters. Even so, one engine company had spotted the fire before Schaffer, and seven companies were on the scene within forty-five minutes. But by midnight the blaze had jumped the river, and within hours it was too big for anyone to contain.

The true culprits were too many and too nebulous: the location of the city—set on the edge of the prairie—beset the fire with a strong, hot wind that whipped up sparks and spread the flames; the materials of which the city was built (the sidewalks, some of the streets, most of the homes, and even many of the big downtown buildings were made of wood beneath a thin facade of brick); and the drought that summer (only an inch of rain fell between July 4 and October 9) that emptied the wells and left a flammable city drier yet. Making matters worse, the "Saturday night fire," which

I depicted through the eyes of Gabriel, Anders's cousin, was one of the worst fires in Chicago up to that time, and had damaged some of the fire department's equipment and left many of the firemen (there were less than two hundred of them) exhausted. In hindsight, these factors make the Great Fire seem almost inevitable.

When I understood these facts about the fire, I realized that it was the perfect metaphor for a certain kind of love triangle. While Emmeline, Fiona, and Anders are close friends, they have kept some really important truths about their relationships with each other secret, and secrecy has made those truths doubly powerful, doubly combustible. The denial of feelings, the unfairness built into these relationships, have heightened all the yearning, desire, loyalty, and sense of betrayal that we see them experience over a handful of days. Like a city built of wood, these characters are tinder just waiting for a match. How could they not set the world on fire?

While the fire was a horror, many who witnessed it also described it as having a terrible beauty—it was a "grandly magnificent scene" in one eyewitness account. Not only were the circumstances perfect for a fire, once it got going, it created its own weather. Fire whirls, which are created when hot rising air meets cool descending air and cause a tornado-like vortex, probably occurred, enhancing the already brutal winds and dominating the sky. This was why flaming debris were carried across natural barriers like the river, and one of the reasons why it was such an awesome and frightening sight to behold.

To me, the craziest fact of the Great Fire is that, legendary as it is, it wasn't even the biggest fire in the country that day. That distinction belongs to a fire that devoured the lumber town of Peshtigo, Wisconsin. There were other notable fires in the Midwest on October 8 as well, due to the long dry summer and the strong winds that harassed the entire region, but Peshtigo—which killed at least 1,200 people and perhaps many more, and destroyed 1.2 million acres—remains the deadliest fire in American history. But Chicago was the news story in the days to come, and its myth is the one we retell.

A story of this kind seems especially relevant to me now, following a year of disasters where nature and an environment altered to suit the needs of human civilization came into violent conflict. Not once, but many times. Floods, fires, droughts, and hurricanes are as old as time, but the way people create their own habitat determines how safely they will weather these natural phenomena.

There is a final reason that the Great Fire of Chicago appealed to me as material for a romance: My maternal grandparents met and fell in love in Chicago. My grandmother's parents were both born in Sweden and immigrated as young adults; my grandfather was of German and Irish ancestry. It is family lore that his grandmother witnessed the fire as a little girl, and she used to tell my grandfather and his four siblings of the terrible orange glow that she remembers seeing in the distance from her South Side home.

I hope that this book will be read as a love story, as a story about real friendship, as an adventure, and as a small window onto the way cities—their governments, their geography, their institutions—affect the personal lives of their citizens. None of us can really live alone.

ACKNOWLEDGMENTS

Like all books, this one is a collaboration, and I am indebted to many for their part in making it a real physical object. Most especially to my editors, for making it possible, and then making it readable, and for being such stars to work with. Thank you, Sara Shandler. Thank you, Emilia Rhodes. Thank you, Alice Jerman. Many others lent their brilliance to this project at different stages. Thank you to Josh Bank, Joelle Hobeika, Hayley Wagreich, Romy Golan, Les Morgenstein, and everybody at Alloy Entertainment. Thank you, Eliza Swift, for the original spark. Thank you, Jennifer Klonsky, Erica Sussman, Alexandra Rakaczki, and everybody at Harper. Thank you, Joe Veltre and Hannah Vaughn and everybody at Gersh. Thank you, Adrienne Miller, for being the greatest of readers and advice-givers. Thank you, Ryan Hawke, for all your support and inspiration. When I had just begun writing this book, I met my best friend and partner; by the time it was finished, we became a family. Thank you, Marty McLoughlin, for being everything.

DON'T MISS A SINGLE PAGE
OF THE DAZZLING ROMANCE!

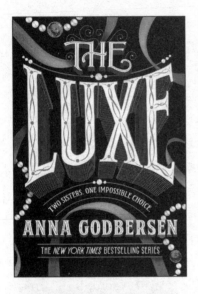

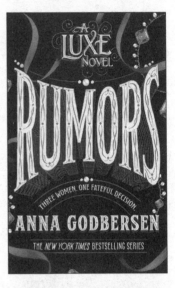

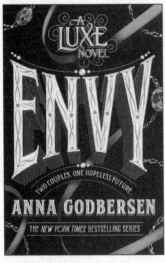

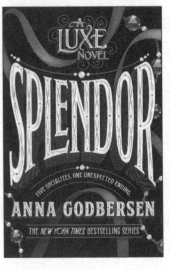